HEROES

Also by Marissa Lete

Echoes
Anomalies

HEROES

MARISSA LETE

Heroes
Book 3 of the Echoes Trilogy

ISBN: 978-1-957204-06-2 (paperback)
ISBN: 978-1-957204-07-9 (hardcover)

Cover art by Donn Marlou Ramirez
Proofread by Stephen Roddewig

www.MarissaLete.com

BOOK THREE

CHAPTER 1

THE FIRST THING I become aware of is the voices. They're somewhere to my right, speaking in low, fervent tones.

"—not going to, after an episode like that."

"She just needs more time."

"It's been three weeks. You know what happened to the last—"

"That was different."

"Hardly."

A pause. Distantly, the words start to make sense. *Three weeks?*

Then the first voice speaks again.

"It's time to dispose of her."

"But she hasn't—"

"That's not a request, doctor. It's a command."

In the tense silence that follows, I become aware of more sounds: the slow beeping of a heart monitor, the sound of air whooshing in and out, the hum of electrical appliances.

Where am I? A hospital?

"Okay," the doctor finally replies, resigned.

"I'll leave you to it, then."

Footsteps retreat. A door slams.

Then a sigh, the sound closer to me now. When the doctor speaks again, she's right above my head.

"I'm so sorry, darling. I didn't want to have to do this."

Then there's a click. A machine cuts off, and the whooshing air disappears. The heart monitor starts to speed up, a warning chime ringing.

My thoughts sharpen as reality finally hits me. She's going to *dispose* of me? Right now? But how? And why? Can't she tell I'm conscious? I'm fine, I just need to—

My eyes fly open.

"Wait!" I yell, raising my hands above my head to push her away. But they only meet empty air.

I jolt upright as the warning chimes on the heart monitor intensify. "I'm okay!" I shout. "I'm awake!"

The heart monitor doesn't stop screaming.

Panicked, I scan the room. To my surprise, the corner I hear the alarms coming from is empty. And then it clicks.

Echoes.

A sigh escapes me.

They're just echoes.

Eventually, the sound of the heart monitor cuts off, leaving the room in a tense silence.

"*Be at peace*," the echo of the doctor whispers, inches from my ear. It sends a shiver down my spine.

Where am I? And how did I get here?

I stare down at the bed I'm lying in, reminding myself to breathe as the world slowly comes into focus. There's an IV in my left arm, and despite the blankets piled on top of me, I'm freezing. The room I'm in is small with no windows, and there's a counter with a sink in the corner. Unlike a normal hospital room, though, there's no TV on the wall, no additional seating for visitors, no second door leading to a bathroom.

I rack my brain, trying to remember how I got here. Before any coherent thoughts can form, the door swings open.

My heart begins to race as a woman in a white coat enters followed by two men in black suits. The sight of them brings flashes of memories.

A barn. Darkness. Running away with Maverick beside me, bullets whizzing past us. The images flicker through my thoughts, bringing the picture into focus. *Maverick falling, blood on my hands. The syringe. Then the vans, tires squealing as they race toward us.*

I've been captured. By the ACA—the Anomaly Containment Association. The organization that Alice works for.

"I'm glad to see that you're awake and alert. How are you feeling?" the woman asks, crossing over to me. The men remain by the door, blocking the only exit.

"Who are you?" I demand, ignoring her question. "Where are we?"

"My name is Dr. Gloria Shaw. We're in the medical wing of the Anomaly Containment Association," she answers simply, and I realize I recognize her voice. She's the doctor from the echoes I'd woken up to seconds ago.

I narrow my eyes at her, remembering the conversation I'd overheard. *Dispose of her.*

"What do you want with me?"

"I'm here to make sure you're recovering well. You lost a lot of blood, and you've been out since you got here yesterday."

At her words, I become aware of a dull ache in my left calf. I shove the blankets aside, revealing the plain gray hospital gown I'm wearing and my bandaged leg.

"Luckily, it was just a flesh wound. It should heal up nicely in a couple of weeks. You're feeling okay, then? Any lightheadedness?" Dr. Shaw asks, picking up a clipboard attached to the end of my bed.

My eyes snap between her and the guards at the door. I ignore her questions again, my voice lowering as I ask, "Where is Maverick?"

Dr. Shaw jots something down, then tilts her head at me. "I understand you're concerned about him and your current situation. I can assure you that he's fine, but I can't answer any of your questions about him. You can take that up with security when I release you for questioning."

"Questioning?"

Without answering, she sets the clipboard down, then comes to my side and places the stethoscope hanging around her neck into her ears. "I'm just going to listen to your heart."

Her eyes lock with mine as she leans closer, hesitating— waiting to see if I'm going to resist—before she places the end of the stethoscope over my chest. I wait impatiently as she listens, my gaze flicking to the guards by the door again.

There's no way I could get past them. I might be able to if it was just Dr. Shaw, but even then, the ache in my calf is enough of a warning not to try anything. Plus, where would I go? Dr. Shaw confirmed that we're in the ACA, which means there are probably plenty of guards crawling throughout this place. And I don't have the slightest clue as to the layout. If my suspicions are correct, we're in one of the underground chambers Angelo pointed out when he, Maverick, Wyatt, and Dahlia snuck in to investigate this place.

I squeeze my eyes shut at the thought. How long ago was that? Just a few days? Somehow, it feels like forever.

"Your heart sounds great," Dr. Shaw says, taking the stethoscope out of her ears and replacing it around her neck. "Will you let me check your blood pressure?"

I narrow my eyes. "Are you really asking for my consent? When you'd just as easily have these guards hold me down if I don't let you?"

Dr. Shaw just shakes her head. "That would give me an inaccurate reading. If you aren't going to let me, I can leave and return when you're ready. But if you want to see your friends again, it's in your best interest to cooperate."

"Oh, sure," I scoff. "You're going to let me see my friends. I *totally* believe that."

"You might not, but you should know the ACA is not the soulless organization you believe it to be."

"Is that what you tell yourself so you can sleep at night?"

Unfazed by my words, Dr. Shaw heads to the cabinets at the other side of the room and pulls out a blood pressure machine.

She tears the velcro cuff open, then pauses, looking at me expectantly.

Pursing my lips, I tug my sleeve up and hold out my arm. As she wraps the cuff snugly around my bicep, I think I see a hint of a smile on her lips.

"Don't talk while the monitor is running, and stay still," she instructs, then hits a button. The cuff starts to tighten around my arm.

While I wait, I stare down at myself. For the first time, I notice that my palms are wrapped in bandages, too. Vaguely, I remember smashing the window of Grace's guest house and slicing my hands on the shards of glass as I climbed through. I'd been so desperate to get the syringe—to save Maverick—that I'd barely even noticed. And despite having been shot in the leg, I'd sprinted back to him.

And I saved him.

The pressure around my arm releases, and Dr. Shaw moves to take off the cuff.

"Why go to all this trouble to make sure I'm recovering okay when you guys are the ones who shot me?"

Dr. Shaw turns her back to me to put the device back into the cabinet. "My understanding is that the use of firearms is only as a last resort. No one here *wanted* anyone to get hurt."

I frown, watching her as she heads back to scribble more notes. "Maverick was shot in the stomach. He almost *died*."

Her eyes fix on mine from just above her clipboard. "And yet, when he arrived here, he was miraculously unscathed."

I close my mouth, dropping my gaze.

Sighing, Dr. Shaw re-attaches the clipboard to the end of the bed, then nods at the guards by the door. One of them tugs the door open and exits the room, returning a second later with a wheelchair.

"When a group of unregistered anomalies starts coming after our organization and takes out an entire research facility, desperate measures have to be taken to stop them, regardless of who gets hurt in the process," she says.

"We didn't take out your research facility," I snap, my tone darkening. "Alice orchestrated it all to cover up what she was doing there."

Dr. Shaw opens her mouth to respond but seems to hesitate, a flash of some unreadable emotion crossing her features. Then she shakes her head. "It's not my job to interrogate you. I'm sorry about your injuries. You're safe here at the ACA, and we're going to get you healed up as quickly as possible. As long as you continue to cooperate."

Dr. Shaw waves the guard on, and he rolls the wheelchair to the side of the bed. She grabs a gauze pad and some medical tape from the cabinet above the sink and comes to my other side. Carefully, she removes the IV from my arm and places the gauze over the hole in my skin, then wraps the tape tightly around my arm a few times.

"You're going to be taken in for questioning, now. Can you get into the wheelchair, or do you need help?"

Biting back another snarky reply, I shift in the bed, swinging my legs over the side without a word. The movement intensifies the burning in my calf, but I swallow the pain, refusing to let it stop me. I step down, putting most of my weight on my right leg, then slowly shuffle into the wheelchair. Goosebumps trail across my skin as the warmth of the blankets dissipates, my bare legs now exposed to the chilly room. I almost want to reach for a blanket to cover myself with, but I curl my hands into fists instead.

"I'll let you take her from here," Dr. Shaw tells the silent guard. He nods, then steps behind the wheelchair and starts pushing me.

CHAPTER 2

IN THE HALLWAY, one of the guards walks in front of me as the other pushes from behind. I almost want to roll my eyes at the fact that the ACA sent *two* guards to retrieve me; in my state, even without guards standing in my way, I probably wouldn't be able to escape. I can't even walk. But I suppose after everything they think I've done and how our group almost got away from them, they want to be extra careful.

As we move, I think back to the night my friends snuck into this place and I'd watched their investigation on the screen Angelo set up in Maverick's mansion. The eggshell walls and speckled white linoleum floors are similar to what I remember, but none of the doors we pass have signs or nameplates, so I can't pinpoint exactly where we might be. Angelo had mentioned that there were multiple underground levels here, and the lack of windows tells me this must be one of them.

At the end of the hallway, the room opens up into a large lobby. To our left, I spot a set of elevators, and beyond them, another hallway, but we hang right so I shift my gaze ahead, taking in the rest of the main area. Directly in the center of the lobby, there's a small room, almost more like the size of a closet, with open space all around it. And mirrors have been hung on all of its outside walls.

But no, probably not mirrors. They're windows. Like the one-way windows in interrogation rooms. It must be a security room, designed so whoever is inside can keep an eye on everyone coming and going from this floor without anybody knowing who's watching. Or if anyone is watching at all.

We continue past the security room, arriving at the other side of the lobby where there are several rows of thin plastic chairs that remind me of a DMV waiting room. Past them, there are two hallways on either side, and I crane my neck, trying to get a good look at the place. I don't see any signage or anything that might indicate what kinds of rooms are behind the windowless metal doors, though.

I wonder if any of the other anomalies are nearby. Could Maverick, or Angelo, or Wyatt be behind one of these doors? Will I get to see any of them again?

Earlier, Dr. Shaw had implied I would. But she could have been lying just to get me to cooperate.

There has to be some hope, though. They aren't going to keep us all isolated forever, right?

We turn right down the next hallway and stop in front of the first door on the left. One guard tugs it open while the other pushes me inside.

The room is empty except for a table and one chair. Another one-way mirror is built into the wall, exactly like all of the interrogation rooms I'd seen on TV shows.

Never in a million years did I think I would end up inside one of them.

Inside a secret government facility that's hunting down people with special abilities, at that.

I'm wheeled up to the open side of the table, facing the one-way mirror, before both of the guards wordlessly exit the room.

As I wait, I stare into the mirror across from me, taking in the bags under my eyes and the unruly state of my hair. I want to lift my hands and smooth it down, to straighten out the neckline of the hospital gown, but I don't. I'm all too aware of the fact that I'm most likely being watched, and any movement I make will be observed by someone behind that glass. So I sit still, staring directly into my own eyes, wondering who might be staring back.

Until the lock clicks again and the door swings open.

A man steps through, then pauses to flip through the folder he's holding. "Laura Jones," he says. Not a question. A statement, made with a sigh, like he's just as unhappy to be here as I am.

I don't reply. Instead, I stare. His hair is a dark gray and clipped short, military style. And even though he looks like the kind of man who normally keeps a clean-shaven face, silver-speckled stubble lines his jaw.

As if hearing my thoughts, he rubs at his chin, dropping his gaze.

And then I realize I recognize him. It's the same man I'd seen outside of my house a couple of weeks ago, on the day I was supposed to meet up with Grace. He'd been looking for me, had asked my parents about me even after they'd lost their memories. It had taken me a while to figure out why he would think they knew anything, but then I'd learned that he was working for the ACA, not for Alice. And the ACA didn't know what Alice had done to us, didn't know that she'd taken so many people's memories away.

An image flashes through my mind—the business card he'd handed to Grace that day.

"Neil Oliver," I say. His eyes widen briefly before his expression falls back into practiced composure, and a sliver of hope runs through me. He doesn't know about what really happened twenty-four hours ago, and maybe I can convince him.

The chair screeches in protest as he pulls it out to take a seat across from me. He sets the folder down between us, then unbuttons his suit jacket and leans forward, his piercing gaze fixing on mine.

"How are you feeling, Laura?"

I purse my lips. "Like I got shot in the leg and almost bled out."

He nods. "That was an unfortunate consequence."

"Consequence," I scoff. "For trying not to get kidnapped?"

Neil leans back in his chair, folding his arms across his chest. "Fortunately, Miss Jones, you have not been kidnapped."

"I think we have different definitions of what *kidnapping* means."

"Sure, you might be here against your will," he offers with a wave of his hand. "But there's a difference between criminal abduction and being taken into custody."

"So what you're doing here is legal, then?"

"In fact, it is. But what you were involved in—several counts of trespassing, arson, even manslaughter—isn't."

At his words, a memory tugs at me. *A gunshot ringing in my ears. The bald man, slumping to the ground in front of me. His body going still.*

I close my eyes to blot it out. I can't think about that right now, can't go down that rabbit hole of guilt. I did what I had to do.

Plus, the bald man was working for Alice, not the ACA. They might not even know what happened to him.

At the sound of papers shuffling, I open my eyes again, watching as Neil sifts through the folder. He pulls out a photograph, staring down at it for a moment. Then he slides it across the table, his gaze shifting to my face. "Let's start at the beginning. Can you explain to me what's happening in this photo?"

I glance down, recognizing it immediately. It's the same security camera photo we'd discovered in the warning message the ACA put out about us—the one of me and the anomalies escaping Alice's lab after she locked us inside and set it on fire. Alice had lied to the ACA and convinced them that we were trying to take down the organization. That *we* were responsible for the damages. It was a way to cover up what she was doing, to hide her little side project from the ACA.

And then she'd twisted everyone's memories so that they believed it, too. So that even if the ACA captured us, they wouldn't find out that *Alice* is the one behind everything.

I swallow. How much has Neil learned already? Has he spoken to Maverick? Or Gabe?

We're the only three that know the truth. Me, because of the echoes. Maverick, because I used Alice's healing syringe on him, which restored his memories. And Gabe, since he wasn't with us that night.

The other twelve anomalies believe the lies Alice has crafted. Have they been interrogated yet? And will Maverick, Gabe, and I be able to make a convincing argument against the rest of them?

That is, as long as Alice hasn't decided to mess with their memories again. What if she found out that Maverick remembers the truth and already wiped it from his mind? What if she got to Gabe? A twinge of panic runs through me at the thought.

I stare down at the photo, at my face, which looks strangely calm, despite how I remember feeling that night. It's grainy, and not everyone who was there is fully recognizable, but I can picture their faces, the way everything happened that night. The memory is still there in my mind—an echo, really, because Alice technically erased my memories and replaced them with false ones. I have to look past the lies to see it, but the echo—the truth—is there. Clear as day.

"Where did you get this photo?" I ask, lifting my gaze to Neil.

He frowns, then leans forward, resting his elbows on the table and clasping his hands together. I expect him to ignore the question, but his next words are a pleasant surprise. "It's from security footage at a research facility that burned down several weeks ago. It was sabotaged by the people in this photo."

I fight the urge to glance down at the photo, at my face, which is clearly recognizable despite the poor quality of the image. "Have you seen it?" I ask, tilting my head to the side. "The footage?"

He shakes his head. "The footage was lost in the fire. This is one of the only surviving images."

A short burst of air escapes me, somewhere between a laugh and a scoff. "How convenient."

Neil opens his mouth to respond, but then he closes it, his brows cinching together in an odd way, like he wants to demand real answers from me but can't shake the curiosity also swirling inside.

Good.

"Who managed to recover this photo?" I ask. "Was it Dr. Alice Wight?"

He narrows his eyes, that same hint of surprise from when I said his name flashing across his face. But this time, it lingers.

"What's happening in this photo," I begin, flipping it around to face Neil, "is a group of children are escaping captivity. They were all kidnapped by your very own Dr. Alice Wight and are fleeing the scene after *she* set the building on fire and trapped us inside of it."

His gaze hardens the tiniest bit. "Dr. Wight burned down her own lab? Is that what you're saying?"

"That's exactly what I'm saying."

"Why would she—"

"To cover up what she was really doing there."

Neil leans back, folding his arms across his chest. "Which was?" he asks flatly, like the idea is so far fetched there's no way he'll believe me.

"Figuring out how to replicate anomalies' abilities. Experimenting on them. And hiding the fact that she's an anomaly herself. You might not know this, but—"

The door swings open, cutting off my barrage of words. I frown as another man enters, wearing a similar suit and a pair of glasses.

"I'm sorry to interrupt. But there's a matter that needs your immediate attention." The man strides across the room, handing a piece of paper to Neil.

Neil stares down at it, and I watch his expression shift from annoyance to urgency. He stands, the chair skidding across the floor behind him. "I need to get over there," he says, starting for the door. But then he pauses, his gaze landing back on me briefly.

"I can take over this interview," the newcomer offers.

Neil hesitates, like a part of him wants to say no. But then whatever message was written on that paper seems to grasp more of his attention. "Okay. Just report back to me when you're done."

The man with glasses nods. Then Neil hurries out the door.

CHAPTER 3

I STUDY THE MAN WITH glasses carefully as he crosses the room, moves the chair back toward the table—quietly, unlike Neil—and takes a seat. He's shorter than Neil—younger, too. And there's a softness about his features that makes him appear warmer. More sympathetic.

But I won't get my hopes up about it.

"Good morning. My name is Russell Lee," he says, offering his hand across the table. I stare down at it, setting my jaw. When he finally realizes I'm not going to take it, he licks his lips and drops his gaze.

"Alright, well," he flips open the folder, scans the top page, "Miss Jones." He reaches for the photo Neil had placed in front of me, studies it for a moment, then tucks it back into the folder and closes it. "Do you know where you are right now?"

"Underneath some building in the middle of nowhere," I reply, a hint of malice coating my words.

Russell nods. "And do you know why you're here?"

"Because you think I'm part of a group you believe sabotaged one of your research facilities."

He nods again, but this time it's a slow, sideways nod—the kind of nod a teacher gives when the answer is only partially correct. "Sure, that incident gave us cause to look for you. But it isn't the *only* reason you're here."

I purse my lips, waiting for him to explain.

"You're here, Miss Jones, because of your blood. Because of a special property inside you that makes you different from the rest of the world."

"Because I'm an anomaly."

"Exactly." He leans forward, resting his chin on one hand. "How much do you know about the Anomaly Containment Association?"

"I know you're capturing anomalies. *Containing* them," I say. "I know you shot at me and my friends. Injured—nearly killed—some of us."

Russell waves his hand in the air, dismissing me. "But do you know what the purpose of our organization is? What our goals are?"

"To ruin people's lives?"

Russell's lips twist like he's fighting a smile. Like he finds this amusing. "I understand you don't have the fondest view of the ACA. But I assure you, we don't mean any harm to you or your friends. In fact, the true purpose of our organization is to protect anomalies."

I glance down at my bandaged leg. *Bullets whizzing past my ear. Glass shattering.*

"Well, if you ask me, you're doing a *superb* job."

"However," Russell continues, ignoring my comment, "along with protecting anomalies, we have the responsibility to ensure the safety of the general public. We don't want anomalies to harm anyone—whether accidentally or intentionally. And that means they must be kept under strict regulations."

"So locked up in your underground lab," I say flatly.

Russell studies me for a long moment, all humor gone from his gaze. "This is not a prison, Miss Jones. The ACA serves as a boarding facility for anomalies. We provide a safe place for them to live where they pose no danger to society. At the same time, keeping the existence of anomalies out of the public knowledge helps to avoid widespread panic and keeps them safe from anyone who might want to do them harm."

"So it's not a prison, but I'm not allowed to leave?"

"For your own safety, no," Russell confirms. "But many of the anomalies in custody find our facilities to be more than sufficient for their needs."

"And you're just keeping us here… until what? You're done experimenting on us and decide to *dispose* of us?"

Russell leans back in his chair, folding his arms across his chest. "In the early years of our organization, we feared that permanent residence here was the only option. But you'll be pleased to learn that we've started a new program that allows anomalies to reintegrate into society, and we've seen a lot of success with it."

I search Russell's gaze, puzzling the words out in my mind.

"The program depends on each anomaly's unique circumstances, of course. And on their cooperation," Russell continues with a pointed look. "Unfortunately, not every anomaly is eligible. You'll be evaluated after an initial probation period of one year, and a decision will be made then."

A year? I could be stuck here for a *year?* The thought makes my head swim.

I can't wait that long. Not while Alice is planning something terrible. I'm going to have to find my own way out, and soon.

"The existence of anomalies is still a relatively recent discovery, and we're doing everything in our power to resolve the problem," Russell says. "Until that happens, all we can do is contain it."

I frown. *Resolve the problem.* As in, get rid of anomalies? Develop a way to inhibit our abilities?

That was what Alice claimed to be doing when I first met her—trying to find a way to block anomalies' abilities. She claimed she wanted to prevent us from harming others, to keep people from abusing our powers.

But then you came along, and you showed me a different possibility.

Her words in the barn echo back to me, sending a shiver down my spine.

She'd changed her mind. Decided that the ACA's agenda didn't align with her own anymore. But why? What changed? And how did *I* have anything to do with it?

Russell shifts in his chair, drawing my attention. He leans forward, flipping through the pages of the folder with a sigh. "Now that you have a better understanding of what the ACA actually does, I hope you'll decide to view us in a better light. And agree to answer a few questions for me."

He's crazy if he thinks I'll take his word for anything. But because I don't want to waste any more time in here, I nod.

Smiling tightly, Russell looks back down at the papers in front of him. "Miss Jones, we know you're part of a group of anomalies that have been targeting the ACA. We know that you assisted this group in destroying our research facility several weeks ago. What we don't understand, however, is *why*. What were the intentions behind this attack?"

I shake my head. "It wasn't an attack. At least not from us."

Russell searches my gaze, his features neutral as he nods for me to go on.

"Whatever you think happened that night is a lie. Our group is not targeting the ACA, we didn't even know the organization existed until you started looking for us. Alice Wight set us up—she's behind everything."

"Alice Wight," Russell repeats. "And how do you know Dr. Wight?"

"Well, she kidnapped me. Experimented on me. Hunted me down, then tried to erase my memories of her."

He licks his lips, tilting his head thoughtfully. "Tried to? And failed?"

"Obviously."

"And how did that happen?"

"I… I don't know," I answer, dropping my gaze. It's the truth—I know that I managed to hold on to my memories because of my ability, but I still don't fully understand how it happened. Everything from the past couple of days is a blur.

"It didn't work on me, but it did on everyone else," I continue. "Alice manipulated their memories. That's why they believe they *are* the group that's been targeting the ACA. It's all a ruse she created to keep the ACA from finding out that she's working against them."

Russell's mouth bunches to the side as he considers my words. He grabs a pen from the front pocket of his shirt, then starts jotting notes inside the folder. When he finishes, he closes it and looks up at me. "Thank you for answering my questions, Miss Jones." Then, to my surprise, he stands and tucks the pen back into his pocket.

The room starts to feel suddenly warm. "Wait, that's it? We're done?"

"I believe I've gathered all the information I need."

I shake my head. "You're not going to ask me what Alice has been doing? What else I know?" After what I just told him, Russell should be teeming with questions. Or at least in denial—I wouldn't be surprised if he doesn't believe me. There were twelve other anomalies that probably described a different narrative, after all. But either way, shouldn't he be inquiring further instead of just dismissing me like this?

"I don't think that's necessary."

"Alice is plotting against the ACA," I tell him anyway. "I'm pretty sure she wants to take over, or something. I know you don't believe me, but this is important. She's up to something, and she's already figured out how to replicate anomalies' abilities. If she decides to—"

Russell raises a hand, silencing me. He studies me for a long moment, eyebrows furrowed like he can't make up his mind about something. Then, finally, he says, "Dr. Wight's private research is of no concern to the ACA, Laura." His eyes bore into mine, a warning in them. "And it should be of no concern to you."

And that's when it clicks.

Russell is working for Alice.

Of course.

He's not really with the ACA. That's why he stepped in for Neil in the first place. Whatever urgent matter Neil had to attend to must have been fabricated—Russell had been watching our interrogation, and as soon as he realized I wasn't telling the right story, he stepped in. To keep Neil from hearing the truth.

Alice isn't working alone. I always knew that, but I guess I'd assumed she only had people outside of the ACA working for her. Not people on the inside, too.

How many others are there? Dr. Shaw? The security guards?

Russell clears his throat, and my thoughts scatter. I look up to find him watching me with a clenched half smile.

"Dr. Wight will pay you a visit soon, and we'll get this straightened out," he says, and the air leaves my lungs. "Until then, you'll be taken back to the medical wing to recover."

And with that, he picks up the folder and slips out the door, leaving me alone in the interrogation room, my heart hammering in my chest.

CHAPTER 4

WHEN WE GET BACK to the room I woke up in, the guard wheels me as close to the bed as she can, then offers a hand to help me stand. I stare at it for a moment, then swipe it away and push myself up. I refuse to be completely helpless.

Shuffling on one foot, I make it to the bed, where all the heat has already been sapped from the mound of blankets. I shiver as I pull my legs up onto it and slide the covers back over myself.

Wordlessly, the guard pushes the wheelchair out the door, and I watch it click shut behind her. My gaze lingers on the handle, on the only exit in this windowless room.

I wonder if it's locked. I wonder how hard it would be to leave.

On the way to and from the interrogation room, we passed that guard room and the elevators in front of it twice. Aside from that, there weren't any other guards stationed in the hallways, so the people in that room would be the only ones I'd have to worry about.

But even if I could get past them, the elevators probably require some kind of security badge. Beyond that, I'm sure the exits on the building have some type of alarm system in place. And if I got out, I'd also have to get past the front gates and through the woods—and we're miles from the nearest town.

To escape, I'll need help. Angelo, Wyatt, and Maverick, at least. They're the ones that got in and out of this place without being noticed before, and I'm sure they could do it again.

But where are they? Will I actually be allowed to see them?

If Alice has any hand in making the decision, that's a definite no. She's already got people like Russell infiltrating security. Who else is working for her? Who—if anyone—can I convince of the truth? Neil? But how can I talk to him if Alice has people watching carefully, waiting to interrupt the moment I say the wrong thing?

I don't know. But I need to find a way.

The door swings open, and for a second, my muscles tense. *Dr. Wight will pay you a visit soon, and we'll get this straightened out*, Russell had said.

But to my relief, it's only Dr. Shaw. And she's carrying a tray of food. My stomach grumbles at the sight of it; I can't even remember when I last ate.

Dr. Shaw sets the tray down on an overbed table in the corner, then wheels it up to me and adjusts the height so that it slides over my lap. On the tray is a bowl of oatmeal, an apple, a water bottle, and a little cup with two white pills in it. I narrow my eyes at it.

"They're just painkillers," Dr. Shaw says.

I press my lips together. "Are they?"

Dr. Shaw looks at me like she wants to roll her eyes. "You don't *have* to take them."

"Maybe I won't."

She just shrugs. "Either way, at least eat the food. You need to regain some strength."

Reluctantly, I pick up the apple and sink my teeth into it. I wince as the sour taste fills my mouth, waking up my tastebuds.

While I eat, Dr. Shaw goes to the side of the room and starts pulling things out of cabinets. She washes her hands, then returns to my side with a tray of medical supplies just as I'm sinking my teeth into my last bite of the apple.

"I need to clean your wound and put on some fresh bandages," she says.

I nod, setting the core of the apple down and shifting in the bed. Dr. Shaw pulls the blanket away and props my leg up before working on unwrapping the bandages.

"As long as you're feeling okay, you should be ready to be discharged by dinnertime. But we have to wait on security to clear you, too, so we'll see."

"Wait for them to clear me?"

"Your case has to be reviewed by a few different people before we can let you join the rest of the anomalies. As long as everything looks good, you'll be assigned an advisor who will determine your room and class assignments. Depending on who handles your case, that could go quickly or take a little longer."

"Room and class assignments," I echo. "Like, school?"

Dr. Shaw nods, then picks up a squeeze bottle from her tray. "This might sting a little bit," she says.

I brace myself for a burning sensation as she squeezes the liquid over my wound, but surprisingly, it doesn't hurt much. I glance down, my eyes landing on the red, inflamed skin for just a moment before I lift my gaze to the ceiling.

"Once we get the paperwork sorted out, your orientation leader will come and show you through our facilities," Dr. Shaw tells me, setting the squeeze bottle back on the tray.

Orientation leader. Everything she's saying makes it sounds like I'm going off to college.

"When will I get to see my friends?" I ask.

A few beats of silence pass as Dr. Shaw opens a pack of gauze, then presses it over my wound. Which, unlike the liquid she'd used to clean it, makes me wince.

"That depends on which friends you're talking about. And on where they place you," she finally answers as she begins wrapping my leg in clean bandages. "There are two separate dormitory blocks, placed on rotating schedules. They have different mealtimes, recreation periods, and study areas so that they rarely cross paths. Obviously, some members of your group will end up in the same block as you. But others won't. So I really can't say."

I swallow. "Will I get—"

But I don't get to finish. Because at that exact moment, the door swings open, and a familiar face appears behind it.

Silver hair.

Those crisp, blue eyes.

The room around me seems to shrink, the walls closing in on us.

Alice looks up, her eyes darting between me and Dr. Shaw. Then they drop to her clipboard. "You must be Laura Jones?"

I grapple for words, the sight of her bringing back memories. Her, appearing before me in the barn. Her, conjuring illusions. Trapping me in sinking mud. In my head, taking and twisting things.

"Dr. Wight!" Dr. Shaw breaks the silence, turning to Alice with a smile. "How are you this morning?"

Alice blows out a sigh. "You mean it's morning already?"

"Long night?" Dr. Shaw chuckles as she turns back to my leg, finishing up with the bandages.

"I'm barely done processing the new arrivals. Looks like it's going to be a long day, too."

"You're telling me."

I watch the encounter with wide eyes, still trying to get control of my racing heart.

Small talk. Alice is making *small talk*.

"So what can I help you with?" Dr. Shaw asks. She puts all the supplies she'd used back on the tray, then takes it to the counter.

"I just got a report from security. They want me to run a few tests on Miss Jones here. Double check a couple of things."

My blood runs cold.

"Of course! Can I help with anything?" Dr. Shaw asks, her back to us as she returns the supplies to their places inside the cabinets.

"Actually," Alice replies, "I was wondering if you could check on our patient in Room 9 for me. I haven't had a chance to get over there since late last night, and I'm worried about him. If

28

you want, I can finish up with Miss Jones for you after I run those tests?"

The faucet comes on, and Dr. Shaw pumps a soap dispenser a few times before running her hands under the water again. "Sure! But we're pretty much done here. I just changed her bandages, still no signs of infection. She's got the all clear from me as soon as security gets things sorted out."

"Excellent," Alice says, her eyes landing on me. Something like satisfaction glimmers in them.

Dr. Shaw turns to face us with a smile. "I'll get to it, then. Dr. Wight will take good care of you, Laura. And I'll see you soon."

She starts for the door, and my chest tightens.

"Wait! No," I choke out. "You can't leave me here with Alice."

Dr. Shaw pauses, glancing back at us.

"She's not who you think she is," I continue, eyes wide with panic. "She's not working for the ACA. She's trying to—"

"I'm sorry," Alice's voice rises above my own. But she's looking at Dr. Shaw, not me. She lowers her voice, leaning toward Dr. Shaw. "Security warned me Miss Jones was having some difficulty… adjusting. But we'll try to work on it."

Dr. Shaw's gaze slides to me, full of nothing but pity. "Don't worry, Laura. You're safe with Dr. Wight," she assures me.

She has no idea that with Alice, no one is safe.

CHAPTER 5

SILENCE BEATS LIKE A drum across the space where Dr. Shaw stood only moments ago. We're alone now, and I'm stuck in this room with Alice, and I'm pretty sure that as bad as things already are, they're about to get even worse.

"What do you want with me?" I demand.

Without answering, Alice walks over to the end of the bed and picks up the clipboard Dr. Shaw has been jotting notes on. "How are you feeling? Are you experiencing any pain?"

I frown. "Oh, are you still pretending you've never met me?" For the first time, I scan the edges of the room. My eyes land on a camera in the corner, a little blue light blinking at the top of it.

"Someone's watching us. Is that it? You can't let them find out that you already know me."

At my comment, an amused smile plays on Alice's lips. She sets the clipboard down. "I'm just concerned for your wellbeing, Laura."

"The only person's wellbeing you're concerned with is yourself," I spit. "Is that why you're here? So you can try to erase my memories again and get me to stop telling the truth?"

Alice takes a step toward me, and I recoil a little bit, shifting my body to the opposite side of the bed. Instinctively, I scan the tiny room for an escape route, hoping one will magically reveal itself to me.

She doesn't come any closer, though. She just stops, then shakes her head at me.

"I'm not going to do anything to you," she says, but I can hear the *yet* hanging in the space after her words. "I simply want to ask you a few things."

"Like what?"

"It seems your dear friend Maverick has no idea how you managed to save his life."

I study her, trying to figure out what she's actually getting at. It's probably true—Maverick wasn't there when I took the syringe from the bald man or when I showed it to Gabe, Brent, and Veronica. And he was passed out when I injected him with it. I never got a chance to explain how he'd miraculously been healed because the ACA showed up moments later.

I narrow my eyes at Alice. "And you can't come up with a good guess?"

"Oh, I know you used the serum you stole from Lucas on him," she tells me.

Lucas. The name feels like a punch to my gut. *The bald man.* I killed him, and I never even knew his name.

"What I'm trying to understand," Alice continues, her words slicing through the guilt gnawing at me, "is how *you* managed to keep *your* memories intact."

"Maybe you're not as smart as you think you are."

Her lips tighten at the corners the tiniest bit, and I hold back a smile. Is she actually frustrated with me?

"Or maybe," she says, lifting her chin, "your ability had something to do with it. Tell me, was it voluntary? Or did it happen on its own?"

I don't have a solid answer for that. And even if I did, why would I tell *her?*

"I don't have to tell you *anything,*" I snap.

"You don't," she agrees. "But if you don't tell me, I'll have to find the answers another way."

Another way. Like, by reading my mind? Or something else?

Alice has made replications of my friends' abilities, and I've witnessed her use several of them before. But there are a lot more anomalies trapped here in the ACA, and I have no idea what other abilities might exist. Has she replicated them, too? What else can she do to get answers out of me?

The thought sends a chill down my spine.

"I don't know," I finally say, hating the way the words taste. Like surrender. "I don't know how it happened."

Alice tilts her head thoughtfully. "You have no guesses?"

I shake my head, squeezing my eyes shut. I think back to that moment, with Alice in my head. I remember feeling trapped, unable to do anything while the scenes played out before me. Memories fading away. Or changing.

I'd realized what was happening, known that Alice was erasing things. But I'd been unable to stop it.

Something had made that change, though. Something had tethered me to my true memories. Had allowed me to find them again.

The echoes.

I open my eyes. "It was like my ability just kicked in. Took over," I tell Alice.

Her mouth bunches to one side. "Interesting."

Then, without warning, she moves toward me. I flinch, trying to back away, but there isn't anywhere for me to go. I start to roll in the bed, ignoring the pain that shoots through my calf as I swing my legs over the side, but Alice snatches my arm, tugging me back. She grabs my other one, pinning me to the bed with surprising strength.

"What are you doing?" I shriek.

Her eyes meet mine, bright with curiosity even as I struggle against her.

"I want to see if you can do it again."

And then the world slips away.

ALICE IS IN MY HEAD.

I don't know how, but I can feel her there, edging between my thoughts, sifting through my memories. In the space behind my eyes.

Nothing else exists. Just me and her as she digs through my past, searching for something.

Then a scene opens up before me. A memory.

Rain pelts against the windshield, the wipers beating a steady rhythm across it, straining to keep the water at bay. A flash of lightning streaks across the sky, followed by a clap of thunder.

I'm sitting in the back seat as Mom drives. I reach out to turn the AC vent toward me, hating the way the sticky summer air paints moisture across my skin.

Vaguely, I remember this day. I was thirteen, and we were on our way to… a doctor's appointment?

Mom starts humming along to a song on the radio. I squeeze my eyes shut and try to pretend the noise doesn't exist.

I want to ask her to turn it off. Car rides are one of my only breaks from the echoes, from the constant noise. But I don't want to start that conversation. So instead, I cross my arms and stare out the window.

Around me, the edges of the scene start to fade, drifting off into a misty haze.

I recognize what's happening right away this time—the intrusion of Alice as she wipes the memory clean.

I try to grasp at it, but there's nothing to hold on to. I can't stop her. I can't fight her off. All I can do is watch as the memory slips out of my grasp.

When the scene is gone, I can't seem to remember what I was reaching for. It was *something*… but now there's nothing. Just darkness all around me.

But it isn't completely dark, I realize.

There, in front of me, is a sliver of light. A fleck of gold, shimmering in the empty space.

I reach for it, my fingers brushing against it.

Flashes race through my head: *Rain pelting against the windshield. Mom in the driver's seat, humming. An appointment with Dr. Owen that changed everything.*

I don't remember this. But as I watch it unfold before me, I realize that I *do* remember this. It was gone for a moment.

And now it's back.

Like it never even left.

THE WORLD DROPS BACK into existence. The tiny room, the bandages around my leg and hands. Alice standing over me, fingers white around my wrists.

Her eyes shoot open, and she lets go of me, stumbling back like she's just witnessed something horrifying. For a moment, her eyes are wide, her mouth hanging slightly open.

Then, in an instant, she composes herself, quickly schooling her features back to neutral. Like nothing happened at all.

She takes a step forward. Resets her posture.

"Very interesting," she says, her gaze landing on mine.

I stare back at her, almost wanting to laugh. I've never seen Alice like this before, like she doesn't know what to do.

"You can't erase my memories," I say. I almost can't believe it myself, except I've witnessed it twice now. I thought it was just a fluke, a one-time thing. Something achieved out of desperation, but maybe it wasn't.

Alice lifts her chin, swallowing. "It seems there is more to your ability than even you know."

I feel suddenly triumphant. "You can't wipe my memories and stop me from talking. You can't keep me from telling the ACA the truth."

Alice just shakes her head. "That's the least of my worries, Miss Jones." Then she turns her back to me, reaching for the clipboard again.

"Oh, right. Because you've infiltrated security. You've got people who are loyal to you everywhere in this place, don't you? Tell me, did you manipulate their memories, too?"

Ignoring me, Alice flips through the pages, searching for something.

"I'm not going to stop. I'm going to keep talking until somebody believes me. Until they take you down."

"I am not your enemy, Laura."

"That's the biggest lie I've ever heard."

Alice drops the clipboard, her mouth drawn into a thin line. "I know we got off on the wrong foot. But I want you to know that everything I do, I do to protect the future of our kind."

"Protect us," I scoff. "Why does everyone think they're protecting us? When everything you've done has hurt us?"

"Some sacrifices are necessary to ensure a better future."

"A better future? Where you can exploit people without facing consequences?"

"Where anomalies get to be free," she snaps, her tone going dangerously low. "You clearly aren't ready to accept it yet. Someday, Laura, you'll see. Someday, you'll understand."

I bite back another angry reply, her words racing through my mind. *Where anomalies get to be free.* So she wants to take down the ACA? Get them to stop holding anomalies captive? Maybe that's a good thing.

But maybe it's not. Maybe, despite my distaste for being stuck in here, the ACA is right. We are safer here, and the world is safe from us.

Alice isn't stuck here, though. She chose to work here, and she's free to come and go as she pleases. Why does she care about our freedom?

There's something else she's not telling me. What, I don't know, but right now, she's just playing a game. Trying to get into my head. Pretending to be the good guy.

But she's not. She's done nothing but hurt me and Maverick and everyone I know. She wants power, and she'll do anything to get it.

"I will *never* understand," I tell her. "Not after what you've done."

Alice just nods, like this doesn't surprise her. Then she turns her back to me and starts for the door. When she gets to it, she pauses, sighing. "That's unfortunate for you, dear."

That cool, calm, and collected composure is back.

She knows she still has the upper hand here. That there's not much I can do to stop her while I'm stuck here.

But that look on her face the moment after she left my mind—the confusion, the fear—plays back in my mind. It was barely a few seconds, quickly replaced by no emotion. But it was enough to give me a glimpse at her true feelings.

When the door closes behind her, a smile slips onto my face.

Because for the first time ever, I've managed to throw her off. To do something that wasn't part of her plan.

For the first time ever, I've caught Alice by surprise.

CHAPTER 6

I DON'T SEE DR. SHAW again until the next morning. I've already been awake for what feels like hours when she opens the door, the same nurse that came in periodically yesterday to check on me trailing behind her.

The nurse is carrying a tray of food, which she promptly sets down on the overbed table beside me. She pushes it over my lap, and I take in the contents of the plate: a pile of yellow mush that might barely pass as scrambled eggs, a single floppy slice of bacon, and a black speckled banana. I try to remind myself that my stomach was growling a few minutes ago.

"Thanks for bringing that, Liz," Dr. Shaw says, smiling warmly at the nurse. Liz nods, then slips out the door, and Dr.

Shaw shifts her attention to me. "How are you feeling today, Laura?"

"Oh, just wonderful," I deadpan. "I've been cooped up in a room by myself for a whole day with nothing to do."

Offering a pitiful smile in response, Dr. Shaw heads for the back counter and begins washing her hands.

I pick up the fork and poke the mound of scrambled eggs with it, debating whether I'm hungry enough to actually eat any of this. "Can't you guys afford to put TVs in these rooms? Or, wait, would that be giving us too much access to the outside world?"

Dr. Shaw just ignores me as she dries her hands on a paper towel. She grabs a thermometer from the counter and comes to my side, turning the device on and placing a plastic covering over the end. Then she holds it up and I open my mouth, letting her slide the end under my tongue.

"Well the good news is," she tells me while we wait, "we're ready to discharge you as soon as I finish checking your vitals and make sure your wounds are looking okay. We'll have to bring you back once a day so we can change your bandages and keep an eye on your recovery, but hopefully in a week or two you'll be good to go."

When the thermometer beeps and she removes it from my mouth, I say, "So security finally decided to clear me?"

"They did," Dr. Shaw replies, turning to put the device away.

"Alice must have figured out how to keep her secrets, then," I mutter.

Dr. Shaw doesn't respond, but when she turns back to face me with the blood pressure machine in her hands, a small line has appeared between her brows. I stare at it, wondering if she's just thinking hard about something or if her interest is piqued because of my comment.

I've wondered about Dr. Shaw a lot since I last saw her. I'd deduced that she's not working with Alice—Alice had pretended not to know me in front of Dr. Shaw yesterday and had deliberately sent her away before talking freely with me—but that doesn't necessarily mean she's going to believe anything I say. Or be willing to help me.

If I can convince her of the truth, however, she might be able to help me. I need to talk to Neil, and Alice isn't going to make that easy for me. But if Dr. Shaw believes me, she might be able to pull some strings that could get me to him.

"She's not who you think she is, you know," I say, lowering my voice.

Dr. Shaw's eyes fix on mine for a moment, and she seems to hesitate. Like she wants to say something, but can't decide if it's a good idea. Eventually, she seems to shrug it off and nods at my arm. "Can you roll up your sleeve?"

Deflating a little, I oblige, letting her velcro the cuff around my bicep.

"Please don't talk while I run the test."

So I don't. But when the cuff finally loosens and Dr. Shaw removes it, I try again. "She's just pretending to work for the ACA. While she plots to take over."

Dr. Shaw lets out a frustrated sigh, shaking her head as she turns to put the machine away. "If you think that telling me these lies is going to get you out of here, you're wrong," she says. "Security has already warned me about your antics."

"Security is being controlled by Alice," I shoot back. "And if you believe anything they say, you are, too."

That seems to make Dr. Shaw stiffen. *Bingo.*

Slowly, Dr. Shaw gets back to work gathering fresh bandages, but her movements are more rigid. When she comes back to start on my leg, I study her face, searching for any cracks in her composure. I certainly have her attention now, but I can't tell if I've convinced her of anything.

"Alice is an anomaly," I try. "She's been hid—"

"Enough," Dr. Shaw says, her eyes flashing in warning. She holds my gaze for a long moment. Briefly, her eyes flick toward the ceiling. Then back to me.

I frown. What was that about?

My eyes drift to the ceiling, above her head.

The camera.

Her back is to it, her face hidden from its view, but that must have been what Dr. Shaw was trying to get me to notice.

We're being watched. And Dr. Shaw doesn't want whoever is on the other side of the camera to hear this conversation.

Why? Because she believes me, but doesn't want Alice to find out? Or because she's worried about getting in trouble for simply listening?

Either way, maybe it's for the best. If someone that works for Alice is watching and they hear me telling Dr. Shaw the truth, they'll know they need to step in and do some damage control. Alice has already erased and twisted the memories of the anomalies she kidnapped—how easy would it be for her to do the same to Dr. Shaw? Or anyone else I try to tell the truth to?

At that thought, a sinking feeling settles into the pit of my stomach. Because if Alice's allies are always watching, ready to cover it up every time I open my mouth, how am I going to convince anyone of what she's doing?

And how am I ever going to get out of here?

****

WHEN SHE'S FINISHED looking me over, Dr. Shaw signs the paperwork to clear me, and twenty minutes later, my "orientation leader" comes to get me. When the door swings open, I'm surprised to see a girl close to my age appear behind it. Her hair is chopped into a pixie cut, and she's wearing a beige uniform, smiling warmly at me.

"Laura?" she asks, hovering in the doorway.

"That's me."

Somehow, her smile gets even wider. "I'm Alexis."

I almost want to roll my eyes. She seems way too happy for someone about to show me the harsh realities of my new life trapped inside a secret underground government facility.

"I brought the clothes they issued you," she says, crossing over to me and holding out a stack of clothes the same color as her own. "I'll wait in the hall while you change, but just let me know if anything doesn't fit and I can grab you a different size."

After the door clicks shut behind her, I stare down at the clothing in my hands. They're essentially just a pair of plain beige scrubs, no different than a prisoner's uniform. Well, at least they're not bright orange.

Tossing the blankets to the side, I slowly start to move my legs, shifting my seat toward the edge of the bed. My calf stings a bit as I move but seems to be in better shape than it was yesterday.

I pull the hospital gown over my head and toss it to the ground, then carefully put on the clothes Alexis brought, which

I'm happy to discover fit perfectly. When I'm fully dressed, I stare down at myself for a long moment, sighing. Grace would probably gag at how drab the whole uniform looks, but I'm just grateful that it's comfortable.

"I'm ready," I call through the door. Alexis comes back in, this time holding a pair of crutches.

"Dr. Shaw said you might want these."

"Thanks," I reply, taking them from her. I place one under each arm, the movement already familiar from when I twisted my ankle while running from the bald man and had to use crutches for a few days. I slowly shift weight onto my right foot, using the crutches for balance as I stand.

"Take your time getting used to them if you need to. Whenever you're ready, we can get started," Alexis says.

"I'm ready."

"Alright, then!" she cheers with a clap of her hands.

This time, I do roll my eyes.

Alexis holds the door for me as I limp out into the hallway. Just outside of it, there are two guards standing at attention, but they don't say anything as we pass by. They simply fall into step behind us, keeping a watchful eye on our backs. Alexis leads me down the hallway, slowing her pace to match mine. My muscles are stiff after lying in bed for so long, and it takes me a minute to get into a good rhythm.

"So you're an anomaly, too, then?" I ask.

She nods. "I've been here since I was nine."

Nine. I look her up and down, trying to guess how old she is. Nineteen? Twenty? That means she's been here for what? At least ten years?

"They didn't let you leave?" I ask.

"I didn't want to." The words almost make me stumble. "After I graduated, they offered me a job helping new arrivals adjust and tutoring some of the students," she explains.

I frown. "And you didn't want to go back to your family? Your life?"

Alexis just shrugs. "This is my life now."

Before I can formulate a response, we reach the end of the hallway, then head through the lobby toward the elevators. I take mental notes as Alexis places her palm on a scanner just beside them before pressing the button to go down. Since it isn't a badge or ID card that lets you call the elevators, if I want to escape, I'll have to convince someone who has access to help me.

"Besides," Alexis says as the doors slide open. "You'll like it here. Just wait and see."

CHAPTER 7

THE FIRST FLOOR ALEXIS shows me, the lowest one on the elevator panel, is essentially a recreation center. It's set up similarly to the floor we just came from: a main lobby—this one with lockers lining the walls—with a guard shack right in the center, and four hallways branching off of it in different directions. One leads to the basketball courts, another to a track that surrounds a weight and exercise room, the third to a pool, and the fourth to a series of small conference rooms for studying or working on group projects.

Surprisingly, it doesn't suck. The whole place reminds me of the pictures Grace showed me after touring a college last summer. It's smaller, of course, and the lack of windows makes it feel a little claustrophobic, but the facilities are nice.

And full of echoes.

Even though the floor is pretty empty right now, in almost every room Alexis shows me, noise from the past lingers. Shoes thumping along the track. Balls bouncing across the basketball courts. Water splashing in the pool. The mix of voices and activity bustling around me seems strange considering we've only seen one group of students. The class was on one of the basketball courts, dressed in identical gym uniforms and playing some kind of kickball game. I'd craned my neck through the window, hoping I might spot someone I know, but Alexis had tugged me along before I could make out any faces.

Now, I follow her back toward the elevators.

"Each block gets access to this floor at different times of the day, and it alternates each week," Alexis says. She holds her hand up to the palm scanner. "You're in Block A, so this week, you get access between lunch and dinner. Which means," she glances down at the schedule in her hands, "you'll be able to hang out here during your free period. Which is right before dinner."

"Great," I reply without a hint of enthusiasm. The elevator's doors open, and I shuffle into it, sighing as I lean against the back wall. My arms are already tiring from carrying my weight on the crutches, and I can feel the cuts under my bandaged hands starting to get warm. "How many more floors do you have to show me?"

"Just two," Alexis tells me. She glances at her watch. "We should finish up right before your next class, too."

Oh, goodie.

The next floor up consists of the dormitories and cafeteria. And this floor, unlike the others, is split into two sides by a wall that runs down the center, right between the two elevators. Block A on the left and Block B on the right, each with separate hallways for the male and female dorms.

The cafeteria is at the back of the lobby, and although the food serving area is closed off, there are a couple students sitting at the lunch tables, reading or working on assignments. Alexis explains that everyone has one free period a day, and during it they can hang out here, at the media center, in the gym, or anywhere else they have access to during that time period.

Next, she shows me to my room, a small space with a bunk bed, two desks and chairs, and a closet at the back wall. All of the furniture is plain, and there aren't any decorations or personal items lying around. In fact, the only sign that someone else is living here is that the bottom bunk's sheets are pulled back rather than neatly tucked. Everything else just reminds me of a dorm room before a college student has moved in and made it their own.

It's better than the prison cell I'd been imagining, though. So at least there's that.

And then we're on to the last floor—the classrooms and media center. This floor is split in half just like the last one, except here, there's one room that both sides have access to: the media center. It's surprisingly large, with various study nooks and group tables alongside multiple rows of bookstacks, and there are doors on either side that automatically open and close depending on which block has access to the center at that time.

True to her word, by the time Alexis finishes walking me through my class schedule, a bell rings and the hallway starts to fill with noise. Voices echo through the space around me, past and present, and as they amplify, my stomach churns. It's been weeks since I've been to school, but I'm instantly transported back, right into those wide, echoing halls.

"Laura? Are you okay?" Alexis's voice draws my attention through the noise. She's standing in front of a locker, holding out a stack of books.

I swallow, taking them from her. "Yeah," I manage. "It's just… loud."

"They're changing periods right now, but everyone's going to be back in class in a few minutes," she assures me. She gestures for me to follow her, but I don't think she understands. I don't think she knows what my ability is.

I take a deep breath, steeling myself. I've done this before. I did it for over a year, and I survived. It sucks, but I know I can figure out how to tune the noise out.

And this is the ACA. They know about anomalies, know that I have this ability. It won't seem crazy to them if I ask for a break from the noise no one else can hear.

At least that's one good thing.

CLASS DRAGS ON, the hands of the clock hanging above Mr. Sutton's head inching forward in slow motion. His voice and the echoes of his voice from previous years all blur together as I stare at the second hand circling and circling and circling. Third period is right before lunch, but I could feel my stomach starting to grumble halfway through second period. Maybe I should've eaten the mushy scrambled eggs after all.

I lean forward, resting my elbows on the desk, my leg bouncing in place. Mr. Sutton drones on, and I spot a few of the other students—none of whom I recognize—resting their heads in their palms or staring at the clock, too.

It all feels so… normal. So *wrong*. Right now I should be escaping, or finding a way to stop Alice, or looking for Maverick. Where is he? In a classroom just like me? Or does Alice still have him locked in a room somewhere while she once again manipulates his memories?

The thought puts me even more on edge. If she makes him forget again, I don't have a way to fix it. I'd used the only syringe I'd managed to get a hold of to save his life, and now, I have nothing.

And instead of looking for him or attempting to convince Neil of what Alice has been doing so the ACA can stop her, I'm sitting in an economics class with a bunch of other anomalies, listening to a lecture about supply and demand.

It feels like some kind of sick torture.

When the bell finally rings and students begin to gather their things and stand up from their desks, I join them, closing my still empty notebook and stacking all of my books into a pile. I shuffle into the crowd, getting lost in the bodies and the noise that forms walls around me.

Out in the hallway, I head for my locker, where I stare at the keypad for too long, trying to remember the code Alexis gave me. What was it again? 4952? The light flashes red. 4295? That doesn't work either. 4592?

The light finally flashes green, and I manage to tug the door open just before a voice appears behind me, making me freeze.

"Laura?"

I whip around, heart leaping into my throat as I take her in, dark curls and wide, hopeful eyes.

"Dahlia!" I exclaim, throwing my arms around her. "Oh my gosh, are you okay? Where's Brent?"

Dahlia turns her gaze across the room and I spot him stuffing things into a locker. A sigh rushes past my lips.

"You don't know how glad I am to see you guys," I say. They might not remember Alice or the truth about how we ended up here, but they remember me. And they're here.

"We're glad to see you, too," she replies. Then her eyes dart around the room, almost in awe. "This place... isn't what I expected it to be like."

A short laugh escapes me. "You're telling me."

She offers a small smile, then gestures at the elevators. "We'd better get to the cafeteria before they run out of the good stuff."

I wonder what she means by "good." If the food I'd been brought in the medical wing is any indication of what to expect, mealtimes aren't going to be very exciting. But I nod, stuffing the pile of books into my locker and closing the door. Brent joins us as we head for the elevators and shuffle in with a few other students.

When we step off on the next floor, Dahlia leans in and asks under her breath, "Have you seen any of the others?"

I shake my head. "Not yet. Have you?"

Dahlia nods. "Veronica and Maren are in the same block as us. And a few of the guys, too. But everyone else must have been placed on the other side."

"Have you seen Maverick?" The words rush out of my mouth, desperate. But Dahlia just shakes her head.

"No one has seen Maverick. Or Wyatt," she says, dropping her gaze.

A lump forms in my throat at the sound of his name. *Wyatt.* The last time I saw him flashes through my head. *Falling to his knees, surrounded by ACA guards.* We'd left him there, back at the barn. In the end, it didn't make a difference—we all got captured anyway. But the memory of his strained face, of him shouting *Run!* while he tried to maintain the illusion of darkness for as long as possible sends a jolt of pain through me.

Are Wyatt and Maverick still being kept by security? By Alice? Or were they simply placed in the other block?

When we make it to the cafeteria, we get in the lunch line. Despite the fact that Dahlia said she hadn't seen Maverick, I scan the room, searching for him. I notice Veronica sitting at a table with a couple of anomalies I don't know, and I spot the boy named Aaron I'd briefly met just a few paces ahead of me and Dahlia. I don't see Maverick, though, and my heart sinks a little.

But then my eyes land on a different familiar face.

Gabe.

He's sitting at a table by himself, already shoveling food into his mouth. The last time I'd seen him was before he left to go to the ACA—to turn us in, like we'd planned, in hopes that the ACA would show up to find Alice holding us captive and realize it was her behind everything all along.

"Oh, and *he's* here, too," Dahlia says, her eyes darkening as she notices who I'm looking at.

My eyebrows knit together for a moment, but then I realize why she's angry. She thinks Gabe is the reason we all got captured. Which is technically true, but she doesn't remember that we had planned for that. It was supposed to work in our favor, and if Alice hadn't thwarted our plan, we'd have all escaped—with our memories intact.

And that makes me wonder… does Gabe remember the truth? Or did Alice mess with his memories before anyone could hear the truth out of him, too?

Someone taps my shoulder, and I look up, realizing the line has moved several feet. I catch up, then glance back at Gabe. I want to go to him, to ask him what he remembers. But I'm all too aware of the guards stationed around the room, any of whom could be working for Alice. If they see us talking, what would they do? I don't know, but luckily, with Gabe, talking isn't the only way to communicate.

Gabe. Can you hear me? I think the words pointedly, hoping this cafeteria doesn't have too many other thoughts swirling around, drowning out my own. *It's me, Laura. I need to know if you remember the truth.*

To my surprise, Gabe's eyes lift, landing on me. Hope bubbles in my chest; he can hear me.

Alice ruined our plans. You remember who Alice is, right?

I hold his gaze for a long moment, waiting. If Gabe remembers the truth, we can work together. He might be able to listen in and find out the best escape route, and together, we can get out.

But then he frowns, and my heart sinks. He drops his head, shaking it. Then he stands, picks up his already empty tray, and turns his back to me as he goes to put it away. Without another glance, he disappears around the corner toward the men's dorms.

Distantly, I recognize the person behind me nudging me to move up in line again, but I can't move. I stand there, frozen, staring at the corner Gabe disappeared behind.

Alice must have gotten to him, too. He probably believes he really did leave our group and turn us over to the ACA. He doesn't remember Alice at all.

I squeeze my eyes shut, trying to block it out, but the feeling of walls closing in around me only intensifies.

If she got to Gabe, then she's going to get to Maverick, too.

Which means I'm completely alone.

CHAPTER 8

THE REST OF THE DAY fades into a blur. I slip in with the crowd of anomalies, wordlessly attending my classes and trying my best to tune out the echoes surrounding me. During my free period, I head for the study rooms on the bottom floor and find a nice, relatively quiet corner to sit in, where I blankly stare down at my growing pile of assignments for too long.

Everything about this place feels odd. It reminds me too much of high school, of my life before finding out that I was an anomaly. At that time, I'd been so focused on hiding my ability, on trying to fit in with normal society.

But this isn't normal society; everyone here is an anomaly. Alexis told me there are currently eighty-eight anomalies here, and yet, no one I've spoken to has mentioned anything about their abilities. Everyone just seems to be going about their life like nothing's wrong. Like it's completely normal to be stuck inside a boarding school run by a secret government institution trying to hide the existence of anomalies from the rest of the world.

But it's not. And there are so many of us—we could take down the ACA. We could get out of here and go back to our normal lives. Angelo, Maverick, Wyatt, and Dahlia already managed to sneak in and out of this place unnoticed, and we could totally do it again. Angelo could easily hack the hand scanners, and Maverick and Wyatt by themselves could keep anyone from stopping us. I don't know what other abilities might be in our midst, but I'm certain there are plenty more that would just make it easier.

So why hasn't anyone tried to leave? Why is everyone just living their lives, going to classes, making friends, and acting like it's okay for the ACA to keep us here as prisoners?

The bell rings to signal the end of my free period, and I snap my books closed and head for the lobby. As I shuffle into the elevator, I search for familiar faces, but I don't see Dahlia or Gabe here. I'm starting to recognize some of the classmates I've been seeing more frequently—they're in my grade and we have similar schedules—but I don't say anything to them.

When the elevator doors open, we pool into the cafeteria. After getting a tray of what looks like lasagna and some mushy vegetables, I sit at the table near the back I'd shared with Dahlia during lunch. But a few minutes later, when someone plops their tray down across from me, it isn't her.

Instead, it's a girl, probably around Dahlia's age, but she's several inches taller and a pair of glasses frames her face. Her bright red hair reminds me of Leo.

She extends a hand, flashing a warm smile. "I'm Georgia! You're Laura, right? We're roommates!"

I shake her hand, nodding. "Alexis mentioned you earlier when she showed me the room."

"Don't worry," Georgia says, finally taking a seat. "I already switched out our bedding. Alexis told me you wouldn't be able to climb to the top bunk." Her gaze flicks to the crutches resting against the edge of the table, then back to me. "I tore my ACL a few months ago and had to be on crutches for a week, so I understand how bad it sucks."

"I sprained my ankle not that long ago, too," I reply. I leave out the part about how it was because I'd been chased by a man with multiple abilities in the pouring rain after he caused our car to crash, though. "It was not fun."

Georgia picks up her fork and turns her attention to the sad excuse for lasagna, poking at it like it's a lab specimen. "How'd you get hurt this time?"

"I got shot."

Georgia's eyes widen, her gaze lifting from her tray to mine again. Her voice drops several notches, and I can barely hear her over the cafeteria noise when she asks, "Like, with a gun?"

I bite my lip, holding in the sarcastic reply forming on my tongue. *No, a paintball left me in crutches.* But I might not want to start off on bad terms with the person I'm going to be living with, so instead, I just nod.

Georgia leans forward, intrigued. "Were you hunting, or something?"

"*Being* hunted," I reply. "By this lovely organization I'm now trapped in."

Georgia's face pales, and she drops her attention back to her food. She glances up a few seconds later, her gaze skirting the edges of the room, hesitating on the guards stationed near each corner.

Right. We're under constant surveillance, and I should probably be more careful about what I say.

"How long have you been here?" I change the subject, hoping to ease the tension.

Georgia relaxes, but doesn't meet my eyes as she responds. "A little over four years."

"Wow. That's... a while."

She just shrugs. "Honestly, it doesn't even feel like it's been that long. I'm just glad I'll be able to get out before my junior year. Mr. Hammond is letting me practice during my free period so I can hopefully make the swim team once I go back to school."

Swim team. School. Her words echo in my head, so strange and out of place in this underground cafeteria. After everything that has happened with Alice, none of it makes any sense.

"So they didn't let you out after your first year? Why?" I ask.

Georgia's eyebrows pull down. "No one gets out after a year. That's just when they do your evaluation, let you know if you're eligible yet."

So Russell was sugarcoating it when he mentioned it would be a year. "How long do you have to wait after that?"

"Depends on the person, but usually another four years. Everyone has to be here at least five years. And for some, it's longer."

My gut twists like I've just been punched. A year was bad enough, but *five?* I might suffocate.

"You're a senior, right?" Georgia asks when I don't say anything for a minute.

I nod, picking up my fork to push what vaguely resembles a green bean around on my tray.

"So you'll have to do all of your college from here," she says, eyes full of pity. "That bites. You'll miss out on the whole college experience."

I just shrug. I'm not planning on being stuck in here for that long, but I don't tell her that.

"I mean, we could throw a rager in the dorms to show you what it would be like," Georgia goes on. "My friend managed to sneak in this old bluetooth speaker we could play music from. I think she knows a few drinking games. But we'd be missing the most essential component of a college party: the alcohol. I don't think security has ever allowed a single drop of it to enter the premises. But we could pretend, I guess."

The absurdity of Georgia's plan makes me snort out a laugh. "To be honest, I have absolutely zero interest in having any kind of *college experience,*" I tell her. "But thanks for being willing."

"So you aren't planning to go to college? What do you want to do, then?"

"Well I am planning on going to college," I reply. "Just the learning and studying parts. Not so much the partying."

Georgia's mouth tugs to the side, and she looks at me like that's the saddest thing she's ever heard. "Those are the boring parts, though."

I drop my gaze, still stirring the pile of mush on my plate mindlessly. "I just don't know if I can—"

I don't get to finish, because another tray plops down on the table, interrupting me. I glance up, and another girl slides in next to Georgia. She tosses her long dark hair over her shoulder, then looks over at me with bright brown eyes and smiles.

"I'm Katie," she says, offering a hand.

"Laura," I reply as I shake it.

"Katie is one of our suitemates," Georgia tells me.

"Whatever Georgia told you about me is a lie," Katie says instantly. She leans across the table, then gestures for me to come closer like she's about to tell me a secret. When she speaks again, her voice drops to a whisper, and at the same time, a burst of laughter bubbles up across the room, drowning out the words.

My eyes dart over Katie's shoulder to the source of the sound, where no one is laughing today. Just an echo.

Katie leans back and grins at me. Georgia slaps her on the arm. "Why would you tell her about that?" she shrieks.

I look between them. I have no clue what Katie said, but I don't want to ask her to repeat it, so I just force a smile and mutter a barely-audible, "Wow."

And it works, because then Georgia shakes her head and starts talking again. "All I said was that he's pretty cute. That doesn't mean I *like* him."

Katie crosses her arms. "Sure it doesn't."

"You're the one that's been ogling at him every meal break the past two days."

Katie throws her hands up defensively. "It's been a while since I've been on a date, okay? And he's better looking than the rest of the guys in this place."

Georgia rolls her eyes, but then replies, "He is."

They both stare off into the distance, somewhere over my shoulder. I follow their gazes, scanning the room for whoever they must be talking about. When I finally realize who they're staring at, I throw a hand over my mouth to stifle a laugh.

"Are you talking about *Gabe?*" I ask, turning back to face them.

Georgia's jaw drops. "You know him?"

I nod. "We were friends. He—" I bite my lip, trying to decide if I should tell them what his ability is. I wonder if he's even listening to anything we're thinking, especially after the way he'd so abruptly left at lunch when I'd tried to get his attention. After a moment of hesitation, I settle on, "He's gay."

Katie slumps back in her seat. "No…"

"Yeah…"

Georgia buries her face into her hands. Katie starts to laugh.

"I guess that's the end of that, then," Katie says.

Georgia shakes her head, joining in on the laughter. "I guess so."

"Doesn't mean we can't admire him, though."

Katie and Georgia dissolve into laughter. I decide I'm definitely *not* going to tell them what his ability is, then. He'd enjoy listening to the praise.

After we finish eating—or pushing the food around on our trays until it looks like we've eaten, rather—Katie and Georgia invite me to come hang out with them in the gym. We have free time for the rest of the evening, and our block gets access to the recreation floor between 7:00 and 8:30. But I refuse, patting my crutches and telling them I should really rest my leg. It's true, but it's equally true that I'd rather be alone, somewhere quiet.

Luckily, our dorm room is just that. There are minimal echoes, and as I sit down at the empty desk, spreading the textbooks and worksheets I'd been given today across it, I sigh in relief. For the first time all day, I feel like I can focus.

I stare down at the pre-calculus worksheet assigned by Mrs. Brigs, letters and numbers dancing across the page. Beside it is a packet of my assigned readings for English. I apparently have some catching up to do.

But none of that is important. I slide the schoolwork to the side, then tear several blank pages out of my notebook. I spread them out in front of me, jotting notes on one, sketching the layout of the ACA on another. I write down the names of all the people I've met, make notes about whether I think they're working with Alice or not.

And, for the rest of the evening, I attempt to plot my escape.

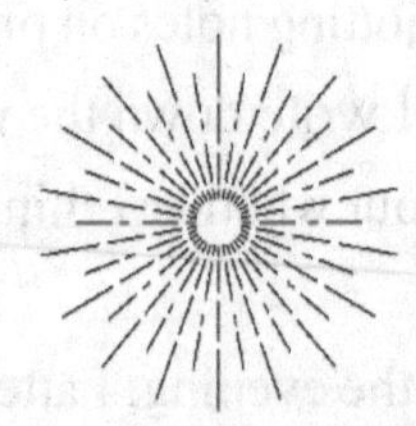

CHAPTER 9

A BELL JINGLES FROM somewhere nearby, jerking me into awareness. Across the room, a door swings open and two figures slip through. The bells attached to the handle jingle again as it shuts, and I frown at them.

Where am I?

I shift my gaze to the counter on my right, taking in the glass display case with tubs of ice cream inside, then to the menu hanging on the wall behind it, and I suddenly recognize the place. *Coffee and Cream.* The little ice cream and coffee shop in downtown Shorewick.

Is this a dream?

"What can I get for you today?" someone asks from behind the counter. A girl in an apron and pink hat bearing the *Coffee and Cream* logo emerges, and I realize I know her. It's the same girl who recognized me and knew my usual order even though I thought I'd never been here before. The one I'd asked about Maverick when I still didn't know who he was or why I couldn't remember him. *Elle.*

Across from Elle, one of the two figures leans over the glass display case, searching. "Do you have cookie dough? Yes! I'll take a scoop of that. On a waffle cone."

I watch as Elle scoops the ice cream, trying to figure out why this voice sounds familiar, too. Then, as she's lifting the cone over the counter to hand it to the customer and I finally take a good look at the girl with dark, wavy hair wearing a gray hoodie, I freeze.

Me.

It's me, at the counter. I'm watching *myself*. Which means that the figure standing next to me must be…

"I think I'll get a hot chocolate," Maverick's warm voice says.

"Whipped cream?" Elle asks.

"That would be great."

"What he means to say is that he wants more whipped cream than hot chocolate," the other version of me adds—the version of me that's there, with Maverick in the coffee shop, while I stand in the shadows watching. Is this an echo? A memory I'd lost?

"*Extra* whipped cream. Got it," Elle replies with a wink, then turns to the counter behind her.

The echo-Maverick turns to the echo-me, one eyebrow raised.

"What?" my echo asks, grinning up at him. "Don't pretend like that's not how you prefer it."

He shakes his head, laughing softly. "Oh, it is. I just didn't realize we'd crossed the line of ordering for each other yet."

The echo-me rolls her eyes, bumping him in the arm. "I didn't order for you. I just *clarified*."

"Ah, right. *Very* different," Maverick replies with a smirk, bumping the echo-me back.

I watch from a distance as they wait at the counter, the past versions of me and Maverick, smiling and unaware of me in the corner. This must have been the first time we'd come to this ice cream shop. Maverick told me we eventually became regulars— that's why Elle recognized me when I stumbled in here that evening after being chased.

"Whipped cream with a side of hot chocolate, here you go," Elle says, handing a foam cup to Maverick. "Can I get you guys anything else?"

"No, I think we're good," Maverick replies, pulling out his wallet.

As he pays, the echo-me wanders over to the other side of the coffee shop, picking a seat at the long table in front of the window with a view of main street. I follow her, stopping at the opposite end of the coffee shop where I can watch from an angle. The rest of the room is empty except for a mom and two young kids huddled in the back, finishing off the last bits of their cones.

Outside, the sidewalk is littered with a few stray leaves, skittering in the wind. It's bright, probably around mid-afternoon, and the street is busy with cars and people window shopping at the downtown businesses. The echo-me bites into her ice cream cone and closes her eyes, savoring the taste.

"Is it good?" Maverick asks, slipping into the chair next to the echo-me and throwing a lazy arm around her shoulders.

"It's actually *really* good. Like ridiculously good."

"Really?"

"I'd offer you a taste, but I kind of want it all to myself."

Maverick chuckles, letting his arm drop as he leans forward and takes a long swig from his cup. "Mmm. The hot chocolate is pretty good, too."

"Not as good as this ice cream," the echo-me says, mouth already full with another bite. "I think my lifelong quest of finding the best cookie dough ice cream in the world is over. This is it."

Maverick leans back, an amused smile playing on his lips. "Really?"

"I will never eat another brand again," the echo-me replies, going serious.

Maverick's eyebrows lift. "This just in, citizens of Shorewick," he says, bringing his fist to his mouth like a microphone and fluctuating his voice to sound like a news reporter. "Local teen claims downtown ice cream shop has the *best* cookie dough ice cream in the *entire world*. Yes, you heard that right. No need to travel to Italy or France to find it. It's right here in your own backyard!"

The two echoes of me and Maverick dissolve into laughter, and even from several feet and so much time away, I find myself smiling.

"I don't know if you're hilarious or just crazy," the echo-me laughs.

"Who says I can't be both?"

They both laugh again, softer this time. And then something changes in my echo's face. Her eyes drop, and the smile fades.

Maverick's eyebrows pull together in concern. "What's wrong?"

The echo-me squeezes her eyes shut. "I'm sorry about last night."

"What do you have to be sorry about?"

"Freaking out. Leaving the movie early. I just…" she trails off, wincing.

Maverick shakes his head, lifting his hand to tuck a stray piece of hair behind my echo's ear. "Laura, you don't owe me an explanation."

"I feel like I do. I ruined the date."

"You didn't ruin anything."

"I know how bad you wanted to see the new *Space Phaser* movie, though. And we didn't even make it halfway—"

"I wanted to see *you*," Maverick says firmly.

My echo opens her eyes, meeting Maverick's gaze. In an instant, the night they're talking about flashes through my head.

Going to dinner with Maverick. Grinning, laughing, having a magical time. Then the movie, the noisy lobby, and the echoes. The sounds of tonight's movie and last year's movie and all the movies playing in the years before, thundering in my ears, pounding against my skull. I run to the bathroom, try to breathe through it. But I can't get myself to go back into the theater. I can't handle it.

I text Maverick. Tell him my parents will come pick me up and he should enjoy the movie. But he finds me in the lobby instead, asks if I'm okay. I burst into tears.

Because how can I keep doing this? Trying to be normal, pretending I can do normal things. How can I date someone and go to school and have friends and exist with all of this past noise clogging up my brain?

Maverick probably thinks I'm crazy. I should tell him I can't be with him. I should tell him to leave me. I should tell him the truth, but I can't. I don't want to.

I like him. I feel something for him, something new and bright. If I tell him the truth, he'll think I'm crazy. But if I don't, he'll probably still think I'm crazy.

He should just leave me here. Put an end to this.

But instead, he wraps his arms around me. Holds me until the tears slow.

"Let's get out of here," he whispers. And I let him pull me up, walk me to the car, open the door for me. And then we just drive. Through the glimmering lights of downtown, out into nowhere, past neighborhoods and schools and in circles until we're completely lost. Until the tears dry and I forget everything. Until I'm laughing again.

"I like you, Laura," Maverick says now, in the coffee shop. He looks into my eyes, and I realize with a start that I'm no longer watching the echo-me from a distance. I *am* her. "I like spending time with you," he continues. "And I don't care if we're in a movie theater or watching something at home on the couch or just driving in circles for hours. *You* are the part that matters."

"Maybe you *are* crazy," I say.

Maverick shrugs. "Crazy for—"

"Don't even finish that sentence, you sap!" And just like that I'm grinning again. In an instant, I notice the taste of the cookie dough ice cream lingering on my tongue. I can smell the rich scent of coffee now, feel the warm air of the room on my skin.

And I feel it, crisp and real, like I'm living inside this moment, when Maverick slides his arm around me again, tugs me close. When his lips touch my temple.

And then I feel nothing.

* * * *

I OPEN MY EYES TO A dark room. Around me, things slowly start to take shape. The bunk bed above me where Georgia is probably still fast asleep, the two desks on opposite ends of the room. The clock in the corner with the numbers 5:46 displayed in glowing red.

A dream. It was a dream.

But it wasn't.

I close my eyes, replaying the echo in my head, trying to hold on to every second of it.

It was a memory. Like the echoes that have flashed through my head whenever Alice has tried to steal my memories. Sometimes I'm in the echo, experiencing the memory firsthand, but this time, I was simply watching it happen from a distance.

Except for the end. I bring my fingers to my temple, where I can still feel the echo of Maverick's lips on my skin.

I remembered him. Just this one small moment, this tiny piece of the puzzle when there are thousands still missing. But it's something, and it wasn't just an echo. For a moment I was there, with him, in the coffee shop. I was the *me* before I lost my memories.

And there was something there. A warmth, a hope. A burning in my chest. And a fear, too. That things wouldn't work out between us. That I'd lose Maverick.

It isn't much different from how I feel right now.

Because I have no idea where Maverick is. And I'm terrified of what Alice could be doing to him.

CHAPTER 10

LATER THAT MORNING, two guards come for me just as Georgia and I are leaving the suite for breakfast. They meet us outside the door, one of them pushing a wheelchair. The other tells me that it's time for me to go to the medical wing to get checked out by Dr. Shaw, then gestures for me to sit.

"I'll walk," I say firmly. I wave at Georgia. "I'll see you in class."

She waves back, and I follow the guards, the rubber soles of my crutches squeaking on the tile floor as I limp along with them.

Wordlessly, they take me through the double doors and up the elevator to the medical wing. As we move, I discreetly try to take in more of my surroundings so I can add to the maps I've started drawing. I look for signs, people, anything that will tell me what the hallways I haven't been on are used for. I scan each door we pass, wondering if there's a way out behind one of them. Right now, the only way up and out of this place that I know of is the elevators, but there's got to be an emergency stairwell somewhere in this place, too, right?

The guards lead me into the room across the hall from the one I'd woken up in two days ago. It's similar to the other one but looks more like a doctor's office than a hospital room. There's a medical exam table instead of a bed, and a significantly less number of devices hung on the walls and piled in the corners. Before the guards can even exit the room, Dr. Shaw appears in the doorway.

"Good morning, Miss Jones," she says, smiling at me. She steps past me, patting the exam table. "Have a seat. How are you feeling today?"

"Oh, lovely," I deadpan, carefully pulling myself onto the table, then stretching out my legs.

Dr. Shaw crosses over to wash her hands, then comes back over to me, getting to work taking my vitals.

"How are you adjusting?" she asks as she pulls the thermometer out of my mouth.

"You mean to being in prison?" I scoff. "Real great."

"I assure you, Miss Jones, this place is far better than any prison."

"I'm pretty sure the food isn't."

Dr. Shaw lets out a small chuckle. "Touché." She puts the thermometer away, then gets to work tugging my pant leg up to expose my calf. "How's your leg feeling?"

"Better, I guess."

"Good." She starts unraveling the bandage—which stings a little bit, so I grit my teeth. "It's healing up nice, no signs of infection. You're lucky."

"Oh, I'm *so* lucky. I got shot in the leg and then locked up in a government institution for doing nothing wrong. I have the best luck ever."

Dr. Shaw shakes her head, pulling out a cream to rub over the wound. I hiss when it burns.

"I hope that the longer you're here, you'll realize that we really just want to help you."

"Ah, yes. Protect me from the crazies out there who want to experiment on me. When one of them's working for you."

Dr. Shaw swallows, then shoots me a warning look. *Right.* The cameras.

I clear my throat. "If anyone here wanted to help me, they wouldn't stick me in a classroom with a million echoes lingering everywhere. It's just as bad as public school in real life."

Dr. Shaw freezes, her wide eyes boring into mine. "What do you mean, echoes?"

"My ability," I say, and Dr. Shaw doesn't move, her attention fully grasped. "I hear echoes of the past. I can't turn it off, and they're everywhere in this place. I can't focus."

Dr. Shaw searches my face but doesn't say anything. Her eyebrows droop slightly, like she can't quite make sense of something.

"When I was in public school, I just kind of dealt with it. But since I'm here—and you guys know about my ability—can't you do something about it? Make some kind of accommodation somehow?"

Finally, a frown tugs at Dr. Shaw's lips. "You're still hearing noise from the past?"

"That's what I just said. Wait, why does that surprise you?"

Dr. Shaw drops her gaze, and I feel a knot beginning to form in my stomach.

"We didn't tell you yet because of your tendency to be… difficult," she begins slowly. "But all of the anomalies brought to the ACA are required to take medication that suppresses their abilities."

The knot in my stomach twists tighter. "Suppresses their abilities?"

Dr. Shaw nods. "It isn't a permanent solution, but as long as subjects continue to take the medication regularly, it inhibits the mutation responsible for anomalous behavioral patterns. Everyone is required to be on it before they can be placed in rehabilitation with the others."

I just stare at her, puzzling the pieces together. It all suddenly makes so much sense—why the ACA lets the anomalies all live together and doesn't seem worried about them trying to escape. Why no one has even tried.

And it explains why Gabe didn't respond to me in the cafeteria. His ability is being suppressed. He can't hear people's thoughts anymore. But still, why didn't he even acknowledge my presence in some way? Was he just being cautious? Or did Alice replace his memories, too?

I lift my gaze to Dr. Shaw, the knot in my stomach shifting into something fiery hot. "You told me they were just painkillers."

"They were," Dr. Shaw nods. "The pills I gave you *were* just painkillers. The suppressing agent can only be given intravenously, once every two weeks. We put it in your IV. You've been on the meds for over twenty-four hours now, so they should have started working…"

My hands ball into fists, angry. They gave me this medication without me even knowing about it. And Alice…

My blood runs cold. Alice had come to my room shortly after I woke up, and she'd tried to take my memories again. The moment flashes through my head, bringing a new wave of terror.

If my ability had been suppressed, if the medication *did* work on me, I might not have been able to resist her. I might have lost all of my memories, ones that I'd barely managed to hang on to in the first place. I might have completely lost touch with the truth and ended up as just another oblivious member of the ACA. I wouldn't know anything about Alice.

The thought fills me with horror, but seeing Dr. Shaw's puzzled expression brings another thought, too.

"But they aren't working," I say, the anger slipping out of my tone.

Dr. Shaw just stares at me, and I can almost see the cogs turning in her head. "I'm going to need to run some tests," she says.

I swallow, thoughts racing through my head, too. Why wouldn't the suppressors work on me, when they work on everyone else here? Does it have something to do with the fact that Alice couldn't erase my memories?

You're different, Laura. You aren't like the rest of them.

Her voice from back in the barn before she'd attempted to take my memories away echoes through my head. What did she mean? Is it my ability? Does it work differently than everyone else's, and that's why the suppressors don't work on me?

Dr. Shaw clears her throat, going back to re-wrapping my leg. "In the meantime, you won't be allowed to go back to your room until we figure out what's going on."

I wince at the thought of being stuck in a medical room for an entire day again. "Why can't I? My ability is *hearing echoes of the past*. It's not like I can do anything that hurts anybody."

Dr. Shaw heads to the counter, where she starts to remove her gloves. "It's just policy. I'm sorry."

I sigh, frustrated. As I wait for Dr. Shaw to finish jotting notes onto her clipboard, my mind whirls around this new piece of information.

The ACA is giving all of the anomalies medication that suppresses their abilities. That's why they've set everything up almost like a rehabilitation center—they bring anomalies in, monitor them for a period of time, convince them to keep taking the suppressors, and then, if they oblige, let them go back to their normal lives with regular check-ins. They're treating anomalies as if we're ill, as if having an ability is some kind of sickness that needs to be cured.

Isn't it a sickness, though? For my entire life, I've wished that I didn't have to hear echoes all the time. I've wished that I could just live a regular life and not have to deal with always hiding such a big part of me. And so many of the other anomalies I've met have struggled with their abilities.

Gabe once hinted at the fact that he couldn't enjoy being in a relationship with anyone because he hears their constant thoughts. Maverick accidentally erased his father's memories of him when he was younger. Veronica told me she can't ever tell if people genuinely care about her or if somehow she has unknowingly manipulated them into feeling that way.

What would their lives be like if they didn't have to deal with their abilities? What if it *is* a sickness that can be cured? How would their lives change?

Dr. Shaw turns to me, holding a small flashlight. "Let me just check one more thing before I leave," she says. She leans close, shining the light into my eye. "Look up," she instructs, and I do. At the same time, I feel her hand brush against mine, which is resting on the table. In a flash of a moment, she slips something into my palm, then moves the light to my other eye, leaning back slightly.

"What—" I begin, but Dr. Shaw shoots me a glare. It's the same look from before, like there's something she's trying to communicate discreetly. Then her eyes flick up into the corner, just for a flash of a moment, and I snap my mouth shut. She doesn't want whoever is watching to know about this.

I tighten my hand around the object, pretending it isn't there.

Dr. Shaw flicks the flashlight off, then turns her back to me, jotting something else on the clipboard. When she turns around, her expression is neutral, like nothing happened.

"Just wait here for now. Someone will come to get you once we've cleared this up."

And then she's out the door, and I'm left alone, clutching my fist around an unknown object.

After waiting a couple minutes so I don't look suspicious, I slowly unravel my fingers, keeping my hand low by my side out of view of the camera. In the palm of my hand is a rolled up piece of paper, and slowly, I manage to open it up. When I start to read, my eyes widen.

Wait 25 minutes, then meet me in the supply closet. Make a right, it's the 2nd door on the left. Do NOT try to go anywhere else, or we'll both be in trouble.

CHAPTER 11

MY HEART POUNDS AS I stare at the door, waiting. Counting.

Has it been twenty-five minutes? I don't know. There's no clock in this room, and what if I'm counting too fast? Too slow? What if I open the door and guards are standing in the hallway? They'd stop me in my tracks, and what if I don't get to talk to Dr. Shaw? What does she even want to tell me, anyway?

I suck in a deep breath and let it out slowly. Maybe she wants to help. She seemed surprised by the fact that my ability is still working despite the medication they gave me, but why would that make her want to meet with me in secret?

I don't know. But I won't find out if I just keep standing here, staring at the door.

So I tug the handle.

To my relief, the hallway is empty. There are cameras in all the rooms, and I'm certain there are some in the hallways, too, but maybe that's what Dr. Shaw was taking care of when she left. Maybe that's why she told me to wait twenty-five minutes.

I tighten my fist around the scrap of paper, repeating the words over and over in my head so I don't forget them. *Make a right, it's the 2nd door on the left.*

It's only a few yards away. A windowless metal door, just like the rest of them. I press one hand against the wall to support my weight—I'd left the crutches behind—and limp down the hall. Then I tug it open and slip inside, holding the door handle as it closes so it doesn't make any noise.

The room is dark. I'm tempted to feel along the wall for a light switch, but I don't want to risk someone noticing. I don't want to risk anything with the ACA. Despite their front that they care about anomalies, I'd watched Maverick get shot and almost die by their hands. *I'd* almost died by their hands. I doubt they'd kill me if they found me hiding in a supply closet, but my heart pounds at the thought anyway.

Keeping my hands on the wall, I move further into the room but stop when I bump into some kind of shelving unit. "Dr. Shaw?" I dare to whisper, but I'm met with silence.

Am I too early? Has it even been twenty-five minutes yet? Or was my counting off? What if Dr. Shaw didn't have enough time to take care of the cameras, and what if the wrong person saw me wander in here? They could be sending guards after me right now, and Dr. Shaw could get caught because of it. She's the only person in this entire organization that seems like she might actually listen to me, and if she's gone, what chance do I have of convincing anyone that Alice is the bad guy?

Finally, the door behind me creaks open. I whirl around, eyes landing on the figure stepping through the crack. She reaches for a switch on the wall, and then the room floods with light.

"Oh!" Dr. Shaw jumps when she sees me. She puts a hand to her chest, breathing out the shock. "I didn't think you were here yet."

I swallow, a flush of relief coursing through me, but then the heart pounding is back. I still don't know what she wants.

Dr. Shaw turns the deadbolt on the door, then faces me again.

"We don't have much time, so I need you to listen carefully and answer all of my questions as quickly as possible."

I nod.

"I've had my suspicions about Dr. Wight for a while now, so I want to hear what you have to say about her. But we cannot speak about it outside of this room. Dr. Wight has most of our security personnel in her pocket, as well as a bunch of other staff members. If anyone suspects I'm listening to you or notices anything is off, both of our lives will be in danger. Do you understand?"

I nod again.

"I know Dr. Wight is up to something. I believe if we can figure out what's going on and take it directly to the head of the ACA, we can convince her to take action and stop Dr. Wight. But I need you to tell me everything you know."

I nod a third time, then clear my throat, my mind spinning. Where do I even start?

Apparently we don't have enough time for Dr. Shaw to let me think, because she starts asking questions before I can open my mouth. "You mentioned before that Dr. Wight is an anomaly. Is that true?"

Another nod. "She can heal. Instantly."

"Seriously?"

"It's how Maverick survived getting shot in the abdomen."

"What do you mean?"

"She figured out how to replicate anomalies' abilities. So that anyone can use them."

Dr. Shaw's eyebrows furrow. "How?"

I swallow. "I don't know. She was keeping anomalies locked up—"

"How do the replications *work*?" she clarifies.

"Some kind of injection," I reply with a shrug. "The effects are only temporary."

Dr. Shaw rubs her chin. "The empty syringe we found at the scene where you all were captured—Dr. Wight told me she was going to analyze it herself, but she never followed up. But that's what saved Maverick. That's why there was so much blood on him, but no injuries. It healed him."

"Exactly."

Without missing a beat, Dr. Shaw moves on to her next question. "You mentioned before that everything was orchestrated by Alice. What did you mean?"

"The anomalies that got captured—that the ACA thinks burned down Alice's research facility—we aren't some crazy group trying to take down the ACA. Alice framed us, made it look like everything was our fault. But we were just escaping captivity. Alice set her own lab on fire."

"Why?"

"To cover up what she was doing there?"

Dr. Shaw drums her fingers against her thigh. There isn't enough room in this supply closet to pace, but she shifts her weight back and forth on her feet as she thinks.

"What is her goal? What is she trying to accomplish?"

"I think she's the one that wants to take down the ACA."

Dr. Shaw's lips pull into a thin, concerned line. "And do what?"

"Take over the world?" I offer, a smile playing on my lips. But then it turns grim.

You showed me a different possibility, Alice had told me. *A future where anomalies aren't seen as a mistake or something that needs to be eliminated. A future where we're the ones calling the shots.*

The memory tugs at me, sending a shiver down my spine. It makes more sense now that I'm here in the ACA, now that I know they've been suppressing anomalies' abilities. The ACA does see us as a mistake, as something they need to control and regulate. We could be dangerous if allowed to exist in regular society, and that's a valid point.

But is shutting down the problem the right answer? Forcing us to take medication to suppress our abilities and then reintegrating us into normal society? It's the safe response. The practical one. But there are so many amazing and useful things we can do. Alice can heal—I'd seen her ability save Maverick's life when he was moments from death. With replications of her ability alone, how many lives could be saved?

A lot. But saving people doesn't seem to be Alice's goal. She wants power. Control.

"What do y—" I begin, but before I can finish, Dr. Shaw's watch starts beeping.

"We need to leave soon," she tells me.

"What do we do now?"

"I want to hear more about what you have to say. We'll need to find some proof and come up with a plan to expose her. But we'll have to do it in secret. No one can know."

"Okay."

"For now, you'll go back to the medical wing. I have to take your case up with security—and Dr. Wight—before you can return to the others. Once you do, though, I'm going to arrange a meeting. I'll send word somehow, but you have to pretend that none of this happened. You have to promise me you won't tell a soul."

"I promise." I agree.

"You should leave first. If anyone is in the hallway, they'll think you simply tried to escape. They'll put you back in your room, but they won't hurt you. I'll leave when it's clear so they don't spot us together."

I nod, and Dr. Shaw places a hand on my back, nudging me toward the door

"Before I go," I say, pausing as a thought sparks. I curl my fingers around the door handle but don't pull it. "When you arrange the meeting, can you bring Maverick, too? He might be able to help us. He knows more about Alice than I do."

Dr. Shaw winces. She shakes her head, then gestures for me to keep going, to leave.

My heart sinks. It had been a long shot, and I hadn't even expected any of this in the first place, so I shouldn't be too disappointed. I shrug the feeling off as I turn to face the door again. But then, as I tug it open, Dr. Shaw mutters something under her breath, and hope burrows under my skin.

"I'll see what I can do."

CHAPTER 12

I SPEND THE REST OF the day alone, cold and on edge, with nothing but the echoes to keep me company. The medical wing isn't as heavily trafficked as the classrooms or the dormitories, but twice I hear Dr. Shaw's voice speaking with patients in this room—one boy who had come down with a sore throat and a girl who had injured her knee during gym class. Dr. Shaw sounded like a school nurse, gently asking questions, offering treatment options, wanting to help the students feel better.

And now, Dr. Shaw wants to help me. If she can convince the ACA of what Alice is doing, we can put a stop to it.

And Maverick.

I'll see what I can do.

Dr. Shaw hadn't been very optimistic, but what if she does bring him?

The thought both thrills and terrifies me. The last time I saw Maverick, he'd barely gotten his memories of me back. The syringe we took from the bald man had just saved his life, and we'd barely had time to share a few words before the ACA showed up to capture us.

And now I don't know what we are to each other anymore. He'd kissed me a while back, before losing his memories, and despite not remembering him, I'd begun to trust him. But after Alice made him forget about me, we'd barely been acquaintances. He'd been hanging out with Veronica, and I'd tried my best to avoid him and get over it.

But then, when he'd gotten his memories back, the way he'd looked at me—the way he'd thrown his arms around me and held me close, so tight like he was hanging on for dear life—had brought those feelings back. Had made me want to be close to him and get to know him again.

So what are we now? Do we just go back to the way things were before he'd lost his memories of me? Will we be together? Or will it be too weird? What if he still has feelings for Veronica?

I'm anxious and excited to see him again, but at the same time, I'm also terrified. Because none of it will matter if Alice has twisted his memories again. He won't remember me or what we were, and he won't be relieved or happy to see me. He'll just be really, really confused.

And I don't know if I can bear seeing him like that again.

✳ ✳ ✳

THEY DON'T LET ME GO until after dinner. Dr. Shaw drops by, explains that I'll have to be brought in for some additional testing at some point but that my ability poses little threat to security. She tells me that they'll do their best to make accommodations so that I can still participate in classes, and then a guard escorts me back to the dormitories.

I've already eaten dinner, and I've got free time for the rest of the evening, so I decide that maybe I'll try and get some schoolwork done. Or some more escape plotting.

I head for my room, the quietest spot I know of in the ACA, but when I get there, it isn't very quiet anymore. In the corner, I can hear echoes of music playing from a tinny speaker and three distinct voices chatting—Georgia, Katie, and a third person I don't recognize.

"*I can't believe you got away with this!*" Katie's echo exclaims. The room fills with giggles.

"*I can't believe I didn't think to do it until now,*" the voice I don't recognize says. Then I hear the crinkling sound of a bag of chips being opened. "*Come on, Georgia, I know ranch is your favorite flavor.*"

"*What if somebody finds out what you did?*" Georgia's nervous echo replies.

"*What are they gonna do? Put me in isolation? For stealing snacks from the staff's vending machine? Come on.*"

"*There's no way they're going to know it was Penny, anyway,*" Katie's echo adds.

"*Unless they check the cameras that are literally in every hallway of this place.*" I can almost hear the glare in Georgia's voice.

"No one ever checks the footage," the voice—Penny—says. *"Half the time, there aren't even any guards in those shacks. I've checked a couple of times."*

"It's true," Katie agrees. *"And even if they do, you won't be on the footage, so eating a bag isn't going to hurt you."*

There's a moment of hesitation, but then a bag of chips crinkles from Georgia's direction, followed by the sound of a chip crunching between teeth.

Then Katie's echo launches into some theory about the personal life of one of their teachers, and I let out a steady breath. I tuck that bit of information about the guards—from a year ago, so I don't know how reliable it is now—away, then rub the bridge of my nose. The music playing, the conversation—it's not going to be great for getting anything done. I need to find somewhere quiet where I can focus.

I gather my books, tucking them under my arm, then take a few steps, testing how it feels to put weight on my leg. It doesn't hurt too bad, so I ditch the crutches and head out into the hallway. As I pass through the double doors, I spot a couple groups of students lingering in the cafeteria, just passing the time by hanging out. The room is full of noise there, too, so I turn for the elevators. I check my schedule, then take the elevator up a floor to the media center, which my block has access to until 8:30 today.

Even in the media center, there are several students mulling about. Most of them are studying quietly on their own, but a few groups are gathered, talking softly amongst themselves. It isn't complete silence like I want, but even so, it's much quieter here.

I scan the room, searching for a place to sit. In addition to the desks and tables littered across the central area and between bookstacks, there are study nooks built into the outer walls of the room, each with a divider separating them from each other. They aren't as good as private study rooms, but they create semi-secluded spaces for students to study, which is as good as I'm going to get in this place.

I head for the back of the room, spotting a nook that's tucked into a corner as far away from the main area as possible. I don't notice that it's already occupied until I make it around the corner and a figure hunched over the desk comes into view. I stop in my tracks, then back up, already scanning the wall ahead for a different nook. But then I do a double take.

"Gabe?" His name passes my lips as barely a whisper, but he turns his head at the sound of it, his gaze landing on me. His eyes widen for a flicker of a moment, then darken.

"What do you want?" The clipped edge of his tone almost sounds like a warning.

"I don't—"

"If you're going to go off on me about the whole betrayal thing, save it," he cuts me off. "I've already heard it, and you don't know what you're talking about."

I frown. "*Betrayal* thing?"

He meets my eyes. "I know you're mad because you think I betrayed you and turned everyone in to the ACA. That's not what really happened, but I'm not going to argue with you about it, because it's not going to get us anywhere." When he finishes, he slams the book in front of him closed and starts to gather his belongings. "You can have this spot. I'm not dealing with this today."

As he moves, I just stand there, staring at him with wide eyes. I turn the words over in my head, trying to make sense of them. *That's not what really happened.*

When Gabe starts to shove past me, I grab his arm to stop him. Two words, saturated with disbelief, barely make it past my lips. But they stop Gabe in his tracks. "You remember?"

His eyes flick back and forth between mine. "Wait. *You* remember?"

We blink at each other.

"Alice did this," I finally say, voice dropping to a whisper. "Our plan to stop her—it didn't work."

"You remember." It isn't a question this time. Gabe backs away, drops his things on the desk, then sinks back into the chair, running a hand over his face. "I'm not going crazy."

I sigh, too, stepping into the small space of the study nook. I drop my things beside me and lean against the wall, sinking to the floor across from him.

Gabe still remembers. Which means that Alice hasn't messed with his memories.

But why? I'm sure Gabe has been thoroughly interrogated about the situation, and it might be a red flag if he changed his story out of the blue. But Alice has a bunch of staff working for her, so I doubt it would be hard to cover up.

Maybe she doesn't want anyone knowing she's actually capable of twisting memories—that would just prove our claims to be true. So does that mean Maverick's memories are safe, too?

"You're going to have to tell me what you're thinking from now on," Gabe says, and I jerk my gaze up to find him staring at me intently. "Reading minds is a little harder without the built-in radio in my head tuned to everyone else's frequencies."

A smile tugs at my lips. "I was just thinking about what my new roommate said about you yesterday," I tell him. "But I guess you'll never know the details."

Gabe folds his arms across his chest, frowning. "Rude."

"It's time you start learning what it's like for the rest of us," I wink.

He laughs softly, but the smile fades quickly. "What happened to you all out there?"

I rub my fingers together, staring at the floor. "It was all a set up. Alice must have known we were coming somehow. Dahlia was there, but no one else was. And then Alice showed up, and she—" I squeeze my eyes shut, reliving the memories. The strange, dreamlike state she'd put me in. Watching my memories disappear, then figuring out how to hold on to the echoes of them. "She didn't just erase everyone's memories. She warped them, somehow. Made everyone believe that they really *were* the rogue group of anomalies the ACA was looking for, so that when they did show up, Alice wasn't tied to it at all."

Gabe lets out a long breath. "I figured that part out when that kid—Aaron?—cornered me in the bathroom to give me a piece of his mind after everyone got here." Gabe pulls his fingers to his mouth, and I notice the cut on his bottom lip. "He was angry at me because I'm the one that went to the ACA and turned everyone in. Which, I suppose, is true, but that was part of the plan. He wouldn't even listen to me, just kept raving on about how awful I was for ruining the plans to take down the ACA."

"Wow," I sigh. "I'm sorry."

"It was even more confusing when I tried to discreetly ask Veronica about what happened in gym class. She didn't know who Alice was, and then she started accusing me of the same thing—I had betrayed everyone and it was my fault everyone got captured. I thought I was going crazy."

A realization dawns on me. "That's why you left when you saw me in the cafeteria."

He nods. "You were, like, glaring. I thought you were about to come yell at me, too."

I shake my head. "I was trying to communicate with you telepathically."

Gabe laughs, a little too loud, and then covers his mouth. We freeze, poking our heads around at the library. Luckily, no one seems to have noticed.

Gabe turns back to me, voice low. "So Alice changed everyone's memories except yours?"

"She tried to take mine, too. But my ability stopped her somehow."

Curiosity lights Gabe's features, but he doesn't inquire further. Instead, he says, "When I got here, I had to pretend like I was betraying everyone. It was the only way I could get them to listen to me. And then, when I realized what was going on, I tried to convince security of the truth, but…"

"They didn't listen to you," I finish.

He runs a hand over his face. "I didn't know what to do. I'm so glad you still remember."

"I'm glad you do, too."

Gabe sighs, leaning back in his chair. "Except now we're stuck here, and we're no closer to stopping Alice."

"Actually, we might be," I reply. Gabe meets my gaze, hopeful.

So I tell him about Dr. Shaw. That there might be a chance to fix this.

Even if it might be a long shot.

CHAPTER 13

IN THE MORNING, there's an envelope under my door with my name scribbled across it. I rip it open, unfolding the slip of paper inside.

11:30 P.M. Study Room 406.

My heart pounds at the thought of it, and only partly because I'm afraid that someone might catch us. I'm pretty sure the anticipation has more to do with whether or not I'll see Maverick.

Just like yesterday, two guards show up at my dorm as I'm heading to breakfast, then take me to the medical wing so Dr. Shaw can take my vitals and change my bandages like usual.

Neither of us mentions the note, but it hangs heavy in the air between us.

When I'm finished in the medical wing, instead of joining the regular classes with everyone else, I'm given a tablet with headphones that's hooked up to the cameras in my classrooms so that I can watch from a distance. There's even a chat box available so that I can still participate and ask questions.

So, for most of the day, I stay in the quiet of my dorm room, listening to the lectures in peace, grateful for the accommodation. It reminds me of being homeschooled, except I actually get to go spend lunch with friends, and it's nice. Before I know it, it's dinner time, so I ditch the assignment I'd been working on and head for the cafeteria.

When I set my tray down—which holds a slice of grayish meatloaf, some mashed potatoes, and a roll tonight—someone slides in across the table, and I look up to find that it's Gabe. He sighs heavily.

"I miss the personal chef at Maverick's."

I smile. "You and me both."

He shaves off a piece of the meatloaf with his fork and brings it to his mouth. Grimaces. "If you guys get back together, do you think you can convince him to let me move in permanently?"

"Honestly, I don't think you even need to ask him. Just pick a room on the other side of the house, and he'll never notice."

We both laugh at that, and then Georgia and Katie appear at the table, eyeing Gabe as they slide in on either side of me. I haven't seen him at all since last night, so they haven't officially met him yet.

"Katie, Georgia, this is my friend Gabe. Gabe, Katie and Georgia," I say, gesturing at each person as I say their name.

Gabe flashes a grin, nodding at each of them. "Very nice to meet you both."

"It's nice to meet you, too," Katie replies, grinning back. I remember our conversation at dinner two nights ago and suppress a smile.

"So how do you two know each other, anyway?" Georgia asks, pushing her tray to the side and leaning forward on her elbows, curious.

"We, uh…" I begin, but I trail off.

"Went to school together," Gabe offers.

"Oh, yeah? Where?" Katie asks.

"St. Martin," I say at the same time Gabe says, "Westview."

An awkward pause ensues.

"School band, I meant," Gabe continues, throwing me a look. "Well, district band, really. Since we were from different schools. But we went to a bunch of competitions together."

Georgia nods as if it actually makes sense. "What'd you guys play?"

"Flute."

"Trumpet." We both speak at the same time again. I shoot him a glare.

"She played the flute. I played the trumpet," Gabe clarifies. "We just sat next to each other."

Katie frowns. "The different instruments usually sit in their separate sections, though. And trumpets are on the opposite side as the flutes."

Gabe shakes his head, unfazed. "Not in Mr. Pierre's class. He put everyone in random places, said it helped with the sound distribution or something. Kind of a lunatic if you ask me."

I have to cover my mouth with my fist to keep from laughing.

Katie just raises an eyebrow doubtfully. Then she shrugs. "Well, I actually play the flute, too," she says, turning her gaze to me. "They let me bring mine here, so maybe we should duet sometime!"

"That's an amazing idea!" Gabe says, grinning again.

I scowl at him. "Too bad I didn't bring mine," I say. "Gabe has his trumpet in his room, though, so maybe you guys can play together. In fact, we still have a bit before we have to go to class. Maybe you should grab it now?"

Gabe lifts an eyebrow in challenge. "I like that idea. Except for one teeny tiny problem," he says. He makes a show of checking his surroundings, then leans across the table conspiratorially. "We've been lying to you guys. Laura and I didn't meet through school band. Actually, we're both part of a secret group dedicated to freeing anomalies, and we've come to bust you guys out."

A beat passes. Then two. I gape at him, shooting daggers with my eyes. Why would he say something like that?

But then Katie throws her head back and laughs. Slowly, Georgia starts to chuckle, too. "Now I don't even know what to believe," Katie says.

"I prefer it that way," Gabe replies with a wink.

Shaking my head at the absurdity of this conversation, I turn my attention back to my food. I take a bite of the mashed potatoes—bland—then move on to the roll, which is pleasantly not awful. Gabe puts Georgia and Katie on the edges of their seats with some story about the time he went skydiving—which could be another tall tale—and I half-listen, debating whether I even want to try the meatloaf.

And then an echo catches my attention.

"I'm Georgia! You're Laura, right? We're roommates!"

Her voice comes from across the table, and I snap my gaze to the empty space beside Gabe, confused.

Then, to my surprise, I hear my own voice reply, *"Alexis mentioned you earlier when she showed me the room."*

"Don't worry, I already switched out our bedding. Alexis told me you wouldn't be able to climb to the top bunk." A pause. *"I tore my ACL a few months ago and had to be on crutches for a week, so I understand how bad it sucks."*

"Laura, are you okay?" Georgia's voice. This time, from my left. From the present.

"I…" I trail off.

"I sprained my ankle not that long ago, too. It was not fun," the echo-me continues.

"You look like you just saw a ghost," Katie comments.

"How'd you get hurt this time?" asks Georgia's echo.

I blink a few times, trying to turn my attention back to the present. I meet Katie's concerned gaze, then Gabe's. His eyebrows furrow as he studies me, and I wish he could still read my mind.

"I just… don't feel well," I lie. But suddenly, I don't. Because it doesn't make any sense.

I stand and pick up my tray, muttering, "I'm going to go back to the dorm," under my breath, then stumble toward the tray return station.

Around me, the room seems to grow louder, voices and clinking dishes and laughter piling up, bouncing off the walls. As if there are suddenly more echoes than there should be.

A hand touches my shoulder, and I turn sharply, sending the still-full cup of mashed potatoes toppling onto the ground. Gabe ignores it, his eyes searching my face.

"What's wrong?" he asks.

I open my mouth. Close it. Open it again. "The echoes. Something's... different."

He shakes his head, not understanding.

"They've always been from a year ago. Or two years ago, or three. But from the same date, same time." I say.

"And now they're not?"

"I just heard a conversation I had with Georgia two nights ago."

Gabe studies me for a long moment. "What does it mean?"

I squeeze my eyes shut. "I don't know. I just... can't think right now. It's too loud in here."

Nodding, Gabe takes the tray from my hands. Then he bends down to pick up the mashed potatoes cup. "Go get some rest," he tells me. "We'll talk tomorrow."

Nodding, I turn toward the hall my dorm is in. When I step around the corner, the noise dulls enough for me to start breathing normally again. Back in my room, I lay down on my bed and stare up at the bottom of Georgia's mattress, my heart racing.

An echo from two days ago. It was from the same time of day, which is normal, but I've never heard an echo more recent than a year ago—not counting all of the crazy memory-echoes that have happened since Alice started screwing with my head, of course. But this one was different. And all of a sudden, things had gotten so much louder in the cafeteria, as if I was hearing all the echoes that have ever happened there.

And the other night, I'd had that strange dream-echo of Maverick. Where, for a moment, I'd stepped right into it and remembered everything about that day clearly.

I shake my head, trying to clear it. Maybe the suppressing medication Dr. Shaw gave me has a different effect on me than everyone else. Maybe instead of getting rid of it, it's somehow making my ability work differently.

That's the only reasonable explanation.

Right?

***

11:21 GLOWS IN RED numbers across the dark of the room. Above me, I can hear Georgia snoring softly.

The last couple of hours have ticked by in slow motion. I stayed in my room, listening to every thump and shuffle from the past, wondering if the sounds are from a year ago or more recent. Hoping that it's the former.

Thankfully, I didn't hear my own voice. Or Georgia's. Just someone coming into the room, then climbing into bed a few minutes before Georgia walked in to head to bed.

Maybe the recent echoes are gone. Just a small, temporary fluke.

I hope.

Slowly, I slide out of the covers, then pull on my shoes. I glance back at the clock—11:25—then reach for the door handle. I freeze when the hinges creak, but Georgia shows no signs of waking up, so I continue.

When I open the door to the suite, I twist my head both ways in the hallway. No one is there, so it should be safe to proceed.

Except for the cameras. I just hope Dr. Shaw managed to find a way to shut them off.

I tiptoe down the hallway, checking both ways again when I get to the end, and then move toward the elevator. Warily, I watch the one-way mirrors on the guard shack, hoping that no one is actually inside.

In my orientation, Alexis had explained that we're not allowed to leave our rooms past 10 PM, so it'll definitely be a red flag if somebody spots me. But again, Dr. Shaw must have arranged things to avoid that.

I press my clammy palm to the scanner in front of the elevator, and to my surprise, it flashes green. The doors open a second later, and I step inside, feeling claustrophobic.

I hold my breath all the way to the bottom floor.

When the doors open, I duck my head and make a beeline for the hallway on the right. Study Room 409 is the second room on the left. It's a small room with a conference table, six office chairs, and a whiteboard that someone has left a few math problems scribbled across.

And it's empty.

I scan the walls for a clock but find none. Then I start to pace, feeling warm.

What if I left too early? What if someone spotted me from a camera and is on their way here right now to reprimand me? Or what if someone runs into Dr. Shaw on her way here and she never shows up?

The endless possibilities race through my head, making my hands shake. I pull them to my chest to steady them.

And then, eventually, the door opens.

I stop pacing, lift my gaze. When I see Dr. Shaw, relief floods through me. She made it; no one discovered our secret meetup and tried to intercept.

But then, behind her, another figure emerges, and my heart stops. He freezes at the sight of me, golden eyes going wide.

Maverick.

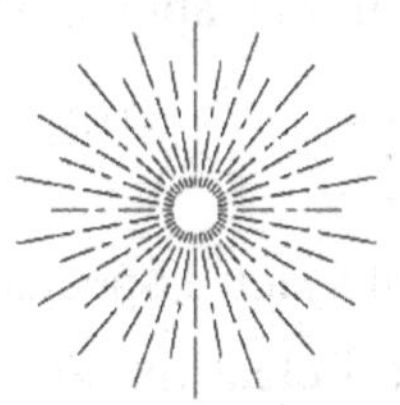

CHAPTER 14

"LAURA?" MY NAME IS barely a whisper, a breath of disbelief. And then he's crossing the room, reaching for me. "You're okay," he says into my hair as his arms tangle around me. I return the embrace, fingers balling into the loose fabric of his shirt

"You still remember me," I say, almost a question.

He pulls away—just barely—to look me in the eyes. Blinks at me like he can't grasp the idea that I'm here, in front of him. "Of course I do."

I deflate, then, the relief flooding through me like a dam has just burst. Tears spring into my eyes. "I was worried Alice was going to take your memories away again," I tell him.

Maverick tugs me close again. He doesn't say anything else, but he doesn't have to. I can hear what he's feeling in the hitch of his breath, in the slight trembling of his arms around me.

Behind us, Dr. Shaw clears her throat. Maverick whirls around to face her but stays close, curling his fingers around mine.

Dr. Shaw crosses her arms. "Is this why you wanted me to bring Mr. Schall?"

Maverick's eyes narrow, and he shifts on the balls of his feet, putting himself between us defensively. "What is going on?"

"Miss Jones said you'd be able to help us."

"With what?"

"I don't know. Why—"

"He *can* help," I interject. Especially now that I know his memories are still intact. I clear my throat. "Maverick, I've told Dr. Shaw about Alice and what she's been doing. She wants to help us stop her." I turn my gaze to Dr. Shaw. "Maverick is one of the only other people that remembers the truth about Alice. And before the ACA got involved with everything, she blackmailed him into working for her. So he knows more about what she's been doing than anyone else."

For a long moment, they just stare at each other, Maverick's jaw twitching and Dr. Shaw's eyes narrowed. Then, finally, Dr. Shaw speaks. "Working for her?"

I don't miss the flicker of guilt that passes over Maverick's face before he replies. "She was forcing me to erase people's memories. So she could get away with kidnapping anomalies without getting caught."

I drop my gaze to the floor, feeling bad for him. For everything that's happened to him.

"And what do you know that could help us?" Dr. Shaw asks.

Maverick opens his mouth, then hesitates. Like he's at a loss for words. I'm not sure what Dr. Shaw told him before she dragged him here, but he must not have been expecting this.

"Maverick knows the truth about Alice," I offer. "And another friend of mine remembers, too—Gabe Jackson. You said before that if we can convince the head of the ACA of all this, maybe she'll do something to stop Alice. We just need to get her to listen to us."

But Dr. Shaw just shakes her head. "Three testimonies isn't enough, not against the twelve who are claiming a different story. We need solid evidence. What proof do you have of what Dr. Wight has been doing?"

Maverick frowns. "Her laboratory. That's where she held everyone captive, where—"

"The one that burned down and left no recoverable evidence?" Dr. Shaw interrupts.

"Nothing?"

Dr. Shaw nods. A few beats of silence pass.

Eventually, Maverick says, "What about all of the people's memories Alice forced me to erase? No one remembers any of the anomalies she kidnapped because of what she made me do—not their families, not their friends. Isn't that proof enough?"

"Unfortunately, I don't think so," Dr. Shaw replies. "The case workers believe you chose to erase all those memories in order to leave your old lives behind and band together without getting caught. There's no way to prove that Dr. Wight *made* you do it."

Maverick runs a hand through his hair.

"What about the syringe?" I ask. "You said you saw it, so it's here somewhere. Couldn't you take it and analyze it? Show it to the head of the ACA?"

"There still might not be a way to tie it to Dr. Wight," Dr. Shaw replies. Then she shakes her head. "And either way, it's still in her possession. If I start poking around and she realizes what I'm trying to do, she'll put an end to this in an instant."

We let the thought soak in. Alice has already shown us that she's capable of altering memories, twisting the game in her favor. If she catches wind that we're working against her, I have no doubt she'll do it again. In an instant, she could ensure that Dr. Shaw, our only ally right now, doesn't remember a bit of anything we've talked about.

A scary thought occurs to me. "What would stop her from doing the same thing to the head of the ACA?" I ask. "Even if we do go to her, we do convince her, wouldn't Alice just erase her memories? What would be the point?"

An unsettling silence falls over the room. Dr. Shaw begins to pace, and Maverick brings both of his hands to his forehead, rubbing his eyes.

Then Dr. Shaw pauses. "We need to show the head of the ACA that Dr. Wight is an anomaly. Then we can get her to lock Dr. Wight up right away, and she wouldn't have a chance to fight back."

Maverick starts to nod, but I bite my lip.

"Alice isn't working alone," I tell them, looking up. "We had a few run-ins with a guy working for her. He always had multiple different abilities up his sleeve to try and take us down, and I… got rid of him." I stumble over the words with a shudder. "But I don't think he was the only one."

"She has a backup plan. People that will come for her in case anything happens," Dr. Shaw says.

I nod. This is Alice we're talking about. She has a plan for everything.

But again, this puts us back at square one. We can't go to the head of the ACA because Alice will come after us. We can't get rid of her because she has fail-safes in place to make sure she'll get out. So how do we stop her?

Dr. Shaw suddenly stops, tilting her head thoughtfully. "You said the replications of anomalies' abilities are administered through an injection. And that the effects are only temporary, right?"

I nod.

Dr. Shaw drums her fingers against her arm. "That sounds similar to the way the suppressors work. Several years ago, I managed to locate the mutation—the sequence of DNA that is responsible for anomalies' abilities. We figured out how to suppress that sequence, but it only lasts a couple of weeks before we have to reinforce it."

"And it can work both ways," Maverick says.

Dr. Shaw nods. "Dr. Wight moved to her new facility before I could finish researching the possibilities, but I always suspected there was a way to replicate abilities. If you can separate out the mutation, then insert a dose into another system and find a way to make it bind with the host, you can create a temporary mutation in another person. It seems Alice managed to do it, but—"

"She needs the DNA of the anomalies to make it work," Maverick finishes.

Dr. Shaw nods. I glance between them, turning every word over in my head.

"There's a finite supply of the replications," Dr. Shaw continues. "If Alice can't get her hands on DNA samples, she can't create more."

"She needs *us*?" I ask, finally getting the gist of it.

Maverick nods. "Our DNA."

"Your blood, most likely," Dr. Shaw adds.

"So we cut off her supply? So she can't make more replications?" I ask.

"Exactly," Maverick replies.

Dr. Shaw's mouth bunches to one side. "Everyone from your group has been placed on the suppressing medications. Any samples Dr. Wight collects while you're here wouldn't be viable for making replications."

"Either way," Maverick says, "she probably has plenty of samples already stored up. She had everyone locked up for months, so there could be a lot."

"We'll have to get rid of those, then," Dr. Shaw says.

"How?"

"We figure out where she's keeping them," I say, my eyes widening. "And destroy them."

Maverick frowns. "How are we going to do that?"

"You're going to have to let us go," I say, meeting Dr. Shaw's gaze.

She stares at me for a long moment, her lips pursing. "I don't know if—"

"It's the only way," I insist. "Alice has people working for her, people who can use *our* abilities at a moment's notice. If she catches you or anyone else snooping around in her stuff, you won't stand a chance. We might, though, because at least we have our abilities to combat her. This is a job for us. For anomalies."

Plus, if Alice manages to capture any of us and tries to manipulate our memories again, I know that she won't be able to mess with mine. I might be the only one, but at least we won't completely lose.

Dr. Shaw paces the room once, twice, then three times. Then she sighs heavily. "I can't just let you go."

"Then don't," I reply, the plan already solidifying in my mind. "Stop giving us the suppressors. Make it look like a fluke. We'll escape on our own once they wear off."

"How would you do that?"

"We'll need Angelo. And Wyatt. And I'm sure Gabe would help. With their abilities and Maverick's, no one will even know how we left. Then we can track down Alice, follow her around until we see where she's keeping everything. We get rid of the samples, then send a signal to you that it's done."

"I can't just let you go, though," Dr. Shaw says, frowning. "Anomalies on the loose are considered a danger to society, and if the ACA even suspects I'm involved in your escape—even if it does look like an accident—I could get fired. Thrown in jail."

I swallow hard, hating that it has to come down to this. "Then we'll come back when we're done. If we're back in custody, we can explain that we did it ourselves. Make sure you take none of the blame."

This seems to be worthy of consideration. Dr. Shaw continues to pace, weighing her options carefully. "How do I know you'll actually come back?"

It's a fair point. "Just… trust us?" I reply lamely.

But Dr. Shaw shakes her head. "I will figure out how to ensure *one* of your other friends doesn't get the suppressors. But the others will stay here, and if any of you don't come back, there will be consequences. I'll make sure that none of them *ever* get out of this place."

Her words make my heart sink. For how helpful she's been so far, I wasn't expecting her to be so brutal. But I guess it's fair. Dr. Shaw's loyalties are with the ACA, not us. She wants to help us so she can stop Alice from whatever she's doing, not so she can set us free.

"Okay," I say.

And just then, Dr. Shaw's watch starts beeping, bursting the tension that has suddenly filled the room.

"We have to get going," she says.

I let out a sigh. There's never enough time.

"The next dose of suppressors won't be administered to anyone from your group for another week and a half, so nothing will happen until then. While you wait, think really carefully about who you want to bring. I'll be in contact soon."

We both nod like children being given instructions for a ball game.

"We'll need to stagger the times we leave so no one sees us together. Mr. Schall, you'll go first. I'll leave after, then Miss Jones last," Dr. Shaw says. Then she nods at Maverick.

Maverick hesitates, meeting my gaze. There are a million unspoken words hanging between us, but we don't have time for them. He gives me the briefest nod, then starts to turn for the door.

"Wait!" I lift my gaze to Dr. Shaw, eyes wide and desperate. "Can I have a moment alone with Maverick?" The words are out of my mouth before I can even think them through.

Dr. Shaw's gaze flicks between us a few times, scrutinizing. Then she sighs, the expression turning to pity. "You have five minutes. If one of you doesn't start back to your dorms before then, you run the risk of getting caught and ruining this entire plan."

We both nod, afraid to say anything else.

"Don't get any ideas," she says, shooting each of us one last glare.

Then she slips out the door, and finally, we're alone.

CHAPTER 15

THE AIR SUDDENLY feels thick, like I might choke on it. Everything goes quiet except for the thundering of my heart in my chest. I wonder if Maverick can hear it, too.

I face him.

"Maverick—"

"Laura—"

We both stop. Wait. Just moments ago, I'd felt the weight of all the unspoken words hanging over us, and I'd been desperate to have more time with him, more time to speak them. But now my brain can't seem to form a single word.

His amber eyes burn into mine, searching, full of emotion. The look seems to unravel me at the edges.

"You saved me," he finally says.

I manage the slightest of nods. "I had to."

"The gunshot wound. My memories. How did you…" he trails off.

"We found a syringe after you guys got captured," I explain. "It had one of Alice's replications in it."

Maverick runs a hand through his hair. That dark, messy hair. Suddenly I want to run my fingers through it, too. "You saved my life."

I shrug. "Technically, Alice did. It was her ability that saved you."

"I'll have to thank her for it the next time I see her."

I grin, and then we both laugh. When it tapers off, he drops his gaze to his hands.

"I used to have a scar," he says, running his thumb over his palm. "Right here. When I was fourteen, I sliced through my palm while doing the dishes." I follow his gaze down to the clean, unmarred skin on his hand. "Seven stitches. And now, the scar's just gone."

A smile tugs at my lips. "I was more worried about the gaping hole in your abdomen, but I'm glad we managed to kill two birds with one stone."

Maverick smiles back briefly, but then it fades and his eyes go serious. "You got your memories back, too, then?" There's a hitch in his voice, a hope hidden in the space between his words.

"Not exactly," I reply. "I still don't have my memories of you." *Except for that day at the coffee shop.* But I keep that to myself, afraid that if I speak the words, they'll turn out to be false.

Disappointment flickers in his eyes, but it's there and then gone.

"My other memories—the ones Alice tried to mess with—are still there," I continue. "I don't know if it was necessarily that I got them back, just that Alice couldn't take them in the first place."

"Really?"

I nod. "I think it was because of my ability."

Maverick stays quiet for a moment, thinking. "And you, me, and Gabe are the only ones who know the truth?"

"Yeah." I wring my hands restlessly. "I was afraid Alice would try to manipulate your memories again after we got here. Once she realized you got them back. But she hasn't."

"Yet."

I swallow. "I don't think she will." I wish the words sounded more confident. "It would be too suspicious if one or all of us randomly changed our story, don't you think? And we're not a threat to her here—she's already gotten away with everything. So she has no reason to."

"Hopefully," is all Maverick replies.

For a long moment, we just let that hang in the air between us, consuming our thoughts. Then Maverick meets my gaze, setting his jaw.

"I'm going to get you out of here, Laura."

I shake my head. "*We're* going to get out of here. Together. And we're going to get everyone else out, too."

He runs a hand through his hair again, wincing. "It's my fault you got dragged into all of this."

My eyebrows furrow. "No. It's not."

He squeezes his eyes shut, hands balling into fists at his sides. "I should have done more to prevent this from happening. I should have left you behind when your parents got kidnapped."

I frown. "I wouldn't have let you do that."

He shakes his head. "But if I had just investigated Alice's office on my own, instead of bringing you with me, maybe Alice wouldn't have taken them. None of this would have happened."

That night flashes through my head: meeting Maverick after school, staking out Alice's office, bandaging Maverick's arm up after he got shot. *His mouth on mine.*

"You can't do that—tell yourself things would have been different. You don't know that."

"But it's true. If I hadn't—"

"If you hadn't *what?*" I interject, my face suddenly flushed with heat. "Met me? That would have prevented all of this too, right? Is that what you want?"

"No. But—"

"But *what,* Maverick?" The harshness of my tone surprises me. "I'm an anomaly, too. This is my problem just as much as it is yours. If we'd never met, they might have found me anyway. I might be lying in bed in one of those dorms right now, or I'd have been locked up in Alice's lab. None of this would have happened. We wouldn't be here, in this room, trying to figure out how to stop it all."

Maverick doesn't respond, just rubs his eyes, looking exhausted.

"It's too late for the *what if* games. We're here now, and we need to focus on stopping Alice," I tell him. "Getting out of here."

Maverick sighs heavily, steeling himself. "Alice is smarter than us. She's got way too many tricks up her sleeve. I don't know how we're going to do this without her finding out."

His words feed the knot in my stomach. "We have Dr. Shaw helping us," I offer.

"Is she really on our side, though? You heard her threats if we don't come back."

And he's right. She only cares about taking Alice down. After we do that, what will happen? Before we got here, Gabe and I had assumed getting out of the ACA would be pretty simple. But we didn't know about the suppressors. Now, we don't have our abilities to rely on.

"I know we can find a way out of this, too," I say. "On our own."

"And if it doesn't work?"

"Well, the food sucks. But we're not in any danger here. Word on the street is that after five years, they'll let us go."

"*Five years,*" he repeats. "Stuck underground, with nothing to do but whatever the ACA says I can."

"It could be worse," I say, but the words taste bitter. Five years is a long time.

Maverick rubs his hand over his face, shifting back and forth on the balls of his feet. Then he leans back against the wall, staring down at his hands. "At least, for once in my life, I'm incapable of hurting anybody."

I cross over and lean against the wall beside him, sliding to the floor. Our five minutes is probably long over, but for some reason, my desire to stay right here with Maverick outweighs my fear of whatever else might happen. He sits down next to me, and I hug my knees.

"I wish my ability was gone, too," I say. But something twists in my gut as I say it, making it feel like a lie. If my ability was gone, Alice would have been able to take my memories away.

Maverick tilts his head. "Yours isn't?"

"The suppressors don't work on me," I reply, realizing that part was never explained to him. "No one knows why."

Curiosity lights his features for a long moment, but then he just shrugs and bumps my shoulder. "I always knew you were special."

Alice's words drift through my head again. *You're different, Laura.*

"I never wanted to be," I say.

"I don't think any of us did. At least, not in the ways we got stuck with."

"Pretty rude of the universe, isn't it?"

"I've filed a few complaints."

That makes me smile. Then I bite my lip, looking up at the ceiling. "What would you be doing with your life, if you weren't an anomaly?" I ask.

He considers it for a moment. "Maybe I'd go to culinary school. I've always loved to cook," he says.

"You weren't going to do that before?"

"No," he says simply. "After everything that happened, I decided I wanted to go into a field where I'd be able to do some research… figure out what was wrong with me. Maybe find a way to fix it."

"That's a pretty drastic change," I reply.

He shrugs. "I've always liked science, too. So it was fine."

"Well, maybe the ACA will let you do an internship while you're here," I reply with a smirk.

Maverick rolls his eyes. Then he tilts his head at me. "What about you?"

I fold my fingers together, thinking. "Honestly, I have no idea. I've never really thought about it."

A smile tugs at the corner of his lips. "You actually told me once that you wanted to be a truck driver."

I clap a hand to my mouth to stifle a laugh. "Seriously?"

He nods.

I drop my head to my knees, hiding my face from him. "I thought I'd never told anyone that before. Gosh, it probably sounded so stupid."

But Maverick just says, "Why would it be stupid?" I lift my gaze, meeting his serious expression. "It's a respectable career and an important one."

"True. But can you really picture me in the driver's seat of an eighteen-wheeler?"

"I don't see why not. You already drive like a grandma, so you'd probably be good at it."

I jab him with my elbow. "I do *not*."

"You may not remember it, but I've been on many car rides with you. And I can attest to the fact that you do, in fact, drive *under* the speed limit the majority of the time."

I let out a playful huff, crossing my arms. But he does have a point. "I like to take my time, because cars are one of the few places where I don't hear a ton of echoes."

Realization passes over his features. "That does make a lot of sense."

"I did consider being a truck driver for a while, though. Then I could just be on the road, in the quiet for a long time. But really, I just thought it might be one of my only career options."

Maverick frowns. "There's got to be something else, right?"

"I thought maybe I'd find a career where I could work from home. Or do something outdoors. But nothing in either of those realms sounded very interesting to me. A job that involves driving would be kind of fun."

"You could become a chauffeur for some rich person."

I raise an eyebrow. "Oh yeah? Do you have one in mind?"

Maverick rolls his eyes. "I wasn't talking about *me,*" he says. "Though, I would totally pay you a ton of money to drive me everywhere if you wanted to do that."

"How much? Will benefits be included? I'll have to compare it with other options first…"

Maverick bumps me in the shoulder, laughing. "When we get out of here, we'll discuss the details."

"Yeah, and I should probably finish my high school diploma first. Will that bump up my starting salary?"

"I'll have to compare you with other candidates, so we'll see," he replies with a wink.

I throw my head back, laughter bubbling up from deep inside. It feels strange, in this room, under these circumstances. But I take it.

When I finally calm down, I glance back at Maverick, finding him staring at me, his eyes lit with a new intensity.

"I've missed you, Laura," he says, his voice heavy. "Even when I didn't know it, didn't remember you, I missed you. Somewhere in my heart."

I smile back sadly. *I've missed you too,* I want to say, but the words won't leave my lips. They feel too real, too fresh. Like a wound that hasn't completely healed.

For a moment, Maverick's eyes drop to my mouth, and I wait, wondering if he's going to lean closer. But then he sighs and looks at the door.

"We should probably get going."

And all at once, the bubble around us pops. We aren't two lovers, stealing a moment together. We're anomalies, in the ACA, trying to figure out how to get our lives back.

Maverick stands, then offers me his hand and I let him pull me to my feet. For a moment, we hesitate, not knowing how to say goodbye. But then Maverick pulls me close, his arms tightening around me like he never wants to let go.

Until he does.

"I'll see you soon," he says. Then he slips out of my grasp, and the door closes behind him. And all I can do is hope it won't be the last time I watch him go.

CHAPTER 16

THAT NIGHT, FOR the first time in what feels like months, I slip into sleep easily and don't open my eyes again until morning. When I finally wake, I blink at the hazy gray room as the edges of my surroundings start to sharpen.

Above me, the mattress groans, and a moment later, Georgia drops to the floor beside me. When she spots me looking at her, she claps a hand over her mouth.

"Sorry!" she squeaks. "I didn't mean to wake you!"

"No!" I reply quickly. "You didn't." I glance at the alarm clock on the desk across the room. 8:17 glows back, and for a moment, I wonder if we both accidentally slept through the alarm. Classes are supposed to start at eight, so—

"I know it's early for a Saturday," Georgia says. *Saturday.* Somewhere in the mess of things, the days of the week got away from me. "On weekends, breakfast doesn't start until nine, but Glen makes custom omelets for anyone who comes early."

At the mention of food, my stomach rumbles.

"You can sleep in if you want. Ash and I like to go every weekend, though. Gotta eat decent food every chance we can get, and Glen's omelets are the best thing you'll get inside these walls."

I sit up, stretching my arms above my head. "Oh, I'm definitely in then."

A few minutes later, we step into the hallway where a girl is leaning against the wall, waiting for us. She looks a little older than Georgia and Katie—probably my age—and her dark, wavy hair barely reaches her ears.

"You must be Ash," I say with a smile, extending my hand. "I'm Laura."

For a moment, Ash's eyes widen, almost like she's scared. Then she seems to shake herself out of it. She nods at me but doesn't return the handshake.

"Nice to meet you," she mumbles, avoiding my gaze.

Before I can process the behavior, Georgia tugs the suite door open, calling after us, "You guys coming, or what?"

Ash offers me a small smile, then turns to follow her. I drop my extended hand and take up the rear.

As we walk, I can't help but notice that there are less guards stationed in the hallways this morning. The spaces that are usually crowded with noise during heavily trafficked times of day are quieter, too. I guess even the ACA takes weekends off.

In the cafeteria, the only other people are three boys sitting at a table—two of whom I've never seen before. But the third boy I recognize. *Aaron.*

I don't actually know him very well, because after breaking him out of Alice's burning laboratory and then bringing him to Maverick's mansion, he'd left with Wyatt a few days later. But the fake memories Alice gave me paint a picture where he stayed with us the entire time, and we all worked together to plot against the ACA. Which explains why he must have been so angry at Gabe, but I picture the cut on Gabe's lip and frown.

Aaron looks up, catching me staring at him. He ducks his head, the slightest nod of acknowledgement, then returns his attention to the guys across from him.

I wonder what he's thinking. What Alice made his memories of me into, and what she did to him the entire time he was gone. I'd learned later that the anomalies who went with Wyatt got captured by Alice not long after leaving.

My eyes linger on Aaron a little too long, and I don't notice when Ash comes to a stop in front of me. I bump into her, and just as I'm opening my mouth to say "sorry," she jerks away from me, recoiling as if I've just burned her. My eyes widen, and she takes several steps back, shaking.

"Ash," Georgia says, putting her hands out as if reaching for her. But she doesn't move any closer.

Ash seems to snap out of it, letting out a breath. But she looks suddenly pale.

"I'm so sorry," I say. "I didn't—"

"It's okay!" Ash rushes to say. "I just—" she stops abruptly, and I think I see a glimmer of tears forming in her eyes. "I'm going back to my room." Then she puts her head down and starts back the way we came, almost at a run.

"Ash!" Georgia calls, but Ash is around the corner before she can say anything else.

I stare after her, my heart pounding. "I didn't mean—"

"It's not your fault," Georgia hurries to say. "Ash has only been here a few weeks, so she hasn't gotten used to not having her ability yet."

I replay the fear in her eyes, the way she'd recoiled from me so quickly. "What was her ability?" I ask, my voice barely audible.

Georgia looks at the ground. "When she touches someone, she sees their deepest fears."

A shudder runs through me. "I didn't know," I whisper.

Georgia touches my arm. "It's okay. She knows that. She probably just got scared. She'll forgive you."

I swallow, my gaze shifting to the kitchen area behind the food warmers, which is empty except for a big, burly man at the back of the room. The smell of vegetables simmering reaches my nose.

"Do you think he'll let me get one to take to Ash?"

Georgia beams at me, then gestures for me to follow. "I think that's a great idea."

By the time we get back to the suite, my mouth is watering. I'm holding a steaming plate in each hand—one with ham, onions, and green peppers for me and one with spinach and tomatoes for Ash. Georgia taps on her door.

"Hey, Ash. We brought you an omelet," she calls through the door.

The door opens, and Ash glances between us, then down at the omelet in my left hand.

"Ash, I'm sorry. I didn't know—"

"It's fine," she cuts me off. Then she steps back, letting the door open wider. "You guys can come in."

So we do. Her room is the mirror image of mine and Georgia's—the same drab bedding, musty gray walls, and wooden furniture—except somehow, it seems even more empty than ours. In our room there are a few pairs of dirty clothes on the floor, some papers on the desk, and the sheets are bunched up from being slept in. But Ash's room is pristine, and the bed is made without even a wrinkle. Like no one has touched it in years.

As we move inside, I hold the omelet out to Ash. "I convinced Glen to make an extra one for you. I didn't want you to miss your only chance for something actually edible."

"Thank you," she replies with a grim smile as she takes the plate.

I follow Georgia deeper into the room, pulling a chair out from one of the desks. Georgia takes the other, and Ash sits on the bed. For several minutes, we just eat in silence, savoring the flavors of the fresh-cooked meal. Then, eventually, Ash sets her plate down on the bed and clears her throat.

"I'm sorry I freaked out like that," she says, rubbing her arm uncomfortably.

I shake my head. "Georgia told me about… your ability. I'm sorry I bumped into you. I should have been more careful."

"You couldn't have known."

I don't know how to respond, so I just drop my gaze to my shoes.

After what feels like hours, Ash finally speaks. "I'm still not used to this... place. Not having my ability. It's nice, but... sometimes I just forget."

I nod. Georgia gives her a reassuring smile. "It took me three months to get used to actually having to walk across the room to get things," she says. Then she looks at me. "Telekinesis. That was my ability. What was yours?"

Was. The word swirls around in my head.

I steel myself. "I hear echoes of the past everywhere I go. All the time."

"Wow. And they just found you?"

I shrug.

"It must be nice for both of you to not deal with it anymore," Georgia says.

Ash nods. "It is. It's just hard to believe it's actually gone, after so many years."

They both look at me, waiting for my response. "Well, actually..." I trail off. "My ability isn't gone. The suppressors just don't work on me."

You're different, Laura.

"For real?" Georgia's eyes widen.

I nod. "That's why I didn't come back until late the other day. They had to run some tests."

"Oh, and that's why you weren't in class anymore?"

I nod. "They're letting me listen in from our room so I can actually focus."

"Well I hope they find a medication that works for you," Ash offers.

I nod, but slowly. As much as I've always wished there was some kind of medication that could stop me from hearing the echoes, things feel different now. It feels wrong to want that.

I bite my lip. "Do you ever wish you still had your ability?" I ask Georgia. "I mean, it must be nice to move things with your mind, right?"

Georgia considers it for a moment. "It was. I guess at first I was a little bit sad about it. I mean, I couldn't move anything big, just little things like my phone or a glass of water. But I could literally get something from the other room without having to get up."

"I would get sooo lazy," Ash replies.

"It's for the best that the ACA found me, really."

They both laugh, but I can't bring myself to join in.

Does Georgia really believe that? That she's better off here, being forced to take medication that stops her from using her ability? Because she can move small objects across the room without touching them?

I shift my gaze to Ash, who's smiling now but whose eyes are haunted. The suppressors are going to save her from living a life of fear.

In that way, the ACA is doing something important. Just like with Gabe, like with Veronica, having an ability can be a pretty terrible burden. Giving anomalies relief from that is a good thing.

But the ACA doesn't care about that, do they? They just want to get rid of all anomalies, to keep us from using our abilities. They don't care if it's a gift or a burden—they just want to keep the world from finding out that we exist. They're only concerned about pushing their own agenda.

And in that sense, they're exactly like Alice.

* * * *

WE STAY IN ASH'S ROOM for almost two hours, getting to know each other. I learn that although Georgia doesn't have any siblings, she comes from a big family. She has four aunts and uncles and nine cousins who love to get together on holidays. Every Christmas, the ACA lets her video chat with her family, so she's excited to be able to see and catch up with all of them soon. Ash doesn't mention any family, but I learn that she loves to draw. She pulls out an ACA-issued notebook and lets me flip through the pages, which are filled with sketches of animals. Horses, dogs, cats, even a few owls. And they're all excellent.

A little after ten, Katie finally wakes up and joins us, but she's quick to suggest we all go find something to do outside of the dorms.

"On Saturdays, our block gets the recreation center all day, so we usually like to play tennis for a few hours. Then we'll just hang out in one of the study rooms," she tells me.

"Yes, let's go! We finally have a fourth player!" Georgia exclaims. Then the three of them start to move.

I remain frozen in place, though. I picture myself joining them, spending hours in a place where there are probably years of history to echo back at me, and I can already feel a headache coming on.

"I think I might stay behind," I finally say, and I'm surprised by the tremble in my voice. All three girls pause, turning to look at me. And for a moment I'm back in Shorewick, sitting at the lunch table at St. Martin High with Grace and Leo.

"You're going to miss this one, too?" There was hurt in Grace's eyes as she spoke the words, concern in Leo's as he studied me.

"I just... have a lot of homework."

"Of course you do." A scoff. Then she stormed away.

I eventually lost track of the number of times we had that same conversation.

Now, here in the ACA, I stare at my shoes, almost waiting for the same scenario to play out.

"I almost forgot about your leg," Katie says. "You can come watch if you want, though?"

I haven't used the crutches in a couple days, and my leg feels fine. I shake my head, keeping my gaze pinned to the floor. "It's just, it'll be too loud," I admit.

Katie's eyebrows knit together, but before she can say anything, Georgia reaches out to put a hand on my shoulder. Ash regards me with understanding eyes, and a flash of her recoiling after I bumped into her replays through my head.

"It's totally fine. We get it," she says.

And for the first time in a while, I know I'm not alone.

CHAPTER 17

I DON'T SEE DR. SHAW again until Monday morning. When the guards usher me into the medical examination room and she's already inside, washing her hands in the sink along the back wall, a surge of relief rushes through me. For the past two days, I'd been cared for by Liz, the nurse that sometimes assists Dr. Shaw, and I was beginning to worry that something had happened to her. But she must just take weekends off. Like a normal person.

Dr. Shaw turns and beams at me. "Good morning, Laura! How are you feeling today?"

"Claustrophobic." I plop onto the medical exam table and stretch out my leg, tugging the stiff fabric of my uniform up over my calf. "I don't suppose field trips to the surface are included in my stay here, are they?"

Dr. Shaw just shakes her head as she starts to remove the bandage. As she moves through the familiar routine of inspecting and cleaning the wound, I try to come up with a way to covertly ask her about the plan we made. But I can feel the camera in the top corner of the room, staring down at us. As much as my eyes want to glance up at it, I don't let them. I can't appear suspicious.

"It's healing up nice," she comments as she works. "Does it hurt to put weight on it?"

"Just a little. I haven't been using the crutches much anymore, though."

"That's fine. But I want to make sure you don't push it. You'll still need plenty of rest and elevation when you're sitting."

"And I'm still exempt from gym class, right?"

A hint of a smile plays on her lips. "For at least a couple more weeks."

I smile gratefully. Then I clear my throat. "So…" I start lamely. But I don't get to finish because at that exact moment, the door opens. And when I spot the figure emerging from the doorway, my heart leaps into my throat.

Alice.

A million thoughts rush through my head all at once. Does she know what we are up to? What does she want with me? What if she's using one of the replications she made and is reading my mind right now? What if she's reading Dr. Shaw's mind? I should have warned Dr. Shaw about this. I should have prepared her for it. Alice is going to find out what we're up to. She's going to put a stop to it.

But Alice doesn't look up from her clipboard as she strides into the room. Either she doesn't hear our thoughts or she's really good at pretending. Which wouldn't surprise me.

"Dr. Wight," Dr. Shaw greets. "We just finished up. Are you ready for Miss Jones?"

"Wait, what is going on?" I ask, eyes going wide.

"Dr. Wight just needs you for a little while to run a few tests. Nothing to worry about," Dr. Shaw says with her back to me.

My stomach plummets. I highly doubt Alice just wants to "run a few tests."

"You might miss your first class, but I'm sure you can catch up," Alice says, finally turning her gaze on me. I'm not sure if I imagine it or if there's actually a hint of pleasure in her eyes at my reaction.

Dr. Shaw finally turns to me. "Your wound has healed enough that I think we can move forward with self-care. I'll have some bandages sent to your room. You'll want to change them once a day, or as often as they get wet or soiled. But other than that, you're good to keep an eye on the wound yourself. If you notice any redness or swelling or start to get a fever, let someone know right away. But otherwise, I'll just be checking in with you on a weekly basis from now on."

I stare at Dr. Shaw for a long moment, my mouth hanging open dumbly. "Okay."

And with that, she slips out the door.

Alice looks up at me with a smile, pulling her clipboard to her chest. "If you're ready, we can get going."

I eye her. "Where are you taking me? The torture chambers?"

She doesn't respond, just pulls the door open, holding it for me. Slowly, I slide off the medical examination table.

I follow Alice down the hallway silently, wishing there was some way I could run or disappear. I consider jumping in one of the elevators and running back to my dorm, but I know I'll be followed. Someone will bring me back.

We stay on this floor, heading toward the interrogation room I'd been taken to that first day. We pass it, though, moving further down the hallway until we get to the end. Alice leads me through the door on the left into an empty room with a single table and chair in the center. In the corner is a cart covered in a spread of medical supplies: syringes, vials of liquids, bandages, a box of gloves.

"Have a seat," Alice instructs, pointing at the single chair.

I hesitate in the doorway, a flashback of being trapped in Alice's lab the very first time hitting me. I start to back toward the door.

Behind me, it swings open, and two guards step into the room, killing any hope I had of getting away.

"It wasn't a suggestion," Alice says. I glance at the guards, then bite down on my lip and start for the chair, sitting on the very edge of it.

"What are you going to do to me?"

Alice drags the cart over, then starts pulling on a pair of gloves. "Just a little bit of research," she says.

I look up, scanning the corners of the room for a camera, but there isn't one. And all four walls are made of the same large white bricks as the rest of this place. No one-way mirror for someone to watch from. We're alone except for the two guards waiting stone-faced by the door. Apparently it's only hard to find a place away from the eyes of security in the ACA if you aren't Alice.

"What are you researching?" I ask, watching as Alice removes the cap from a syringe and sticks the needle into a small vial, turning it upside down and slowly pulling the liquid into the syringe. I squint at the vial as she sets it back down, trying to read the label, but it's just a series of numbers and letters that don't mean anything to me.

"*You*, Laura."

"Why? What do you want to know? What is that stuff?" I demand. But she ignores me as she opens a sterile alcohol wipe with her other hand.

"Roll up your sleeve."

I just stare back at her, lifting my chin in defiance.

"We've been through this before, Laura. If you don't cooperate, it only makes this harder for you."

"Fine. Then let's make it harder," I spit.

With a wave of her hand, Alice signals the guards to come after me. I jump to my feet, grabbing the chair as a weapon and backing away as they close in from either side. I glance between them, sizing them up. They're both bigger than me, and with my injured leg, I don't stand much of a chance against them. But I can try my best to put up a fight.

It doesn't end up being much of one, though. When the guard to my left steps forward to reach for me, I swing the chair at him. But instead of hitting him, he just catches it, ripping it from my grasp and tossing it behind him. At the same time, the other guard closes in from behind and grabs my arms, pinning them behind my back. Together they half-carry, half-drag me back to the center of the room, then plant me back in the chair, still holding my hands behind my back. One of them tugs my sleeve up, exposing my arm for Alice.

With a sigh and disappointed shake of her head, she presses the alcohol pad to my arm, rubbing it in a small circle. Then she brings the needle down, and I squeeze my eyes shut, feeling the sting as she injects me with goodness-knows-what.

When she's done, the guards release me, and I shrug them away, trying to hold on to my defiant expression despite my heart thundering in my ears.

"What was that?" I demand, but it's just a repeat of the last time I was in this scenario: Alice ignores me, messing with the tools on her cart. A minute later, she reappears by my side with a fresh needle.

"Now I'm going to take some blood," she tells me, then hesitates for a moment. But I don't fight her this time. I close my eyes as she draws a vial, then backs away.

And then I start to hear them. Echoes. But not the normal echoes—these are different. They're happening in real time, and I hear them *before* a sound is actually made. The *plink* of a plastic cap on the floor seconds before I watch Alice drop it. The sound of the door creaking on its hinges and footsteps exiting the room just a few moments before Alice gives a signal to the guards to leave.

My own voice, once, then twice before I actually open my mouth and repeat the words: "What *was* that?"

Still, Alice doesn't answer. I replay the memory of being trapped in Alice's lab, when I'd experienced this same thing. Back then, I didn't know she was experimenting on anomalies, or even what an anomaly was. But then, later on, I'd learned that

Alice had been replicating abilities. I'd realized eventually what she must have injected me with.

"It's a replication." The words echo to me before I've even decided to say them out loud. "Lily Alen's ability... she sees flashes of the future... that's why I'm hearing... echoes like this." I have to speak in short phrases and pause between each one so I don't get confused by the echoes repeating things back to me before I say them.

"Echoes like what?" Alice asks, eyebrows furrowed.

"Things that are... about to happen... just before they do."

Alice studies me for a long moment, but she doesn't respond. Just waits.

"Why Lily's ability?" I ask. "What is the point of this?" Does she want me to see my future as some kind of cruel joke? Does she even realize that the replication doesn't give me Lily's ability—that it just mixes with the echoes and makes this horrible, echoing jumble of everything right here in the present?

But then Alice's voice echoes to me, stopping the thoughts. I hear it twice, overlapping on itself as she starts to speak the words out loud. "What I gave you wasn't a replication of anyone's ability."

My voice comes out small and weak. "What *was* it, then?"

"A marker I developed to aid my research of anomalies," she explains, her words nearly getting lost in the echoes of the next words already starting. I try my best to listen intently, focusing on her mouth moving right now so that I can make sense of the overlapping words. "It targets the mutation present in anomalies and forces it to multiply, making it easier for me to find it. At the same time, it has a neat little side effect of enhancing your abilities."

In the chaos of the echoes surrounding her words, my mind zones in on only one word. "*Enhancing?*"

"Some anomalies find that their abilities are temporarily stronger. They can use it to a greater capacity, or it simply doesn't drain as much energy from them," Alice explains. I keep my eyes trained on her face, trying to ignore the strange pit forming in my stomach. "Other anomalies find themselves able to control their ability for the first time." She pauses, tilting her head to the side thoughtfully. "You seem to be having a unique response, however."

I drop my head into my hands, squeezing my eyes shut as the echoes bounce around inside my skull. Somehow, this feels worse than the first time Alice had injected me with this stuff.

"*What is happening to me?*" I choke out. As the words echo over and over, a wave of nausea rolls over me, and I lift my hands to cover my ears, trying to blot out the noise. When Alice speaks, though, I hear her voice as clear as day.

"You're fighting it."

"Fighting *what?*" I demand.

"Your ability," Alice replies simply, as if it's the most obvious answer in the world.

"This *isn't* my ability," I grit out. An ache forms behind my eyes, pressure building. I can't take all of this noise much longer. Whatever Alice gave me is making the noise around me so much worse, so much stronger. Every echo, every tiny little fraction of a sound seems to pierce into me, splitting me open and tearing me apart.

"You need to listen, Laura."

"I can't *stop* listening," I reply, my voice cracking on the words.

"Then stop fighting it."

"Why would I want to do *that?*"

"Because there's so much more to your ability than you realize, Laura. You just aren't letting yourself see it."

"Why would I want to see it?" My own voice echoes around me, but I don't open my mouth to say it out loud. Instead I just let the words swirl in the tornado of sound around me, circling and circling, moving closer and closer to me at the center.

Why would I? All my life, the echoes have been nothing but a burden. An unexplainable part of me that kept me from living a normal life. A constant reminder that there's something wrong with me. I've always known that because of them, I'll never be able to fit in with society, even though all I've ever wanted is to just be normal and have friends and do the things people my age do. And for a while, I thought I could pull it off.

But now, the echoes are swallowing me whole. Sucking me in and trying to pull me toward something.

Alice is right. I *am* fighting them. Because I have no idea where I will end up if I let go.

I'm not sure I have much of a choice anymore, though. I feel like I'm dangling from a cliff by one arm, trying desperately to cling to this root of normalcy.

And I can't hold on forever.

So I close my eyes, releasing my hands from my ears, embracing the wall of noise around me.

And then the world starts to shift.

CHAPTER 18

AS THE ROOM AROUND me fades away, my new surroundings start to take shape.

A house at the end of a cul-de-sac with music thumping inside. A girl sitting alone on the curb out front, her chin resting on her knees.

Me.

Before I can even start to wonder what's going on, a series of images flash through my head at triple speed. Somehow, I'm able to make sense of them all.

New Year's Eve. A party. Grace, begging me to go with her. Finally giving in. Then the loud, booming music. People playing games and dancing. Laughing. Standing in the corner of the room, watching everyone enjoying themselves. I should be enjoying myself, too, but I'm not. So I slip out the door without anyone noticing.

A warm hand lands on my shoulder. All at once, the world sharpens. I notice the bite of the chill in the air, the hardness of the cement under me. In an instant I'm no longer watching myself sitting on the curb from a distance. I'm there, in the memory, simultaneously participating in and observing it, because I don't recall this at all.

"Hey." The sound of Maverick's voice fills me with warmth.

I glance up, a grin spreading across my face. "I didn't think you were going to make it."

He sits down on the curb beside me, scooting in close, his arm pressing against mine. "Mom went to bed early, so I figured it was safe to sneak out for a few hours."

"How's she doing?" I ask, eyebrows creasing with concern. *Last month he told me about her diagnosis. Early onset of Alzheimer's.*

Maverick drops his gaze. "I think the new meds might be helping. A little bit. But only time will tell."

I reach a hand out, folding my fingers into his. "I'm so sorry."

Maverick pulls me closer, tossing an arm around my shoulders. "Goodness, you're freezing. How long have you been out here?"

"I don't know."

"Party's that bad?" he asks with a laugh.

I shrug, fixing my gaze on my shoes. "Everyone else seems to be enjoying it."

Maverick glances up at the house behind us. Multicolored lights flicker in the windows, and from somewhere inside, the crowd starts cheering.

"You can go inside if you want," I tell him. "You don't have to stay out here with me."

But Maverick just shakes his head. "I didn't come here for the party."

My cheeks burn, and I fiddle with the strings on my hoodie. Maverick pulls me even closer, squeezing me tight.

"Let's go for a walk, get some blood flowing," he mumbles into my hair. When I nod, he stands, then offers his hand. I let him pull me to my feet. "The greenway runs through this neighborhood just down the road," he says, pointing.

Sure enough, the entrance to the greenway is only six houses down from us, and as we step onto the gravel path, the bare trees groan in the wind above our heads. The moon is behind a mask of thick clouds tonight, but the greenway is lit by lamp posts every hundred yards or so. They dot the path ahead of us in an orange glow.

Maverick tugs his phone out of his pocket and wakes up the screen. "Eight minutes until the new year starts," he observes.

"Don't remind me," I reply.

"Not a fan of New Year's?" he asks with a sideways glance.

I shrug. "It just seems kind of ridiculous to me—throwing big parties and making a huge deal out of the passing of time. There's nothing different about tonight than any other night. Time passes every day, people are only celebrating because one big number is changing."

Maverick nods thoughtfully. "I suppose you make a good point," he offers. "It's kind of fun, though, I think. To look back on the year and see how far you've come. Then look forward into the future and think about where you're going. An ending and a beginning at the same time."

A silence falls over us as I consider his words, the only sound the crunching of our feet over the gravel as we meander along the greenway. "I guess you have a point, too," I finally say. "But I still kind of hate it." What I don't tell him—what I can't tell him—is the real reason I hate New Year's: a new year just means new echoes. New sounds to deal with. More time in the past that the world is going to keep replaying for me.

"Is that why you left the party?" Maverick asks.

I shake my head. "It was just… *loud*," I tell him, then wince at my own words. Of course it was loud—it was a party. Parties are supposed to be loud.

But Maverick just nods and squeezes my hand, like he understands. For a minute, we continue on in silence, his warm fingers curled around mine, our paces matched perfectly. Until he tugs my hand, pulling me to a stop, then steps around to face me.

"Laura…" he begins, trailing off and dropping his gaze. He fiddles with my hand nervously.

"Don't tell me you're about to get all sappy on me because it's New Year's," I joke, trying to ignore the heat spreading through my chest.

Maverick grins. "What if I'm about to get all sappy just because?"

I roll my eyes but can't help but grin back.

"Look," he starts, dropping his gaze. "I just—I want you to know how much I care about you. I really enjoy hanging out with you, and talking to you, and just being around you. It sounds super lame and sappy, I know, but I do. I just…" he trails off, hesitating. "I—"

"Look!" I interrupt, my gaze catching on something drifting past Maverick's face. I hold out my hand, letting the flick of white fall into my palm, where it instantly disappears, leaving my skin wet. I lift my gaze to the sky, then gasp. Above us, more glimmering white flakes hover in the air, catching in the light from the streetlamp. They drift to the ground like rain in slow motion. "It's snowing!"

Maverick releases my other hand, holding his out to catch a snowflake.

I do the same, grinning as another one melts against my skin. "It never snowed in Pendleton," I say. "I've always wanted to see it happen in real life."

"Well, I guess your wish is coming true," Maverick says, smiling at me. But when I meet his eyes, I catch the hint of disappointment in them.

I turn my attention back to the snowflakes drifting from the sky, but suddenly my excitement is masked by the dread forming in the pit of my stomach. Maverick's unspoken words hang in the air between us, searing despite the cold.

I didn't let him finish. I *couldn't* let him finish. But why?

We've known each other for almost three months now, and he's been nothing but kind and thoughtful. I've enjoyed every second I've been able to spend with him, and I can't deny how much I care about Maverick, too. Being around him is easy, like hanging out with an old friend I've known for years. When I'm with him, I feel like I can be completely myself.

At least, almost. There's still a huge part of me that Maverick knows nothing about—that Maverick *can't* know anything about.

Because what sane person is going to believe someone when they say they hear echoes of the past? No one—not even Maverick— will be able to make sense of that. And where could this relationship possibly go without him knowing everything?

I can't keep pretending to be normal forever. And if I let Maverick admit his feelings for me, if I admit my feelings for him… how much more is it going to hurt when this all comes crashing down?

"It's starting to get pretty heavy," Maverick says, still staring at the sky. "We should probably head home before the roads get slick."

Swallowing the lump in my throat, I nod.

As we start down the path back toward the main road, the snowflakes falling around us start to get bigger. Just before we step onto the neighborhood sidewalk, I pause to admire the leaves on a holly bush, which are already covered in a sheet of white.

Maverick stops, too, waiting for me. And without our footsteps crunching over the gravel, I suddenly realize how silent the night is.

"It's so quiet," I whisper thoughtfully, peering at the woods around us. Even though the snow is coming down harder now, it seems to fall without a sound.

"It is," Maverick agrees.

A smile tugs at my lips. All my life, I've craved silence. And here it is, dropping out of the sky.

"Yes, it's very exciting," Maverick teases, nudging me playfully with his elbow.

I nudge him back, but my smile fades. I wish I could tell him that it's true. The silence *is* exciting, because almost everywhere else I go, there's too much noise. Too many echoes.

And then a wild thought flies through my head, unexpected: *What if I did tell him the truth?*

I shoo it away. There's no way I can tell Maverick about the echoes. Not right now. Maybe not ever. I know how that conversation is going to end.

"If we want to drive rather than slide home, we really should keep moving," Maverick says, finally breaking the silence.

"You're right," I reply.

Maverick hesitates for just a moment. I watch as he shifts his hand, almost like he's going to reach for mine. But then his lips purse and he seems to think better of it, tucking it into his pocket instead. He turns his back to me, starting down the path again.

The knot in my stomach tightens.

"Maverick, wait," I say. I reach for his arm, pulling him to face me. His eyes meet mine, and something inside of me starts to unravel.

Tell him the truth.

And I want to. I want to tell Maverick everything, so bad. I don't want to hide anything from him, I don't want to have any secrets between us. I want him to understand why things like parties are so hard for me, why something as simple as quiet snow is so exciting.

So I open my mouth. But when I speak, a different truth comes out.

"I love you, too." The words are in the air before I can think them through.

Maverick's eyes widen, and then so do mine.

"Wait. I mean, *I love you.* Not 'too.' I don't know why I said—I didn't think you were—I mean, I thought you were going to, but you didn't, and I just…" I trail off with a sigh, grateful that it's dark out so Maverick can't see my burning red cheeks.

But Maverick just stares at me, an amused smile tugging at his lips. He takes a step closer, cupping my cheek with his hand. In the hazy lamplight, his hazel eyes meet mine, and the moment drags on, like time has slowed down around us.

"I love you, Laura," he finally says, the faintest whisper into the silent air.

"I love you, too, Maverick."

"See, now it works," he adds with a wink.

I squeeze my eyes shut, laughing as I bury my face into his chest to hide my embarrassment. But Maverick hooks a finger under my chin, nudging me to look up at him.

"You're adorable."

He starts to lean in, his breath warm against my skin. At the same time, the edges of the memory start to shimmer, like a fading dream.

And then it's gone.

CHAPTER 19

MY EYES SNAP OPEN. Bright fluorescent light floods my vision, making me squint them closed again.

A chill runs through me. I can almost feel the icy air still sapping heat from my skin, Maverick's fingers still curved under my chin. The memory lingers like an echo, reaching to hold on to me through the stretches of time.

Until a voice shatters it.

"What did you see?"

I hear it just once. No echoing, no overlapping noise. The future-echoes are gone, and it has only been a few minutes. The last time Alice gave me that stuff, it had lasted for hours.

I open my eyes again, blinking until the shape of Alice comes into focus. She's standing across from me, staring at me like I'm a solution in a beaker and she's waiting for the chemical reaction to take place.

I narrow my eyes. "Wouldn't you like to know?"

"I would." Alice turns her back to me, her hands hovering over the cart of medical supplies. A moment later, she crosses over to the table in front of me carrying a small plastic box. She sets it down, then snaps it open, revealing the contents: five identical syringes, resting neatly inside. She meets my gaze. "And I'm willing to do whatever it takes to get you to tell me."

"What do they do?" I demand, trying to keep my expression neutral.

"I suppose you'll find out, if you don't want to talk," she replies.

"Why do you care so much? What do you want from me?"

"I just want to understand you, Laura. I want to know what you're capable of."

"I'm not capable of anything. I don't know what you think I saw, but it was nothing. It's not going to change anything."

Alice tilts her head the slightest bit. "Then why not tell me, if you think it won't make a difference?"

My hands curl into fists. "Why do you want to know so bad?" I demand. "Because you want to find some way to work around my ability? So you can manipulate my memories like you did to everyone else?"

Alice just watches me, expressionless.

"Or because you want to replicate it? Find some way to use it to your advantage? Well, good luck with that. I'm sure hearing a constant stream of noise is going to be super helpful to you."

My words are full of acid, but when I finish, Alice doesn't seem fazed at all.

"If you aren't planning to voluntarily tell me," she says, "I'd rather get on with this." Then she turns her attention to the box on the table. She reaches for it, her fingers brushing over the syringes as she scans the label on each one.

I follow her movements with my eyes, trying to puzzle out what she's going to do to me. So far, I know she's made replications of Maverick's, Gabe's, Wyatt's, Angelo's, and Brent and Dahlia's abilities. She also must have used a combination of some of those abilities to manipulate the anomalies' memories, rather than just erasing them. So there could be any combination of abilities in this box, and she could easily find a way to get into my head, scouring my brain for the information she wants. If she does that, she'll find out that I'm working with Dr. Shaw, too.

I can't let that happen.

Alice's fingers close around one of the syringes, and she lifts it out of the box. "This should do the trick," she says, moving to tug the cap of the needle off.

"Wait!" I interrupt, hating the twinge of desperation in my voice.

Alice's hands freeze, and her pale blue eyes meet mine expectantly.

I release a long, hot breath, pinning my gaze to the table. "It was just a memory," I tell her, my voice dropping several notches. "One I lost."

Alice lifts her chin, then places the syringe back in the box. "Of what?"

I squeeze my eyes shut, the snowy night replaying before me. The memory had felt so sweet, so genuine. Telling Alice about it feels like a violation.

"Of Maverick," I finally answer.

"From before he erased your memories?"

I nod, still avoiding her gaze.

"Why choose this specific memory? What significance did it have?"

"Nothing," I snap. "It's none of your business."

Alice's gaze flicks down to the syringes between us, then back to me. A threat.

I clench my jaw, hating that she has the upper hand. Hating that this memory, this single moment I just want to tuck away and treasure is in Alice's hands now. But I just shake my head. "I didn't *choose* the memory."

Alice tilts her head.

"It just happened," I say. "I couldn't control it."

"Are you sure about that?" Alice asks, her gaze fixed on my face.

"Yes."

"Is that how it happened that day in the barn, too? The memories just came back, you had no control?"

I squeeze my eyes shut, remembering the odd sensation of memories flashing before me, fading away, changing. At the time, not much of it made sense, but now I can recognize that it was Alice in my head, messing with my memories. I'd seen each one as she sifted through them, watched as they got erased. Then replaced. But somehow, under it all, the echoes were still there.

I finally open my eyes again. "Yes. Everything was just gone, and then back."

Alice steps back from the table, then begins pacing in front of it. "Gone, and then back?"

"I couldn't stop you," I explain. "The memories were gone. But later, they just kind of… came back. I didn't do anything." For several minutes after I'd woken up that morning, my memories actually had been altered, just like everyone else's. I'd felt off, like something was wrong, but I couldn't figure out what. And then I'd heard the dog barking and seen the echo of it, and somehow that had triggered me to remember everything.

"I doubt you did *nothing*, Laura," Alice says. Her eyebrows furrow thoughtfully. "The memories were within you the whole time. You just chose to see them."

"I didn't *choose* anything," I argue. "I had no control over any of it."

Alice gives me a long, pitiful look. "If this was something you couldn't control, Laura, then every time someone has tried to erase your memories, it would have happened the same way. Including the first time."

Her words hang over my head for a long minute, floating in the air. I hear them, see them, feel their impact. But I can't grasp them. I hug myself, letting my fingers bunch into the fabric of my shirt. "I don't understand."

"Your memories of Maverick are still missing. And yet, the memories I took are intact. Why do you think that is?"

"This is different," I say, trying to sound firm, but my voice wavers. "You were changing the memories, not just erasing them. That's why I was able to resist it."

"But that's not true," Alice says. "I had to first erase your memories in order to plant the false ones. They were gone, just as much as the others."

I open my mouth, wanting to argue, but I can't seem to form words.

"Your ability is not what you have made it out to be, Laura. You can't see it because all your life, you've been taught that it's wrong. You've been told that if you want to be like everybody else, you have to suppress it. Ignore it."

I stare at the table, speechless.

"But you're not like everybody else, Laura," Alice continues. "You never were, and you never will be. And the sooner you accept that, the sooner you'll be able to see the truth."

When she finishes, all I can do is sit there, listening to my own heart thundering in my ears. Because despite how much I hate Alice, despite how much I know she's probably just trying to manipulate me, I know there's truth to her words.

Hadn't I been thinking the same thing just before I fell into the memory of Maverick? Hadn't I admitted it to myself already?

So what happens if I let go? If I just allow myself to be who I am, allow my ability to exist the way it was meant to, what will I find? I'm standing on the edge of a cliff again, looking down at an abyss, and being told that jumping will free me.

What's at the bottom of it? Something I couldn't even imagine?

All of my lost memories of Maverick?

Alice lets out a long sigh, dragging me out of my thoughts. I glance up to find her back turned to me, her shoulders slumped almost in defeat. "Imagine how much more anomalies could do if we weren't treated like we were dangerous," she says softly. "If we weren't treated like something is wrong with us." She straightens, turning to face me with a look of pure determination on her face. "The ACA wants to prevent that. They want us to disappear, to stop existing. Because they're afraid of us—of what we could do if we just tapped into a fraction of our power."

I narrow my eyes. "Maybe they're just afraid of what would happen if the power got into the wrong hands."

"Or maybe, they're afraid of what would happen if it got into the *right* hands," Alice says, her eyes brightening. "Imagine what life would be like if everyone had access to our abilities. Imagine how much easier we could build things with the help of telekinesis, how many lives could be saved with my own ability, how much better our infrastructure could be with Angelo's ability. Imagine being able to travel anywhere you want as quickly as you want with the twin's teleportation—even Maverick's ability could help so many lives ridden by PTSD."

I let her words sink in. "Things would certainly be different."

Alice nods, a wistful smile spreading across her lips. "It would be beautiful. A utopia, eventually. Anomalies could change the world… we would be heroes."

I close my eyes, absorbing her words, but don't reply.

"Now you see why I want you on my side?" Alice says, turning her gaze to me. "What I'm working so hard for?"

I meet her gaze, long and hard, but shake my head. "That doesn't make anything you're doing right. The ACA might not have our best interests at heart, but that doesn't make kidnapping and experimenting on kids okay. That doesn't justify the things you've done."

"The things I've *had* to do, because I was given no other choice," she fires back.

I drop my gaze, setting my jaw. "There's always a choice."

"I should have known you wouldn't understand," Alice says sadly. Then she turns her back to me. "Enjoy your ability while you can. Maybe do some soul-searching to find those lost memories. Because I'm going to take them all once I find a way to inhibit it."

And with that, she leaves me alone in the room, her words burrowing under my skin, sending me into a panic.

Inhibit it.

If we don't stop Alice soon, she's going to find a way to erase my memories. She's going to make me a blank slate, like the rest of them, so she can execute her plans without interference. And I'm never even going to realize what has happened.

CHAPTER 20

AFTER MY ENCOUNTER with Alice, I'm constantly on edge. For the next several days, every time I see a guard in the hallways, a wave of anxiety rolls through me—are they there to take me to Alice? Has she found a way to inhibit my ability already?

But each time, thankfully, is just a false scare. The guards stay stationed along the walls, observing from their posts, just doing their jobs. Nobody comes for me in the middle of the night or drags me kicking and screaming to the medical wing.

I can't focus, though. Even in the quiet of my room, listening in on my classes from a tablet without any echoes to distract me, the screen just blurs. Because my conversation with Alice keeps haunting me.

There's so much more to your ability than you realize.

I can't deny it. I can't pretend that she's wrong, because I've experienced so much proof that it's true. The memories of Maverick that I've slipped into—twice now. The echoes I'd heard in the cafeteria that weren't from a year ago. The fact that I've managed to keep my memories both times Alice has tried to take them.

The memories were within you the whole time. You just chose to see them.

But how had I done that? None of these strange occurrences have felt like they were in my control. I don't remember *choosing* to see anything.

That day in the barn, after Alice had twisted my memories, things had simply felt off. And then I'd heard the dog barking, the same sound from when I'd first arrived at the barn, and somehow that had triggered me to remember the truth.

The other memories, the ones of Maverick, have been different. One of them I'd dreamed. And the other one was because Alice had injected me with that serum. So how can I even know that she's right? That somehow, I'm in control? Because maybe I'm not. Maybe it's just random. Something that doesn't make sense.

Nothing about me has ever made sense.

As the days pass and the same thoughts circle in my mind, I start to lose hope of finding answers. Because even when I stare at the walls for hours, trying to get my brain to remember Maverick, trying to convince myself that I can find the memories somehow, nothing happens.

Georgia sneaks me food from the cafeteria during breakfast and lunch because I can only seem to drag myself out of the dorm room once a day for dinner. And even then, I only stay for as long as it takes me to eat. My dorm room feels like the only safe place. Logically, I know that the guards still know where to find me, but behind these doors, in the dark, I can almost pretend I'll be able to hide from them. From Alice. And plus, it's quiet inside.

At least most of the time. On Friday morning, an echo wakes me.

"*I can't believe today's finally the day!*" It's the same voice from the echo I'd heard last week: Penny.

"*I'm so jealous,*" Georgia's echo groans from the bed, her voice muffled by a pillow.

"*Your time will come, don't worry.*"

"*What's the first thing you're going to do once you get out?*"

Penny's echo lets out a long, thoughtful sigh. "*I can't decide. My top choices are: go to my favorite Mexican restaurant, lay outside in the sunshine for hours, or spend all day binging the last few seasons of* Vampire Hunters. *I've been hanging off that cliffhanger in Season 1 for five years now, and I can't stand another minute of it.*"

"*Seriously!*" Georgia squeals. "*I only got to see three episodes of Season 2 and I'm so scared. What if something happens to Liam?*"

"*If they killed him off, I. Will. Literally. Die.*"

"*Before you die, you have to send me word. That way I don't watch it when I get out and die, too.*"

"*I will make sure you know with my dying breath.*"

Giggles fill the room, and then fall into silence. A few sounds drift to me: drawers opening and closing, fabric rustling. The sounds of someone getting ready for the day.

Then, Georgia's voice. "*I'm going to miss you, Penny.*"

The sounds of movement pause. "*I'm gonna to miss you, too, G. But you'll be out of here before you know it, I promise.*"

"*I know. And you'll be around, right? Maybe Dr. Shaw will let me see you when you're back in to get your meds.*"

"*Maybe,*" Penny says. Then she hesitates. "*If I even come back at all.*"

A few beats of silence pass. "*You have to,*" Georgia finally says warily.

Penny sighs. "*Georgia, I've been stuck in here for five years. I don't ever want to come back.*"

"*But you* have *to,*" Georgia insists. "*They won't let you go if you don't.*"

"*I'm not going to tell them I'm not coming back, G.*"

When Georgia speaks again, her voice is laced with fear. "*They'll come for you. They'll find you, and they'll force you to. And then they might make you stay for disregarding the rules.*"

"*They won't find me if I hide well enough,*" Penny replies simply.

"*Penny, this isn't—*"

"*I know you're a rule follower, Georgia. But I'm not.*"

"*It's not about that,*" Georgia snaps. "*It's about you getting away with it. What if you don't? What do you think they'll do to you?*"

"*I* will *get away with it.*"

"*But—*"

"*I can turn invisible, G. How would they ever find me, even if I was right in front of them?*"

"*But you don't—*"

"*I'll hide out until my powers come back. Just two weeks. They won't even be looking for me until I don't show up.*"

The room falls quiet, but even here, in the present, I can feel the tension in the air. Georgia's terror.

"Georgia, I'm going to miss you. A lot," Penny finally says, her voice going soft. *"I wasn't going to tell you, but I decided I couldn't just leave without an explanation. This might be the last time—"*

"Don't say that."

A pause. Then, *"I'll find you once you're out, G. We can get away from all this. Together. But you just need to trust me."*

From Georgia's spot, I hear a sniffle. *"Okay."*

"Come here," Penny says. Feet cross the room. I picture Georgia hugging Penny, though I don't know what she looks like.

And then the door opens. Not an echo.

I glance over, where Georgia is stepping through, smiling at me hesitantly. "I brought you a plate. Pancakes today, which are… well, you know."

I swallow. "Thank you."

Gratefully, I take the plate from Georgia's hands. She even poured some syrup over the bacon the way I like.

As I pick up the fork and start cutting the pancake, Georgia slumps into her desk chair, sighing heavily. "I'm so glad it's Friday."

I nod, but keep listening for the echo. It seems to have been the end of the conversation, though, because all I hear is the sound of the door clicking shut.

"Gabe still wants to know why you won't come eat with us," Georgia tells me.

I roll my eyes. I'd seen Gabe at dinner a few times this week and had explained exactly why. And he, of all people, should understand. Unless he's already forgotten what it's like to hear noise that shouldn't be there all the time. "Tell him I missed him, too."

Georgia smiles. "I will."

I turn my attention back to my food, and as I eat, a comfortable silence falls around us. Georgia just sits with me, lost in thought, and I'm grateful for her presence. I never asked her to bring me food or stay with me while I eat, but she started doing it when she realized I was going through a hard time. And she doesn't expect to have a conversation with me while she's here, either. She just gives me her presence. Lets me have my quiet without having to be alone.

When I swallow the last piece of bacon, I set my plate down and shift in my seat. "I heard an echo," I say.

Georgia tilts her head to the side. "Oh?"

"It was you talking to someone. Her name was Penny?"

Her eyes widen, then drop to the floor. "Penny," she echoes softly.

"It sounded like she was leaving—getting out of here. You were saying goodbyes."

Georgia nods. "Penny left a couple of months ago."

My stomach twists. *Months*. Not a year. I'm still not hearing the right echoes.

"We were roommates for a while, so we got pretty close."

"She sounded really nice."

A faint smile passes over Georgia's lips. "She was. She was wild and… carefree. She used to get in trouble all the time, even dragged me into it once or twice. But she didn't care. She just wanted to have fun."

I smile at the thought of her. Then I bite my lip. "Did she ever… come back?" I try to say the words delicately, worried I might be crossing a line. But Georgia just shakes her head. The gesture looks painful.

A lump forms in my throat. It's got to be awful, losing a friend like that. Not knowing where they might be. But… "She got away, then."

"I guess so," is all Georgia says. She offers a grim smile, and I know that she's trying to be happy for Penny. Even though it hurts.

I wonder if Georgia wishes that she could leave, too. If she's thinking about what will happen once the ACA lets her out. The other day, she'd mentioned how excited she was to go back to school, to make the swim team. But that's only as long as she keeps coming back to let the ACA administer the suppressors. Her ability isn't even something that hurts her, and it would be easy enough to keep it a secret. But the ACA doesn't care. They won't let her have a choice.

None of it feels right.

Penny had found a way out of it, though. And that gives me hope.

Because if she managed to escape the clutches of the ACA, then maybe I can, too.

CHAPTER 21

ON MONDAY MORNING, two guards are standing in the hallway outside of my suite when I open the door to leave for breakfast. I freeze, limbs going tense, when I see them. Because the first thought that runs through my head is that Alice has done it. She's figured out how to erase my memories for real this time, and she's sent the guards to get me. It's over.

The second thought that comes to me is that they're just here to take me to the medical wing to see Dr. Shaw—it *has* been a week. And that makes me relax a little.

Without a word, the guards nod at me and start down the hallway, and I know I don't have a say about it anyway, so I follow them into the elevators. We ride up to the medical wing, and then I'm waiting in the exam room, fingers tangled together anxiously.

When Dr. Shaw opens the door, my shoulders finally relax.

"Good morning," she greets with a smile. "How was your weekend?"

I'm not in the mood for small talk, so I just sigh, pressing my palms to my eyes while I will my heart to stop racing.

"Feeling okay?"

I open my eyes, meeting Dr. Shaw's concerned gaze. "Just… anxious." I hope she gets the hint. I want to know where we're at with the plan.

She gives no indication that we're going to discuss it, so I don't say anything while she goes through the motions of taking my vitals and inspecting my wounds. She seems pleased by the state of my leg, which is healing nicely, but frowns at the cut across my left palm. I'd removed the bandages from my hands a few days ago.

"Is that one bothering you?" Dr. Shaw asks.

I glance down at the red streak across my hand, then shake my head. "Not much."

She sifts through a drawer, then hands me a small tube. Some kind of ointment. "Apply that once a day. Just as a precaution."

With a nod, I tuck it into my pocket.

"Well, Miss Jones, everything looks good. There are a few tests I need to run before you head to class, though, so whenever you're ready, you can follow me."

"Tests?"

Dr. Shaw nods. "Nothing to worry about. Just a bit of research to figure something out."

I wonder if she's being vague because she doesn't want me to know—or because she doesn't want whoever is watching behind the cameras to know. Either way, I slide off the exam table and say, "I'm ready."

She leads me through the door, and I follow her across the lobby, then down a hallway I've never explored before. It doesn't take us long to reach a door with the nameplate "Dr. Gloria Shaw" on it.

"This is your office?" I ask.

Dr. Shaw just pushes the door open.

As I step inside, I quickly realize that I'm right. But it isn't what I expect.

Every available surface is covered in something: stacks of paper with highlighted sections, pens and pencils, notebooks, books lying open on random pages, half-empty water bottles, wrinkled lab coats, and a fake orchid collecting dust. Even the walls are dotted with sticky notes, messy handwriting scrawled across them.

Dr. Shaw strides over to her desk and takes a seat like everything is perfectly normal, then gestures at the chair across from it. "Please, sit."

I have to move a stack of papers to the floor before I do.

"There are a few things I'd like to ask you before we go over the details of your plan," Dr. Shaw says simply.

Instinctively, I glance up at the ceiling, worried.

"No one can watch us in here," Dr. Shaw assures me, and I drop my gaze. "We're free to talk."

I swallow. "What do you want to know?"

Dr. Shaw turns in her chair, reaching for a stack of papers. Despite the mess, she seems to know exactly where the one she's looking for is. She sets it down in front of her, running a finger down the page while she scans it. "The records I've found indicate that you were born in Pendleton, is that right?"

Slowly, I nod.

"Is that where your grandparents are from, too?"

"My grandparents?" I ask, frowning.

"Specifically your maternal grandparents."

I shake my head. "Why do you want to know?"

Dr. Shaw rubs her chin with her thumb. "Part of my job here is to research anomalies. To figure out why they exist. So that maybe we can discover a way to prevent the mutation from developing in the first place."

I study her, my leg bouncing in place. "What does it have to do with my grandparents?"

"The mutation that's responsible for anomalies' abilities doesn't appear to be random. It's inherited."

"From the maternal grandparents?"

Dr. Shaw nods, leaning forward on her elbows. "The mutation passes down through the parents but remains dormant. Until the third generation."

My eyebrows furrow as I think of my grandparents. "What does that have to do with where they're from?"

"We don't believe that the original mutation just happened on its own," Dr. Shaw explains. "We think it was a result of exposure to something—a chemical, a virus perhaps. Which is why the only known anomalies in existence have ties to Pine Springs Valley."

Pine Springs Valley. Shorewick. Garysburg. Bluthtown. Rison.

But not Pendleton. That's on the other side of the mountains.

I stare down at my lap. "My mom's parents are from Drenville." On the other side of the mountains, too.

You're different, Laura.

I look up to find Dr. Shaw scribbling a note onto the paper in front of her.

"What do you think that means?"

Dr. Shaw's mouth twists to the side. "I'm not sure. It might mean that something else caused the mutation—something we haven't thought of. But just as easily, your grandparents could have traveled to Pine Springs Valley and been exposed to whatever caused the mutation while they were there."

I purse my lips as the words settle over me. I'd never really thought about how anomalies came into existence. I'd always assumed we were just freaks of nature, something no one understood. But that might not be true. There might even be a perfectly logical scientific explanation out there for why I am the way I am.

And that makes me feel a little better.

Dr. Shaw turns to put the papers back, then meets my gaze. "Do you mind if I take a quick blood sample from you?" she asks. "Dr. Wight has kept all information on you away from me, and I'd like to do some research without her finding out. To figure out what she's been hiding."

Instinctively, I cross my arms, hugging myself. People poking me with needles has never turned out well so far.

But it's just a blood sample. And Dr. Shaw might be able to make sense of things. She might be able to tell me why Alice said I was different, and the curiosity tugs at me.

I nod.

While Dr. Shaw gets to work preparing to take the sample, she asks, "Have you decided which of your friends you'd like to take with you?"

So it's time for that conversation. I chew on my lip, wondering if she's going to budge at all. I'd discussed the plan with Gabe a few nights ago, and he'd made the point that it had taken both Wyatt and Angelo's abilities to sneak in and out of the ACA unnoticed. It would make things a lot easier if we had both of them for this, too. Even if it means leaving Gabe behind.

I clear my throat. "I don't think our plan will work with just one of my friends. We need to take two if we want to have a chance at stopping Alice. Both Wyatt and Angelo."

Dr. Shaw is quiet for a long moment. "I'm afraid that isn't going to be possible."

"Please, just hear me out. We're not going to—"

"It's not just because I wouldn't let you," she hurries to explain. Her eyes meet mine, wary. "Your friend Wyatt has been in a coma since he got here."

I suddenly feel like I've been kicked in the stomach. "*What?*"

Dr. Shaw opens an alcohol wipe and rubs a small circle on the inside of my elbow. "I've only seen it happen a few times before. But sometimes, when anomalies over-exert their abilities, it causes permanent brain damage."

Her words are like another kick, right where it hurts. "He… he can't…" I choke out.

Wyatt had saved us. Well, he had tried to. We'd been captured anyways, in the end. But he'd used his ability to trap everyone in a mental cloud of darkness, which had given us the chance to get away.

And now, because of that… "Is he going to be okay?"

Dr. Shaw's lips purse. She doesn't offer an answer. Instead, she says, "I'm going to take the sample now."

When she inserts the needle, I barely feel it. Because I'm numb.

Wyatt.

We were barely friends. And his temper had caused our group a few problems. But in that moment, when it mattered, he'd done everything in his power to save us. And now…

"So Angelo, then?" Dr. Shaw asks.

"I—I guess."

Without giving me time to process any further, she launches into the plan. I try my best to keep up, to remember her instructions. The original dose of suppressors they gave everyone will wear off by the end of today, so we'll wait until tomorrow night, just to be safe. I'll need to meet the others in the media center. It's up to us to escape, but once we're past the gates, she'll leave a vehicle in the woods. And she's pinpointed three addresses traceable to Alice for us to investigate.

She hands me a map to the car and the list of addresses. Asks me if I'm ready to go. But I'm not. I can barely breathe.

"I need a second," I say, feeling dizzy.

Dr. Shaw nods, giving me a pitiful look. "I'll go get you some water."

Then the door closes behind her, and that's when I start to hear echoes.

CHAPTER 22

A KNOCK ON THE DOOR. Then Dr. Shaw's echo, from her desk.

"Come in."

The door creaks on its hinges as it swings open.

"Good morning, Dr. Shaw," the newcomer greets. Strangely, her voice sounds familiar, but I can't pinpoint where I've heard it before.

Dr. Shaw makes a noise of surprise. *"Katherine! My apologies, I didn't know you were stopping by,"* she says, her words rushed. I hear shuffling, like she's moving things around on her desk.

"I wanted to give you the update first."

The shuffling stops. "*The update?*"

"*About the new procedures we'll be implementing.*"

Dr. Shaw is quiet for a moment. Then she says, "*Please, sit.*"

Feet move toward the chair I'm sitting in now, and then the woman—Katherine—clears her throat.

"*There's been an incident,*" she begins, pausing to let the words settle. "*An anomaly who was released a few months ago did not show up for his remediation appointment on Saturday. When our agents finally tracked him down late last night, he had full access to his abilities again. He attacked them, killing one and injuring the other.*"

Dr. Shaw's echo curses under her breath.

"*Fortunately, the situation has been handled. But it has made me realize that the reintegration program we have in place is flawed.*"

I hear Dr. Shaw sigh. "*I should have thought about this. We need to monitor the anomalies that have been released better. More check-ins. A mobile unit to administer the medication.*"

"*I don't see that as a permanent solution to the problem,*" Katherine says. "*As we find more anomalies, and as we release more, we'll have to bring in more staff to support that. Which defeats the purpose of this organization—to keep the group of individuals that know about this issue as small as possible. The more we have to expand, the more risk we take of information getting out.*"

A long silence stretches across the room. Dr. Shaw's voice is small when she asks, "*What do you think we should do, then?*"

"*I think that while releasing anomalies is the humane thing to do, we need to recognize that this situation calls for more difficult decisions to be made.*"

"More difficult decisions?"

Katherine's echo shifts in her chair before she answers. *"Anomalies shouldn't be allowed to leave unless their abilities have been permanently suppressed. So there's no chance of something like this happening again."*

"So... we get rid of the reintegration program. Until I finish with my research."

"And that's where we have a problem. We have no idea how long that will take. Or if it's even possible."

"It is *possible,"* Dr. Shaw says, an edge to her voice. *"I'm getting close."*

"You've been getting close for the last eight years, Gloria. Even Dr. Wight has hit a wall."

A beat of silence passes. *"So, what? We just give up?"*

"Of course not," Katherine says, almost gently. *"But in the meantime, our numbers are growing. Soon, we won't have the capacity to hold all of them. We need to make room for new arrivals."*

"We can convert some of the classrooms into dormitories," Dr. Shaw says simply. *"Or use the recreation floor while we get the permits set up for another building."*

Katherine sighs heavily. *"You don't understand. Expanding is not an option, even here. We can't bring in more staff. We're having trouble finding enough personnel with the right security clearance as it is."*

"So what are you suggesting?"

There's a long pause before Katherine speaks again. *"I'm not suggesting anything. I'm letting you know that new procedures are going to be implemented. Anomalies that have been here the longest will no longer be released. But they'll still have to be removed from our facilities."*

My stomach drops when I realize what Katherine's echo is implying.

"Are you serious about this?" Dr. Shaw's voice cracks.

"We don't have another choice."

"You can't just do that," Dr. Shaw protests. *"These are people we're talking about, not animals. They're just children."*

"It's an unfortunate sacrifice that has to be made."

"What about the families?"

"We'll tell them the mutation causes complications. That we couldn't find a cure in time," Katherine says matter-of-factly. As if she isn't gambling with people's lives with those words. *"They will receive a generous stipend for their loss. Enough to keep their mouths shut about all of this, too."*

When Dr. Shaw speaks again, her voice raises an octave. *"So you can afford to do that, but you can't afford to expand?"*

"It's not about the money," Katherine fires back. *"It's about keeping this under control."*

A sound startles me—Dr. Shaw's chair scraping across the floor. *"This isn't what I signed up for."* Footsteps pound across the floor. But when they get to the door, Katherine's low voice cuts through the room, stopping them.

"You know what will happen if you leave."

I stare at the spot by the door where Dr. Shaw's echo must be, my heart pounding for her.

"I can't believe this," she finally says, voice breathy. *"I can't believe you, of all people, would get behind this."*

"I didn't want it to come to this. I really didn't."

"So you're blaming me?"

"*Of course not,*" Katherine says. "*But maybe it will be a good incentive to hasten your research.*"

Dr. Shaw's voice drops to a near-whisper. "*It doesn't have to be this way.*"

"*The decision has already been made.*"

"*Kath—*"

"*You need to leave your heart out of this job, Gloria. You need to go back to your desk.*"

"*Please—*"

"*That's a command.*"

And it's in that moment that I finally remember where I've heard Katherine's voice before. I'd woken up to it that first day here in the ACA.

"*It's time to dispose of her,*" she'd said.

And Dr. Shaw had tried to argue. "*But she hasn't—*"

"*That's not a request, doctor. It's a command.*"

In that echo, it had sounded like the anomaly they were discussing had sustained some injuries, and that she hadn't recovered much in the past three weeks. And Katherine had ordered Dr. Shaw to *dispose* of her.

The door opens, right now in the present, making me jump. Dr. Shaw steps in, and the echoes seem to fade from the forefront of my mind. With the way I've been hearing echoes lately, I don't even know when this one could have been from. A year ago? Or is it more recent?

Dr. Shaw is in front of me, holding a cup, and it takes me a second to notice. I grab it, then let it fall to my lap, where I stare down into the water, watching my reflection shimmer as my hands shake.

"Feeling okay?" she asks, eyebrows drawn.

I can't even shake my head. I have too many things swirling in my mind, and I can't risk forgetting any of them.

Dr. Shaw reaches out to take the cup from my hands. "Maybe we should—"

"No!" I jerk my hand away, water sloshing over the edge of the cup and onto my lap. Dr. Shaw looks shocked, and I hurry to offer an apology, but suddenly her presence makes me uneasy. Sure, Dr. Shaw is helping me, and sure, she'd been against Katherine's plan. But she's still here. Working for the ACA.

I suck in a deep breath, steeling myself. "I just need to go back to my room and rest."

And then I'm standing, almost running out the door. I ignore Dr. Shaw's calls, don't even bother waiting for the guards who are supposed to escort me. I just get in the elevators, rapidly pressing the buttons until the doors close.

And it isn't until I'm back in my dorm room, lying on my bed, panting, that I think of Penny.

That morning—just a few days ago—I'd heard an echo of her talking to Georgia. Excited to leave.

Georgia said she's been gone for a couple of months now. That she hasn't seen Penny since. But did she leave before or after the echoes I'd just witnessed happened? I can't tell because I have no idea which echoes are from when anymore. I don't know *how* to know.

I thought Penny got out. That she escaped the ACA for good. And that had given me hope.

But maybe she didn't.

Maybe she was never going to make it out.

And none of us are.

Because the ACA isn't letting anomalies go—they're *disposing* of them.

CHAPTER 23

I HAVE TO GET OUT.

The thought burns with a new intensity as I go through the motions of the rest of the day. And then the next.

We have to get out.

Ever since I got here, I knew I wanted to escape. I knew that being trapped in here would drive me crazy. But I'd gotten used to the idea of staying. Of being stuck here for the next five years in case that was what ended up happening. I knew that I needed to do something about Alice, but I thought that maybe, once she was taken care of, the worst of my problems would be solved.

I was wrong. *So* wrong.

This isn't just about Alice. This is about the entire ACA. About the fate of all anomalies.

And we have to get out.

It isn't an idea anymore. Or a hope.

It's a necessity.

Because if we don't…

I can't let my mind go there. I can't even consider that possibility, because I won't let it happen. I won't.

The resolve courses through me as I pace back and forth in my dorm room, waiting for the clock to move forward.

Georgia, Katie, and Ash have been hanging out in Ash's room since after dinner, and even when it starts to get late, I find myself alone. And instead of trying to get some rest before it's time to leave, I'm pretty sure I've started to wear a rut into the linoleum.

We're getting out. Tonight. Me, Maverick, and Angelo. And even though the original plan was to stop Alice, we have a bigger objective now. We need to find a way to shut down the ACA. Get all of the anomalies out.

The idea almost makes me want to laugh. Because it's exactly what the ACA thinks we were trying to do before.

When the clock finally nears midnight, I stop pacing and suck in a breath, steeling myself. I double check my pockets to make sure the map and list of addresses Dr. Shaw gave me are still there, then slip out the door. Just like the night I'd met Maverick and Dr. Shaw in the study room, the hallways are empty. Silent.

I ride the elevator up, and when I get to the door of the media center, I hesitate. A drop of sweat slides down my back. What if

Dr. Shaw lied? What if she isn't going to help us, and when I open this door, no one is there? What if—

My thoughts don't get a chance to spiral any further. Because the door opens, and the figure that steps through puts a halt to all of my fears.

"Laura." Maverick says my name like a sigh of relief. He reaches for me, pulls me to him. As I tighten my arms around his back, I wonder when we're going to stop doing this—greeting each other as if we believed the other was lost forever.

When I open my eyes over Maverick's shoulder, I see Angelo. He offers a little wave.

And then I'm hugging him, too.

"You guys are here," I whisper. *We're going to get out.*

And then the urgency takes over. I step back, my eyes darting around the room. "We should get going." I pull the tablet I'd tucked into the waistband of my pants out. It's the tablet I'd been issued to watch my classes remotely with, and it has a bunch of security measures installed to prevent me from using it for anything else. But that shouldn't be a problem for Angelo.

He reaches for it with eager hands, then closes his eyes. The screen starts to flicker.

"I missed being able to do this," he says, sighing.

"I figured maybe you could—"

I don't get to finish, because Angelo is already walking toward the edge of the room to stick his fingers into an electrical socket.

Beside me, Maverick lets out a short laugh. It seems like a strange thing to do at a time like this—laugh. But I find myself joining in

And then it fades.

"Maverick," I say, turning to him. "There's something you need to know."

Concern draws a line across his forehead.

"The ACA… they're not letting anomalies go."

He frowns. "What do you mean?"

I swallow. "They're telling everyone they are. They're making it sound like we can go back to our lives once we've stayed here long enough. But…" I hesitate, unable to say the words. "I heard an echo. I heard that… anomalies don't get to leave. Not the way they make us think."

Slowly, understanding washes over Maverick's features. "You don't mean…"

"They're killing anomalies. Instead of releasing them."

Maverick runs a hand over his head, mouth hanging open.

"Maverick, we need to get everyone out. We need to stop this." My voice sounds small, like a plea.

"We…" He shakes his head. "We can't. Not right now. Not just the three of us."

Despite my best efforts to prevent it from happening, my bottom lip wobbles.

"We need to get out of here," he says, his tone changing. No longer shocked. Determined. "We can't do this without an escape plan. A way to get everyone somewhere safe. And we'll need help—the three of us might be able to get out of here without any issues, but there's no way the ACA won't notice all of the anomalies trying to leave at once."

I drop my gaze, hating that he's right.

Maverick's eyes dart around the room, already forming a plan. "We'll come back. Once we find Alice's replications of our abilities. Maybe, instead of destroying them, we keep them. Use them to help everyone escape."

I start to nod, the plan already forming in my head as he says the words, but before we get a chance to discuss it further, Angelo calls to us.

"I've tapped into the security system," he says. "I'll control the cameras while we leave, so no one will see us on the footage. And I've disabled the alarms."

I nod, squaring my shoulders. "Then let's go."

Angelo leads the way as we exit the media center, then start for the elevators. He presses his hand to the scanner, and the light flashes green. A moment later, the doors open. We shuffle into it, then Maverick and I watch as Angelo fiddles with the control panel. For obvious reasons, anomalies can only get the elevator to go to three floors: our dorms, the recreation floor, and the classrooms. It usually takes someone with more security clearance to get anywhere else, but all it takes Angelo is a bit of focus and the light for the main level flashes on.

I stare at the screen at the top of the elevator. Watch it change from B2 to B1.

"Oh no," Angelo says just before it changes to 1. In a second flat I'm standing over his shoulder, looking down at the tablet screen with him. It's footage from a camera in the main hallway. A guard has just stepped into the lobby, headed straight for the elevators.

Before we can do anything, the elevator chimes and the doors slide open. Sure enough, she's just outside them, and I watch her face start to change when she spots us, eyes widening and jaw tensing.

Maverick reacts first, stepping out in front of us, reaching for her. But she backs away, dodging him easily. A second later she's pointing a gun at his chest.

Maverick freezes, hands going up in front of him, and mine go up too. Images flash through my mind of Maverick and I running, gunshots whizzing past us. Then Maverick falling to the ground, blood staining his shirt.

If she shoots, I don't have a way to save him this time.

"I need backup on the main floor. Immediately," the guard says into a radio clipped to her chest.

"Roger," a scratchy voice responds.

"What do you guys think you're doing?" the guard asks, eyes slowly moving over each of us. Gun still positioned to send a bullet straight through Maverick's heart.

Trying to save everyone, I think, but my lips don't move. Our one shot, our chance at escaping. Gone. Just like that.

When no one answers her, she gestures with the gun for us to move. "Against the wall. Hands on your heads. All of you."

Without a second thought, Angelo and I obey, pressing our backs against it. But Maverick stays where he is, eyes narrowed in challenge.

"Every extra second it takes you to join them is another day you're going to spend in isolation for this," the guard warns.

"And if I don't?"

I watch the guard's thumb move toward the safety switch. "I'll be forced to shoot."

"Please, don't," I say, my voice hoarse. Then Maverick looks at me, and his eyes seem to soften. He takes three slow steps, then his back thumps against the wall beside me.

The elevator dings a moment later, and a second guard steps out. When he spots us, his body goes rigid, his hand moving to the gun on his hip.

"What's going on here?"

"I'm not sure," the first guard responds. "But it appears they were attempting to escape. Would you help me cuff them?"

He nods, moving his hand away from the gun to grab the handcuffs clipped to his belt, then sets his eyes on me. The first guard finally lowers her gun, reaching for her handcuffs, too. And that's when she makes a mistake. She reaches for Maverick first, grabbing his wrist to slide the first cuff over, and her bare fingers brush against his skin. Within seconds, her eyes gloss over and her body goes limp. Then she slumps to the ground, unconscious.

The other guard starts to turn, eyebrows pulling together, but Maverick reaches for him, too. He braces the man as he starts to fall forward, lowering him to the ground gently.

I release a breath, heart pounding wildly in my chest.

"We need to get moving. There are probably more on the way," Maverick says. He bends down to unclip the keychain from the man's belt loop, then reaches for my wrist to unlock the single cuff the guard managed to get around it. Meanwhile, Angelo goes for the tablet he'd dropped.

When we're all ready, Angelo gestures for us to follow him. "This way."

Our pace quickens. That encounter with the guards was close. Too close. If they had simply been wearing gloves or had decided to shoot at us anyway, it would have been over.

Angelo leads us around a bend, then another. We practically run down the hallways, slowing only at each corner for Angelo to double-check that our path is clear. And then we're barreling through the exit, into the outdoors.

The frozen air burns against my cheeks as we make a mad dash for the woods, but I barely feel cold. I focus on each step, trying not to trip in the darkness.

When we finally get to the gate, Angelo works his magic. Maverick manages to catch the guard in the shack by surprise, ensuring he won't remember seeing us, and then we slip into the treeline beyond.

And finally, we're free.

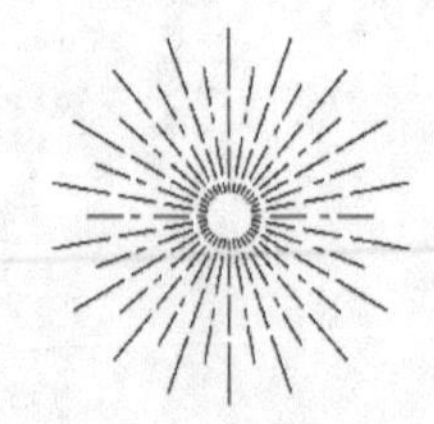

CHAPTER 24

TRUE TO HER WORD, Dr. Shaw left us a car in the woods. It takes almost forty-five minutes of tromping through the trees, going in the wrong direction, checking the map again, then circling back to find it, but when we step into the clearing and spot the small black sedan, a wave of relief washes over me.

I find the key on the driver's side tire, right where Dr. Shaw's note explained it would be, then reach for the door handle. But Maverick touches my shoulder, stopping me.

"I'll drive," he says, extending his hand.

I raise an eyebrow. "Because I drive like a grandma?"

He grins. "Yeah, mostly." When I roll my eyes, he adds, "Plus, I know a place we can stay for a while."

"Your second mansion?"

He shakes his head. "Not exactly."

Shrugging, I drop the keys into his palm. Then we all pile into the car, and Maverick cranks the heat up. Cold air blows from the vents at first, but even it feels slightly warmer than the outdoors. I rub my fingers together, trying to warm them up.

Maverick pulls the car onto the road that runs alongside the clearing and slams the gas, revving the engine. There aren't any other cars around, and we didn't pick up on any signs that we were being followed in the woods, but I guess we can't be too careful. Even though Maverick erased the guards' memories, there could have been others who heard the request for backup, and they might realize something is off. So we speed through the night, and as the minutes tick by, the heater starts to warm the car and thaw my limbs.

Eventually, we turn down a dirt driveway, and I get a strange sense of *déjà vu*. It isn't until I spot the mobile home up ahead, a detached garage to the right of it, that I realize why.

"We stopped here before," I say, glancing at Maverick. It feels like forever ago. But after I'd been kidnapped by Alice the first time and Maverick had broken me out, we'd stopped here to switch cars before heading to his mansion.

Maverick shifts the car into park, nodding. "This is my dad's old home from before he won the lottery. He never sold it, so I inherited it, too."

"I guess this is good," I say, unbuckling my seatbelt. "Since Alice probably knows about the mansion now."

"If she knows about that, she knows about this place, too," he says. "We won't be staying here, just… changing vehicles." When I give him a puzzled look, he continues, "Dr. Shaw might be helping us, but driving the car she gave us might be like drawing a giant target on our heads if she decides to send people after us. So I figured we'd grab one of mine."

I nod. I hadn't thought about it, but Dr. Shaw's loyalties are with the ACA first, so it makes sense.

Maverick opens his door, slipping out of the car, and I follow. Angelo trails behind us, the tablet tucked under his arm. He's been messing with it since we got in the car.

When we get to the garage, Maverick punches a number into a keypad and the door groans as it slides upward. Slowly, a car comes into view, and I recognize it instantly. It's the slim black sports car Maverick had driven when he rescued me from Alice's lab. The one he'd crashed into the Suburban that had been following me on the night of the Halloween dance, too. Which had given me an opportunity to escape.

"Wow," Angelo says, running his fingers over the passenger door, which is still crushed in. He tugs the handle, but it doesn't budge. "Are you sure it runs?"

Maverick nods. "It'll get us out of here. You just have to get in from the other side."

"Must have been some accident," Angelo comments, heading to the driver's side.

"Yeah." Maverick shrugs, glancing at me.

A smile twists my lips. "I can't believe you crashed a Lamborghini for me."

"Well that's because it's not a Lamborghini," Maverick replies with a smirk. "But I did think it would be pretty romantic."

I wrinkle my nose. "It might've been more romantic if it *was* a Lamborghini."

"I'll remember that for next time," Maverick replies, laughing. Then he gestures at the open door. "After you."

I get into the car, climbing over the center console before plopping into the passenger seat. Maverick slips in behind me and cranks it up.

We drive for almost an hour. I stare at the road ahead of us silently, and eventually it changes from two lanes to four. The woods start to thin out, and when we pass a sign that says "Welcome to Garysburg," I can finally picture where we are on a map. Garysburg is about fifteen miles northwest of Shorewick, so even though I'm still far from home, I feel closer than I have in weeks.

Maverick keeps driving until we get into the city center, and finally, we pull into a parking lot. I stare up at the high-rise building in front of us, reading the sign hanging over the awning. *City View Apartments.*

"You rent an apartment on the side?" I ask, raising an eyebrow at Maverick.

He bites his lip. "I don't *rent* it."

"You *own* it?"

"Yes..." he trails off, smiling sheepishly. "Not just one apartment, though."

My jaw drops. "You own the *complex?*"

Maverick shrugs, which is enough of an answer.

"*You own an apartment complex?*"

He scratches the back of his neck. "My dad was a bit of an investor."

A shocked laugh escapes me, and I cover my mouth to stifle it.

"That doesn't make things weird, does it?"

"I mean, maybe a little," I reply with a sly smile. "Not very many eighteen-year-olds can say they own an apartment complex."

"Not very many eighteen-year-olds have superpowers and just escaped a secret government institution, either," Maverick fires back. "So I think that means we're all weird."

"Touché."

Maverick flashes a grin at me before opening the door. When I slide out behind him into the night air, a shiver runs through me. Without the adrenaline pumping, the cold cuts right to the bone, so as soon as Angelo is out, we make a beeline for the front door. Once we're inside the lobby, I take in the pristine marble floors, the sparkling chandelier hanging above our heads, and the massive fireplace with wood crackling against the back wall. But it isn't any of those things that make me pause. It's the Christmas tree in the center.

"It's Christmas Eve," I say, staring. Somehow, even though I'd known the date, I hadn't put it together. Maybe because inside the bland walls of the ACA, there was nothing around to even indicate that a holiday was near.

"Actually, it's Christmas," Maverick says, pausing a few steps ahead of me to nod at the clock. I follow his gaze and realize he's right; it's well after 2 AM now.

I stare at it, thinking of my parents. It doesn't feel like that long ago that I was stuck at Maverick's mansion, missing them on Thanksgiving. And now it's already Christmas?

Sighing, I turn to join Maverick and Angelo, who are already waiting outside the elevator. The doors open as I approach and inside, Maverick presses the button for eight—the top floor.

When we get there, he leads us to the door on the far left and punches a number into a keypad beside it.

Unlike Maverick's mansion, the apartment is relatively small. Hardwood floors and a plush carpet in the living room make it feel homey, and the decor is simple and elegant. Off to the left, there's a kitchen with stainless steel appliances and white marble countertops. And, gratefully, it's quiet.

"There are two bedrooms down the hall," Maverick says, pointing as he moves toward the living room. "I'll take the couch."

Yawning, Angelo starts in that direction. While he disappears through one of the doors, I hesitate in the entrance way.

"You wouldn't happen to have anything to eat, would you?" I ask. I'm not actually that hungry, but the last thing I want to do right now is be alone.

"Hmm, I'm not sure," Maverick says. "Let's look."

I follow him into the kitchen, settling onto a bar stool at the counter. Maverick rummages through a few cabinets, pulling out the things he finds and setting them on the counter in front of me. A can of tuna. A box of cheese crackers. A couple packages of pasta. He goes to the fridge next, finding an expired carton of milk—which he drops in the trash—and a single bottle of soda.

"So, you don't come here very often, then?" I ask.

Maverick shakes his head. "Just another thing my dad left. I guess he stayed here occasionally. I was actually planning to start renting it out, but before I could get the paperwork set up, things kind of… got crazy."

They most certainly did. "Well, at least we have somewhere to stay for now."

Nodding, Maverick opens the last cabinet, then sets a chocolate bar down on the counter. We both stare at the spread for a minute, and then I swipe the chocolate bar and soda.

Maverick frowns. "If you want some real food, we could order something?"

"Do you think any restaurants are open right now?"

His mouth twists thoughtfully. "Probably not. There's a gas station not too far, though."

I rip open the wrapper of the chocolate bar. "This should tide me over until tomorrow."

Maverick slides onto the bar stool next to me, opening the box of crackers for himself. He tosses a few into his mouth, then winces. "They're stale."

I reach over him, sticking my hand into the box, then pop a few in my mouth. It takes a lot of effort to force myself to swallow.

"Yeah, they're… not great," I finally say. "Not as bad as the ACA lasagna, though."

Maverick laughs. "You're right about that." He throws another handful into his mouth to prove it.

"Here," I say, breaking off a piece of my chocolate bar and offering it to him. But he waves it away, reaching for another handful of crackers instead.

We eat in silence for a few minutes, and when I finish the chocolate bar, I fiddle with the wrapper.

"Maverick," I finally say. "I…" I pause, swallowing. "I'm glad we made it out of there."

He nods. "Me, too."

"I didn't think… I was worried that Dr. Shaw wouldn't pull through," I say. The lingering fear makes my voice waver. "Or that Alice would get to you before we could leave."

His eyes meet mine, but he doesn't say anything. Just holds my gaze, trapping me in place.

"I don't know what I would do if I lost you again," I add. And then, almost of its own accord, my hand moves to his face. My fingers brush the stubble along his jaw, and for a moment, his eyes close as he leans into the touch.

Then he's shifting on the bar stool, moving closer. I close my eyes, heart racing in anticipation, and for a flicker of a moment, I feel his warm breath against my skin.

But then it's gone. He pulls away, dropping his gaze. His mouth sets into a thin line, and I see his walls going up. Walls that are shutting me out.

"What's wrong?" I ask, heart sinking.

He lets out a pained sigh, then stands, running a hand through his hair. "I just… I feel so bad. About everything."

Everything. Alice, the ACA, my parents, the anomalies. So many bad things have happened, but none of them are Maverick's fault. Except…

"You're talking about my memories," I say.

He squeezes his eyes shut. "I can't stop thinking about it. Wishing I could go back and undo it."

I swallow. "Maverick, don't be so hard on yourself. You made a mistake. People do that."

"Most people's mistakes aren't directed against the people they love."

My chest tightens. "I've forgiven you, Maverick. I thought I made that clear." That night we'd investigated Alice's office and he'd taken a literal bullet for me, I told him I'd forgiven him. That I wanted to give us another chance. And then he'd kissed me.

But now, he can barely look me in the eyes.

"You did," he finally says. "But then Alice took *my* memories away. Then I finally understood what it was like."

I open my mouth, then close it again, grappling for words. Before I can form any, Maverick continues.

"I stole memories from you, Laura. Without even asking, I removed myself from your life. What kind of person does that make me?"

I shake my head. "The kind of person that is willing to give someone up to protect them. The kind of person who was put in a desperate situation and made the best choice he knew how to."

His jaw twitches. "It wasn't right."

I slip off the bar stool, stepping closer to him. But he backs away, so I stop. "Of course it wasn't," I say. "But you were dealing with a lot of insane stuff. And now, we're dealing with even more. I don't care about that anymore. So why can't we just move past it?"

He pins his gaze to the floor, shaking his head. Starts to pace in front of me.

"Maverick."

"Because I *do* care," he finally says, stopping abruptly. He faces me, his hands splayed in front of him, but he keeps his distance. "I care about you, Laura. And I can't even forgive myself for what I did to you. And what if—" he breaks off, grimacing, as if the next words are too painful.

"What if *what?*"

He sighs heavily, rubbing his face with his hands. "What if I do it again?" When my eyebrows knit together, he hurries to add, "What if I can't stop myself? What if I lose control of my ability?"

"*Lose control,*" I repeat. "What, you think we're going to be holding hands one day and then—oops—you accidentally reach into my mind and wipe out my childhood memories?"

I'd hoped my words might lighten the mood a little bit, but Maverick's gaze just hardens. "Not like that," he says, dropping his head. "What if I'm doing it subconsciously? What if just being around me makes people forget things and there's nothing I can do about it?"

And then it clicks. "You're talking about your mom."

Maverick turns his back to me, pacing again. "She wasn't even fifty yet, Laura. And she died from *Alzheimer's.*"

"That doesn't mean *you* caused it. Sure, it might've been a rare case, but that happens."

"The average life expectancy of a person with Alzheimer's is four to eight years after diagnosis. Sometimes way longer than that. But my mom died less than a year later."

"But you lived with her your entire life," I argue. "If it was happening because of you, wouldn't it have happened a lot sooner?"

"Maybe," Maverick replies. "But maybe not. Maybe it happens over time, little by little. And then one day, the brain just can't take it anymore."

I swallow. "And you're worried it's going to happen to me."

Letting out a long sigh, Maverick turns to me, searching my face. Studying me, like he's afraid I'll just disappear any moment. "I can't risk it, Laura. I can't risk you. I've lost too much already, and I'm not about to add your name to the list."

I stand there, just staring back at him for a long time. What am I supposed to say to that? How can I convince him that his mom's death isn't his fault? It can't be. Sure, it was a wild coincidence, but Maverick can't really be causing people memory loss just by being around them. Just by existing. Right?

"I still feel the same way about you that I always have," Maverick finally says, his voice hoarse. "But I don't want to put you in danger." Slowly, he takes another step back, putting more distance between us. Too much distance.

And suddenly, I can't stand it anymore. In the space of a breath, I move to him, reaching out and throwing my arms around him before he can stop me.

"Laura," he says into my hair, a warning. But he doesn't try to move away. Instead, he seems to melt into me, as if the embrace has snapped all the strings holding him back. And when I lean back and lift my hand to his cheek, his eyes close.

"You aren't putting me in any danger."

His eyes lift to mine, a storm brewing in them. "You don't know that."

"I do." *There's so much more to your ability than you realize, Laura.* Alice's words, however frustrating and irrational they seemed, feel like truth. "You can't take my memories away anymore."

He starts to shake his head, and the spell my closeness seemed to put him under breaks. He shifts away, fingers curling into fists like he doesn't trust them not to reach out for me again.

"Alice couldn't take my memories away—and she tried, twice. Maverick, I figured out how to resist it." My voice sounds like a desperate plea for him to come back, to hold me again. But he just hovers there, inches that feel like miles away from me.

Then he starts to turn away. "Laura, we don't—"

I snatch his wrist to stop him. "I can show you," I say. When he hesitates, I hurry to add, "Try to erase one of my memories."

Maverick jerks his hand away. "*What?*"

"It won't work," I say. "I can stop it."

"Laura, I promised I would never do that to you again, and I intend to keep that promise."

I hold his gaze firmly. Confidently. "Pick something small. Insignificant. Like… like a few months ago, the night I took a walk by myself through Dorton Park. It started to rain, and I saw an owl. It's not important."

Maverick looks horrified. "Laura, I can't—"

"Please," I say, extending my hand. "I'll prove it. And even if it doesn't work, even if you do take the memory, I won't miss it."

His eyes burn into mine, wide and wary. But I keep my jaw set, my hand extended between us. And after several long, tense seconds, his gaze finally softens.

"Are you sure about this?"

"Yes."

"One hundred percent?"

I take a step closer, until I can feel the heat from him on my skin.

Maverick hesitates for so long I'm sure he isn't going to go through with it. But then, slowly, he lifts his hand. Curls his fingers into mine.

And then the echo of the memory starts.

CHAPTER 25

IT'S LATE, AND THE park closed hours ago, so I have to duck under the gate closing off the main entrance. The overcast sky and the warm breeze sifting through the trees carry the promise of a late-summer storm, but I start down the gravel trail into the woods anyway.

It's quiet. On nights like these, after a long week at school filled with echoes, the empty park offers the silence I crave.

Somewhere in the back of my head, a familiar sensation pricks at me. A shadow watching the memory with me. But unlike Alice, Maverick's presence is gentler, more hesitant. He's careful, so different from Alice tearing through the memories with no consideration for the consequences.

It happens slowly, but soon, the scene starts to fade. Emptiness replaces the sensation of wind against my skin; nothingness begins to sweep over my surroundings. But now, instinctively, I know what to do. And as the scene drifts away, I reach for the echo that replaces it. Watch it illuminate the darkness.

Distantly, I feel Maverick slip away, let go of my hand. But I stay there in the echo for a moment longer, my gaze pausing on a spot in the trees, where a pair of eyes peers back at me. *An owl.*

White flashes across the sky, the jagged shape of a lightning bolt reflecting in the bird's pupils.

And then I'm somewhere different.

In my room, mid-morning. By the window, staring through streaks of rain out at the yard below.

It takes me a minute to get my bearings, to realize I've somehow slipped into another memory, but as soon as I do, flashbacks of the night before this day play through my head.

Grace's house. Her end-of-school-year party. Bodies all around me. People we aren't even friends with, but who heard about the lack of parental supervision and flooded the place. Grace soaking it in, grinning the whole night. Me, searching the room for a head of dark hair. His lean frame, warm smile. He'll walk through the door any moment, toss an arm around my shoulders, tell me he got stuck at work or something.

But the clock ticks later and later. I check my phone for the gazillionth time, but still, nothing. I think of typing out another text, but what good will it do after the twelve I've already sent? So I tuck my phone back into my pocket instead.

If I was outside, alone, in the quiet, I might be able to think clearly. Logically. But in this sea of pounding noise, the doubts start to creep in.

Maverick has been distant lately. Which, considering everything that has happened—his mom's death just two months ago, finding out about all the wealth his estranged father left him—makes sense. He's still grieving. Still processing.

But why does he seem to be pulling back from me? For a few weeks now, I've noticed the shift. Him acting distant when we hang out, leaving abruptly with no explanation. Like there's something else pulling at his attention. Or... someone else.

No. Maverick wouldn't do that to me. Would he? I can't let my mind go there.

But maybe... maybe he finally realized that we're different. That I'm different. I knew I couldn't pull it off forever, didn't I? Pretending to be normal, pretending the echoes aren't constantly interrupting my life.

For months now, I've tried to make it work. Maverick likes going out, going places, being around people. And I've gone along with as much of it as I could handle. But still, on days when I've had too much and I need to be somewhere quiet instead of out with him, I can't ignore the disappointment in his eyes.

Back in my room, thunder rumbles, shaking me out of the memories. The sound almost blends in with the knocking on the front door beneath me, but as the thunder fades, I notice it.

I'm on my feet in an instant, racing down the stairs. When I get to the door, though, my hand pauses on the handle. Because what am I supposed to expect? What is he going to say about never showing up last night? Will he pretend everything is fine between us, or finally address the way things are heading? And what am I supposed to say to convince him that I don't want him to leave me, that I can't stand the thought of life without him by my side?

The truth?

Finally, I tug the door open, revealing a disheveled Maverick standing before me. His hair is drenched, even from just the short walk across the street to my porch. But that's just the first thing I notice. As my gaze slowly drifts down, my stomach twists.

His left eye is ringed in dark purple and just beneath it, a thick gash runs from his nose to his jawline. And it looks fresh. In addition, his clothes are wet from the rain, but mud-stained and torn in places, too, like he spent the night running through the woods. He stands with his shoulders hunched, wringing his hands.

"What happened?" My voice is hollow, suddenly wobbly.

Maverick pins his gaze to the ground, a pained expression taking over his features.

I step out onto the porch, shutting the door behind me. "Maverick."

Over his shoulder, a jagged light streaks across the sky. I count the seconds—five, six, seven—before the low rumble of thunder surrounds us. And then, finally, he looks up.

His eyes are full of too much—desperation, hope, loss, *fear*. I can't make sense of any of it.

"What is going on? Where were you last night?"

He winces. "I can't explain."

My eyes trail over the cut on his cheek, down the line of scratches along his forearm. Here I was, wallowing in my insecurities, worried that Maverick might be planning to break up with me, and he shows up on my doorstep looking like he's been fighting for his life all night. What is wrong with me?

"Come inside," I say, turning for the door. "We need to clean that cut, you might need—"

Maverick's hand lands on my shoulder, stopping me. I spin to face him.

"I can't explain," he repeats with a shudder. "And it won't matter anyway."

I start to shake my head. "I don't understand."

But Maverick doesn't offer any explanation. Instead, he just reaches for my hand, rubbing his thumb along my knuckles. He brings it to his lips, breathing something against the back of my hand.

It sounds like *I'm sorry*.

And then everything goes black.

*****

FOR A MOMENT, in the midst of the darkness, I see a light.

Bright. Twinkling. *Just within reach.*

And I watch it fade.

*****

THE PRESENT SLAMS into me like a freight train. Maverick's apartment, standing in his kitchen. The floor suddenly feels like water, shifting beneath my feet. Threatening to pull me under.

Until two hands reach out to steady me.

"Here, sit," Maverick says, pulling the bar stool over. He holds my arm while I sink into it, taking short, shallow breaths. "Are you okay?"

Slowly, I nod.

"Do you remember?"

I blink, the moments right before the echoes took over coming back to me. "Yeah, the park, the owl. I remember all of that," I say, waving my hand dismissively. "But, Maverick, I remembered something else."

The relief that washes over his features is quickly replaced by confusion. "What do you mean?"

I stand, bringing my fist to my mouth as I start to pace. "I saw another memory that was lost. Of the day you took my memories away."

His eyebrows pull tighter together. "Wait, what? How?"

"I don't know, it just came to me," I say. "It was storming, and you showed up on my doorstep with a black eye and a cut on your cheek. Like you'd been in a fight or something."

Maverick watches me pace in front of him, his mouth falling open in disbelief.

"You missed Grace's party the night before, and I was worried about you. I thought you… well," I stop in my tracks, facing him. "In the echo, I thought you had decided you didn't want to be with me anymore."

Maverick shakes his head. "Alice sent her goons after me that night. I'd been refusing to do her requests for a couple weeks, and she had them threaten me. I barely managed to escape." He leans against the counter, drumming his fingers against the marble. "It was that night I realized I was in too deep. That if I didn't do something soon, she'd find a way to target you."

It's easy to recognize that now. To see that all along, we were both fighting with much bigger demons than we ever admitted to each other. But in that moment, in that echo, the idea that Maverick might leave me had felt like torture. And then all of it had faded.

"That day isn't the only thing I've remembered from before," I continue, my feet restless under me as I resume pacing.

Maverick doesn't say anything, just fixes his gaze on me as I weave back and forth in front of him.

"I had a dream a few weeks ago. But I'm pretty sure it wasn't just a dream, it was a memory—the first time we went to *Coffee and Cream*."

Maverick's eyes circle the room as he thinks. "It was a Saturday afternoon, I think?"

I nod. "And the night before, we'd gone to a movie and I tried to ditch. I broke down in the lobby when you came looking for me. When we got ice cream the next day, we talked about it."

"Yeah, I remember that," Maverick says. "But how… you said it was a dream?"

"That time, yes. But that isn't all—I remembered New Year's Eve, too."

His expression tells me I don't have to explain any further—he remembers exactly what happened on New Year's Eve.

"That memory didn't come to me in a dream, though. Last week, Alice injected me with something—some kind of marker she uses that also has a side effect of enhancing anomalies' abilities. I got sucked into the echo right there in front of her."

Maverick shakes his head, eyes full of disbelief. "I don't understand. It made you get a memory back?"

More of Alice's words drift through my head, making my feet pause under me.

The memories were within you the whole time. You just chose to see them.

"It sounds crazy, but she might be right."

"Who's right about what?" Maverick asks.

"Alice," I answer, lifting my hands over my head while my thoughts race. "She thinks that there's more to my ability than just hearing echoes. She thinks that I've been suppressing it—which is why you were able to take my memories away before. And she wasn't able to when she tried because I somehow figured out how to block it." I pause, chewing on my bottom lip. "She thinks the memories you took before are still in me somewhere. Echoes. I just have to find them."

"How… how do you do that?"

I swallow. "I don't know."

Maverick's gaze finds mine, and I can almost see the gears turning in his head. I drum my fingers against my thighs, rocking back and forth on the balls of my feet while I process it, too. Maverick's kitchen suddenly feels too small, so I take a few steps into the living room, stopping in front of the floor-to-ceiling windows looking out over the city. Down below, dots of color speckle the streets—Christmas lights.

How do you do that? How *do* I find the memories? Every time I've done it so far has felt random or seems to have been triggered by something—a dream, Alice's serum, Maverick in my head. But if the memories are just there, waiting to be uncovered, isn't there something I can do to reveal them?

A hand lands on my shoulder, startling me out of my thoughts. Maverick hovers beside me in front of the window, his gaze fixed on a point somewhere in the distance. Then it shifts to my face, and something changes in his expression. Something that sends my heart into a flurry.

"You remember it, though?" His eyes search mine, filled with desperate hope. "The memory you told me to take?"

A faint smile curves my lips at his concern, and I nod. "I went for a walk that night to clear my head, to be in the quiet. I think it was the first week of the school year, and I was still adjusting."

Maverick nods, but his expression doesn't change, like he's waiting for me to continue.

"It was windy," I add. "A storm was blowing in, and there was lightning. I had stopped, trying to decide if I should head back to my car before the rain came, and that's when I spotted the owl in the trees, just a few feet away."

Maverick nods again, slowly, still staring at me expectantly.

I frown. "That's it, that's the memory."

He scrunches his mouth to the side. "What color was it?"

"The owl?" I shrug. "Brown? I don't know. It was dark."

"How dark? Were there street lamps?"

I close my eyes, picturing it. "No."

"How did you get there—walk or drive?"

"I drove, but the gate was closed, so I had to park just outside and duck under it."

"Can you tell me the date? Time?"

I shake my head. "It was near the end of August. I don't know what time exactly, just that it was pretty late."

"After you saw the owl, did you go home? Or did you—"

"Maverick!" I interject, throwing my hands out in front of me in exasperation. "I remember, okay?"

He blinks at me, his jaw working like he isn't completely convinced. But then, finally, his shoulders sag and he releases a sigh. "I just... don't want to hurt you."

I take a step closer, narrowing the already small bridge of space between us. I can feel the heat radiating off of him now, smell the ACA-issued soap on our matching beige scrubs.

"You can't hurt me," I say, realizing just how untrue the words are as they leave my mouth. Because Maverick *can* hurt me—just not in the way he thinks. It will hurt if he turns away from me now, if he decides being near me isn't worth the risk.

But he doesn't turn away. He stays there, hazel eyes filled with too many conflicting emotions to count. I watch them drop to the ground, fix on a point over my shoulder, and then, finally, land on my face. My lips. I see it when something changes in his expression, when a decision has been made. But the moment drags out, suspended in air. Time seems to slow around us, and I swear I can feel the earth moving beneath our feet, see the light particles sparkling down around us.

"Maverick, I—" I start to say, but he doesn't let me finish. And it's okay. Because when he finally closes the distance between us, his hands curving under my chin, his fingers tangling into the hair at the base of my neck, we don't need words. And when his lips finally meet mine, we don't need anything except for this moment, this feeling to say all the things we haven't been brave enough to.

It isn't like the first time we kissed. *Under the stars in my backyard, a shy and nervous brush of lips.* The memory illuminates somewhere in the back of my mind, painting a picture of the echoes I'd heard on that cold, lonely night before I knew who Maverick was.

But no, this is different. And it isn't like the tender kiss we'd shared in Maverick's kitchen back when I'd first decided I could trust him, either. This—here, now—is something else. Something wild and desperate, like everything we were, are, and might be is all right here in this kiss. Maverick's hands tangle into my hair, holding me close, pulling me impossibly closer. He tastes like home, like safety, like exactly what I remember.

And there, in front of me. A spark. A light.

Just within reach.

I know what it is now. An echo. A memory. And if I focus on the darkness, I can see more glimmers of light appearing. Thousands of them, like stars dotting the sky as the sun dips beneath the horizon.

If I reach for them, they'll show me what I lost. What I watched disappear, because I didn't believe I could do anything to stop it.

I know I can do something now. But instead, I leave them be.

I know what I'll find in my lost memories. More of me and Maverick. More self-doubt, more uncertainties. And at the center of it all, this feeling that I've known all along.

Love.

Maverick breaks off the kiss, pressing his forehead against mine while we catch our breath.

"I promise you," I say, "that doesn't hurt at all."

Maverick breathes a laugh, pulling back enough so he can look me in the eyes properly. "I don't know how I survived without you for so long."

"You didn't know who I was for a good bit there, so that probably helped."

His lips twist into a frown. "You didn't know who I was for a lot longer."

I reach around his neck, twisting my fingers into the hair at the back of his head. "Then we have a lot of catching up to do, don't we?"

In answer, he brings his mouth to mine again.

And there, the lights. The memories, *just within reach*.

They'll be there for me, when I want them.

But this.

Here.

Now.

This is what matters.

CHAPTER 26

THE MORNING LIGHT streaking through the blinds and into my eyes is what finally wakes me, but the scent my nose catches a moment later is what makes me clamber out of bed. I stumble to the bathroom, my limbs stiff from a heavy sleep.

Is that… bacon? Some kind of sausage? Pancakes, maybe? Whatever it is, it smells better than anything I've eaten in weeks, and by the time I make it to the kitchen, my mouth is watering.

Angelo is already seated at the bar, a half empty plate in front of him and his mouth full of food. Maverick is at the counter, his back to us as he stacks things onto a plate, and my cheeks warm at the sight of him. I'm not sure what time I finally retreated to bed last night, but we stayed up for a while after our conversation, just chatting. Laughing. *Kissing.*

Maverick turns around with a piled-high plate in his hands and spots me, then flashes a smile that turns my insides to goo. I grin back for a moment but quickly snap out of it when I catch sight of the spread on the counter behind him—several trays filled with pancakes, sausage, scrambled eggs, hash browns, biscuits, yogurt, and fresh fruit. My stomach grumbles audibly.

"I managed to find a restaurant down the road that was open today," Maverick explains. He nods at the empty plate beside the food. "Please, help yourself."

"You don't have to tell me twice," I reply, snatching it up. I move along the counter, piling a bit of everything onto my plate, then join them both at the bar. For several minutes, we eat in silence, too focused on the food in front of us to make much conversation. Then, after finishing his second—third?—plate, Angelo speaks.

"I almost forgot what normal food tastes like," he says.

Sighing, I lean back in my chair, savoring the last strawberry from my own plate. "I'm pretty sure this is the best breakfast I've ever had in my life."

"I don't even like scrambled eggs," Maverick adds, "but I don't even care right now." Proving his point, he tosses another scoop of them onto his plate. We've pretty much cleaned out everything else—there are only a couple of biscuits and a handful of blackberries left.

"I don't ever want to go back to the ACA," Angelo mumbles through another bite.

Even though his tone is lighthearted, I swallow at the comment, my mood shifting. Dr. Shaw's warnings rush back to me, including the additional information I'd learned from the echoes in her office.

"We will have to go back," I finally say. "But not to stay."

Maverick meets my gaze, nodding. "We've got to get everyone out."

"Yeah," I agree, but the thought gives me pause. Because what will we do then? Go into hiding? That doesn't feel like a very permanent solution. If the ACA is killing anomalies, we can't let it continue to exist. They'll keep hunting us, finding more anomalies, and getting rid of them. We have to shut it down completely.

But in order to do either of those things… "We have to find Alice's stash of replications," I say, "without getting caught by her *or* by the ACA, who are both probably out looking for us already."

"Dr. Shaw gave you some addresses we can investigate, didn't she?" Maverick asks. "Maybe if we're lucky one of those will be the place."

Nodding, I reach into the pocket of the beige scrubs I'm still wearing, then pass the paper to Maverick. He glances over the addresses, chewing on his lip as he considers them.

"This one is her office downtown," he says, pointing at the middle address. "We've been there a couple of times already, and I doubt she's been back since."

My heart sinks a little at the information. I'm not sure how Dr. Shaw obtained these addresses, but that means there are only two places for us to look. And we don't know how old this information is, so all of them could be dead ends. Which leaves us with nothing to go on.

"Do you recognize the other addresses?" I ask.

Maverick shakes his head. He walks over to the living room to grab a laptop, then comes back to the bar. Angelo and I watch over his shoulder as he types one of the addresses into an online map.

"This one looks like a residential address," Maverick says, zooming in on the satellite image of a neighborhood. "I never pinned Alice as the kind of person to own a lake house, but I guess you never know."

"It's pretty isolated, which suits her. And look," I say, hovering my finger over the screen. "Is that a boat house?"

"Looks like it," Maverick replies.

"Maybe it's a secret place to store her research," Angelo chimes in.

"Or maybe she just likes going fishing to decompress on the weekends," I say. The joke gets me a few chuckles.

Maverick takes a screenshot of the map, then goes back to the search bar and types in the second address. A business pops up under the search—Redstone Self Storage.

"A storage unit," I say.

Maverick nods. "There's a unit number listed, too."

"It's probably locked, right?" Angelo asks.

"Likely nothing a pair of bolt cutters can't handle," Maverick replies.

"There's gotta be something in there," I say. "No one has a storage unit unless they have something to hide, right?"

"Or just a lot of junk." Maverick shrugs.

"Maybe she has a massive rock collection," Angelo says.

"Or a bunch of creepy dolls."

"*Or,*" I say, dragging out the word for emphasis, "a bunch of vials filled with replications of abilities from anomalies she kidnapped and experimented on."

Maverick and Angelo exchange a glance.

"Nah, I doubt it," Maverick says.

"Nope. Definitely the dolls," Angelo adds.

I roll my eyes before joining them in laughter. As it settles down, Maverick zooms in on the street view of the storage center.

"It's in Rison, about an hour and a half away," he says. "The lake house is in Lackerton, a little closer."

"I vote we check out the storage unit first," I say. "It's more suspicious."

Maverick glances at Angelo, who just shrugs. "I think that's a fair point."

"Creepy doll collection it is," Maverick replies, closing the laptop. "But first, we need to put on some different clothes so we don't look like escaped convicts out in the public."

* ✱ *

TWO HOURS LATER, dressed in various mismatched and ill-fitting clothes Maverick managed to procure from the closet in his apartment, we roll to a stop in front of Redstone Self Storage. There's a large iron fence surrounding the white cement buildings and a gate blocking our path inside.

"Should we just… go in?" I ask. "Or should we wait a bit to make sure no one is keeping tabs on the place?"

"I haven't seen another car for miles, so if we're quick, we shouldn't run into any trouble. Angelo, you can keep an eye on the security cameras, right?"

"Already on it," Angelo calls from the back seat, where he's got a tablet and a laptop spread out on the seat beside him. "I've been working on figuring out how to hack things remotely, and I think…" He pauses, tapping the screen on the tablet. "That should get us in."

On cue, the gate starts to swing open.

I glance back at him. "What would we do without you?"

Angelo considers the question for a moment. "You'd probably have to hop the fence."

We wouldn't have even gotten this far without him, but he already knows that, so I just shrug and reply, "That would *really* suck."

As we pull into the storage area, I scan the small parking area near the front, which is empty. Rows of red metal doors line the buildings, which are sectioned off in a grid-like pattern by narrow roads branching off from the wider road at the center.

"What number are we looking for?" I ask.

"307," Maverick answers.

I search for some kind of sign, but there aren't any, so we just slowly make our way down the main road, scanning both directions at every intersection. Eventually, we spot numbers in the low 300s, so we veer down one of the side roads, scanning each door until we reach 307.

As expected, there's a padlock on the door. We park, and Maverick pulls a bolt cutter—that he apparently had to buy for one of Alice's jobs a while back—out of the trunk. It doesn't take long for him to cut the lock off, and then we all pause for a moment.

"It better not actually be a collection of creepy dolls," I say. Then Maverick takes a deep breath and grabs the handle, sliding the door up.

The light from the sun illuminates the inside of the unit, and I feel a small sense of relief. *Not* a creepy doll collection. No, instead, there are open boxes scattered around the front, a few cabinets at the back, and some office furniture mingled in with it all. Overall, the unit is nowhere close to being full, and everything seems to be fairly organized, which is promising.

"Well," Maverick begins, "if the replications are actually here somewhere, this will be the easiest mission we've ever gone on."

"So either they're not here or something is about to go really, terribly wrong," I reply.

Maverick shrugs. "Might as well get to searching, then."

I follow his lead, stepping inside and reaching for one of the boxes on the floor. Inside it, I find several reams of blank printer paper and nothing else, so I move to the next one.

We fall into a rhythm, used to this type of search by now. Open the boxes, sift through the contents, move on. Next, we go through the cabinets, which are full of files. As I sift through them, I realize the paperwork looks familiar. It's the same paperwork Maverick and I had found the first time we'd searched Alice's office—she must have moved everything here when she ditched the old office.

As I scan the labels on the folders, the disappointment sinks in. I've looked through all of this before. Back then, I'd learned that Alice was researching anomalies and keeping records of them, but I already know that now. It isn't going to help us track down her new research facility.

"I think I found something," Maverick says, pulling me out of my thoughts. I ditch the paperwork in my hands and cross over to him to study what he's holding up. It's a notebook with the ACA's logo printed in the corner. "It has Dr. Shaw's name on the inside," he says, opening the cover to show me. I scan the first page, which is covered in messy handwriting.

"A journal? Maybe Alice took it because she wanted to snoop into Dr. Shaw's personal life?"

Maverick shakes his head, eyes fixed on the paper. He flips the page, scanning the next several paragraphs. "It's full of notes about her research."

I follow his gaze down to the notebook, trying to make out the handwriting. A few words here and there are highlighted—*cause of mutation, exposure to something.*

"This reminds me of my conversation with Dr. Shaw just before we went over the escape plan," I say.

"Oh?" Maverick flips to the next page, still reading.

"She explained some of what she has learned about anomalies to me. She said the mutation we have is inherited. It starts with the grandparents, then lies dormant in the parents and finally causes abnormalities in the third generation."

"Yeah, that's what I just read here. And they believe the original mutation happened because of exposure to something—somewhere between fifty and sixty years ago in the Pine Springs Valley—but they haven't been able to figure out what."

I nod. "That's what she told me, too."

"The interesting thing is this: all the comments about the cause of the mutation and about when and where it might have happened are highlighted. And why does Alice have this journal if Dr. Shaw wrote it?"

"Maybe Alice took over the research? And maybe she knows something about it all that Dr. Shaw doesn't?"

Maverick frowns, flipping to the next page in the journal, still reading. "How old do you think Alice is?"

I shrug. "Her mid-fifties, maybe? She could be older, though. There's no telling how her ability might affect her aging."

Maverick's eyes snap to mine. "So she could have been around when the exposure happened."

"I… suppose."

"And," Maverick continues, rocking on the balls of his feet, "if the exposure happened fifty years ago, and then it took two generations for it to finally create anomalies, then most anomalies would probably be around our age, right? Which seems to be the case…"

"Except for Alice," I finish, eyes widening. We share a look for a long moment, letting the idea settle in. Then Maverick glances back down at the journal, flipping through the next few pages.

"What if Alice started all of this?" he asks. "Maybe she was experimenting, and she figured out how to give herself powers. And then she caused whatever everyone with the mutation was exposed to fifty years ago. What if she *created* anomalies?"

"What would be the purpose?"

Maverick shrugs. "To gain power? Create chaos?"

Alice's words back in the ACA echo through my mind.

Imagine what life would be like if everyone had access to our abilities. Anomalies could change the world… we would be heroes.

"She wants the glory," I say. "To save people. To be the hero. And she wants to use us to get it."

That's probably why she made the replications of our abilities in the first place. She doesn't want *us* to help other people—she just wants to harvest our DNA so she can make the replications and use them for her own benefit. And the ACA is providing a convenient spot where she can contain all of the anomalies until she's ready to execute her plan.

It's only a matter of time before she goes for it. And whatever she decides to do isn't going to end well for us.

We just have to make our move before she does.

CHAPTER 27

WE SPEND ANOTHER half-hour sifting through paperwork, searching boxes, and trying to find anything that might point us to where Alice is keeping the replications of our abilities. But we come up short and we don't want to hang around too long in case someone shows up, so we end up piling into the car with nothing but our new theories of what Alice could be plotting.

"There's still the other address," I say as we pull out onto the main road. "If Alice actually lives there, it would make sense for her to keep her research where she can monitor it closely."

Maverick drums his fingers on the steering wheel. "So we can probably assume that getting in and out undetected will be more difficult than this was."

"Do you think she'll be expecting us? Should we wait?" I ask.

Maverick shakes his head. "If she's expecting us already, it doesn't matter when we show up. She'll be ready. We just have to be careful and hope that the element of surprise is still on our side."

"Maybe she hasn't learned that we escaped yet," I offer. "It is Christmas, after all. Maybe information will travel slower through the ACA because people are off for the holiday."

"That's possible," Maverick replies. "We might as well act now."

"When we get close enough, I should be able to detect and disarm any kind of security system," Angelo says.

"We'll need that. But we'll also need to be prepared in case Alice is there. I'm sure we'll run into a few people working for her."

"The guy that chased us before was always using multiple abilities, so we have to assume they'll be capable of anything," I add.

"Exactly," Maverick agrees. "And if—"

He doesn't get to finish the thought. Because just then, a loud *pop* sounds, interrupting our conversation. Maverick slams the brakes, jerking us all forward in our seats as the tires squeal against the pavement. The car wobbles beneath us as we slow down. Did we blow a tire?

"What happened?" I ask when we finally come to a stop in a patch of dirt off the road's shoulder.

"I don't know," Maverick replies, scanning the rearview, then the side mirrors. "Wait here," he orders, then throws his door open. I crane my neck, searching the road in front of and behind us. Completely empty.

Maverick crouches down beside the left front tire, eyebrows furrowing. "The tires are shredded." He glances at the road behind us. "Are those… road spikes?"

"Who—" I begin, following his gaze, but the rest of the sentence dies on my tongue. Because a figure in front of the car catches my eye at that exact moment, moving so fast that if I'd blinked I might have missed it. I open my mouth to warn Maverick, but before I can even suck in a breath, the figure slams into him, taking him to the ground.

I scramble over the center console, then stumble out onto the street. The man is covered from neck to toe in black clothes and already has Maverick pinned to the ground while he attempts to slide a pair of handcuffs around his wrists. Maverick struggles against him, but the man has a firm hold.

I rush forward, planning to throw my weight against the man in hopes that I might surprise him enough to give Maverick an opening to get away, but when I'm inches away, a strong hand grips my arm and yanks me backward. The shift in momentum makes me stumble, sending me crashing to the ground. Pain shoots up my knees as they collide with the asphalt, stunning me long enough for the person behind me to get a firm grip on me. He tugs my hands behind my back and slides a pair of handcuffs around my wrists before I can even blink.

As the man yanks me to my feet, I glance up to see that Maverick is in a similar predicament. I shift my gaze to the car, curious if they got Angelo, but then one of the men speaks, answering the thought.

"Where's the other one? There were supposed to be three."

"I thought I saw someone in the back," the other one replies.

The man behind me jerks me along with him as he shifts toward the car, craning his neck to look inside. "No one's in there."

"He didn't come with us," Maverick says.

"Shut up," the man holding him orders. Then he glances at the other guy, extending a hand. "Search the area. I'll take the girl."

A second later I'm shoved in their direction, and as I stumble closer to Maverick, I meet his gaze briefly. He gives me the slightest of nods, and even though I'm unsure of what it means, I keep my guard up, ready to spring into action at a moment's notice.

The man who had been holding me before starts to make his way around the car, and the second he makes it to the other side, Maverick moves. Whipping around to face his captor, Maverick swings his legs out in an attempt to trip him, but flinches when the guy points something at him. My stomach plummets when I spot the gun, flashbacks of Maverick getting shot running through my head, but when Maverick's gaze drops to his chest, where a little dart is sticking out of his shirt, I relax a little. It isn't a gun intended to kill.

Maverick starts to sway, his eyes glossing over. I step closer, bracing him against me as he sinks to his knees, which proves to be difficult with both of our hands cuffed behind our backs.

"Laura," Maverick slurs as he slumps all the way to the ground.

"Wake up! Maverick!" I plead, but it's too late. His body goes completely still.

Above me, I hear a click. When I look up, the man is pointing the dart gun directly between my eyes. "Move an inch and you'll get to join him."

I bite back the angry response that forms on the tip of my tongue, knowing that at least if one of us is conscious while they capture us, we might have better odds. But I set my jaw, channeling the anger into what I hope is a menacing scowl.

"I don't see anyone else," the second guard calls as he steps back around the car. "He must be—"

An engine rumbles to life from somewhere behind me, and I crane my neck to find the source. There, tucked behind a tree and almost entirely obscured by the bushes, is a black sedan. It's barely visible from this angle, which explains why none of us had noticed it before.

But Angelo must have.

The car starts to move, and the man behind me curses under his breath. "Don't let him get away!"

The second guy takes off in a sprint across the street, but the car whips out onto the road before he can reach it. It speeds toward me where I'm on my knees, still hunched over Maverick's unconscious body. In a split second, I realize that there's no way we'll be able to load him into the car without all being knocked unconscious. And there's no way I'm going to leave Maverick here by himself, either.

So as Angelo moves closer, slowing down to help us out, I shake my head. "Just go! Get out of here!" I shout.

Angelo seems to understand, because a second later the tires veer away from us and the engine revs as he presses the gas, whipping past us.

Behind me, the man grips my jacket, pressing the cold metal of the dart gun into my neck. A sting follows, and then the world starts to grow fuzzy.

The last thing I see before everything fades to black is the cloud of dust the tires are kicking up as Angelo disappears in the distance.

✳ ✱ ✳

I OPEN MY EYES TO bright fluorescents and a pounding headache. Images of the moments before I fell unconscious swim in my mind, and I will my limbs to move, to pull me upright. It takes a ridiculous amount of effort, but eventually, I manage to sit upright, blinking in my surroundings as they come into focus.

Another white room with no windows. A large, handleless metal door. It's cold, with a musty scent that reminds me of a basement, and there are two cots—the one I woke up on and another, where a figure is lying with their back to me.

My eyes widen. "Maverick?" The sight of him seems to clear some of the grogginess out of my system, and I manage to drag myself to my feet and cross over to him. "Maverick," I say. Our hands are still handcuffed behind our backs, but I use my knee to nudge him. "Maverick, wake up."

Slowly, his eyelids begin to flutter. He opens his eyes a moment later, but squints, turning his head away from the overhead lights. As he twists on the cot, he seems to notice that his hands are restrained and tugs at the handcuffs, grunting.

"Those aren't coming off," I say. The sound of my voice grabs his attention, and his eyes fly open again, zeroing in on me.

"Laura."

"I'm here."

Pulling himself to a sitting position, Maverick gives me a once-over, concern drawing a line between his brows. "Are you okay?"

"I'm fine. Are you?"

He winces as he swings his feet onto the floor. "I think so."

Letting out a breath, I back toward my own cot, sinking onto it to give my wobbly legs a rest. I swallow, the weight of our latest predicament settling over me. "They got us."

Maverick scans the room, his gaze lingering on the door. "Who?"

"These were Alice's people," I say. "Not the ACA." Which is probably for the best. The ACA would've shown up with actual guns and wouldn't have hesitated to use them. At least Alice's men weren't equipped with lethal force.

"How did they find us?"

I frown. "We must not have been careful enough. They were probably watching the storage unit somehow. Or maybe they tracked your car."

Maverick lets out a heavy sigh, cursing under his breath. "Where are we now?"

I just shrug.

Maverick stands, making his way over to the door. He kicks it a couple of times, then turns his back to it, running his hands over the edges as far as he can with his restraints. Then he shakes his head.

"It must be bolted from the outside."

I scan the edges of the room, looking for another escape route, but all I find is an air vent in the ceiling that's both unreachable and too small to fit through. Maverick follows my gaze, then closes his eyes in defeat.

"I guess we just have to wait until someone comes for us," he says.

I nod slowly. "Maybe Angelo will track us down somehow."

Maverick's gaze snaps to mine. "Angelo? Did you see what happened to him?"

"He got away," I explain. "At least, it looked like he made it out."

"Seriously?"

"He stole their car. Unless they had another one really close by, I doubt they were able to catch up with him."

Maverick's expression brightens suddenly. He twists his arms, reaching for something. It takes him a solid minute with his hands still cuffed, but eventually he manages to slide something out of his pocket. It falls to the floor, the screen lighting up as it lands in front of him.

My heart skips a beat. "A phone?"

Maverick starts to laugh, breathless, as he leans against the wall and tosses his head back in relief. "My phone. They didn't think to confiscate it."

"We can call him!" I exclaim.

Maverick grins at me. "Even better. This phone is connected to the same service as my laptop *and* my tablet. Angelo had both of them."

"Which means he might be able to find us," I finish for him.

Maverick nods, his expression going serious again. "As long as—"

Above our heads, the light goes out, plunging the room into darkness. A moment later, we hear a loud *thump* just outside our door.

I stand, moving toward the doorway, grateful when my shoulder bumps into Maverick's and he leans into me reassuringly.

We pause, waiting for something else to happen, but are met with nothing but more silence and darkness.

"Do you think it's him?" Maverick finally whispers.

I swallow. "I really, really hope so."

CHAPTER 28

MY HEART THUMPS in my ears as we wait. I blink several times, trying to get my eyes to adjust to the dark, but there aren't any windows or other sources of light, so it's still nearly impossible to see anything. Eventually, Maverick slips away from me and tries pushing on the door, but it won't budge.

And then we hear a click.

I stiffen, expecting someone to barge in, but the door opens slowly. In the hallway, there's a faint glow, but before I can make out any of the shadows dancing in front of me, a flashlight clicks on and shines directly into my eyes. I squint, craning my neck to see who's standing behind it, but all I can make out is a vague silhouette.

And then he speaks.

"Oh good, you guys are awake."

I blink. "Angelo?"

The light drops to the ground, leaving spots dancing across my vision. Then Angelo circles me, reaching for the handcuffs at my wrists. With a click, they open, and I rub my skin, stretching my stiff arms out in front of me. Angelo places a flashlight into my hands and presses the button to turn it on for me. I raise it at him, still in disbelief at the fact that he's standing in front of me.

Angelo squints when the light hits his eyes, then grabs the tip of the flashlight, redirecting it at the ground. "I wasn't sure if I waited long enough before coming in, so I'm glad the drugs have worn off already."

"You found us," Maverick says quietly as Angelo reaches for his handcuffs next, sliding the key into the lock.

"I found a lot of things," Angelo replies, tossing the handcuffs to the ground. "And I've got both good news and bad news."

"What?" Maverick and I both ask at the same time.

"We don't have much time, so I'll explain on the way. Follow me." He turns for the door, beckoning us as he slips into the hallway. We hesitate in the dim glow of the flashlight for a moment, exchanging a relieved glance. And then, unexpectedly, Maverick pulls me into a quick embrace, pressing his lips to my temple as he squeezes me tight.

"Let's not do this whole getting-captured-together thing again, as romantic as it is," he mumbles into my hair. "Maybe we can go back to ice cream dates?"

I give him a playful shove. "You're the one that keeps getting knocked out first. So maybe just… don't do that?"

He grabs my hand, tugging me through the doorway. "I'll try my best."

As we step into the hall, I spot a figure lying prone on the floor beside the door; Angelo must have knocked the guard out somehow. I shine the flashlight in both directions, taking in the long hallway that bends to the right in the direction Angelo is leading us. I peer into the adjoining rooms as we pass them, noticing the state of disarray the place seems to be in. There are papers scattered everywhere, broken office equipment strewn about, and a dusty, almost smoky scent that lingers in the air, getting stronger the farther we move. When we round the corner behind Angelo, I find out why.

The beam of my flashlight reflects off something bright yellow in front of us: caution tape. It's blocking off the rest of the building, and beyond it, the linoleum flooring is charred completely black. Burn marks stretch up the walls and into the ceiling panels, a few of which are missing completely. *Fire damage.*

Angelo tugs open a door that leads up a staircase, but I pause before following, my gaze lingering on the burned end of the hallway.

"Why does this place seem familiar?" I ask, suddenly certain that I've been here before. And before anyone can answer, it clicks. "Alice's lab."

I frown, confused. This is the place Alice had been keeping all of the anomalies she was researching. After our very first confrontation with her, she'd trapped us all inside and set the building on fire. We managed to escape, but that was what set the ACA on our trail and made them think we were sabotaging them.

Alice made us take the blame so they wouldn't find out about what she'd really been doing here.

Angelo throws a mischievous look back at us. "Apparently it didn't burn down completely."

"Why would she bring us here?" I ask, taking the stairs two at a time to keep up with Angelo's pace.

"That's the good news I was going to tell you about," he says. "Apparently, she's been using the remains of this lab as a place to store her research. Which, I suppose, makes sense. If the entire ACA believes that this place was wiped off the map, they'd never think to look here."

"Wait, are you serious?" Maverick demands.

"The replications are here?" I add, breathless as we reach the landing.

Angelo turns to face us, grinning. "They're up one more floor. Alice brought you guys to the exact place we've been searching for." Without giving us a chance to process, Angelo peers out the small window on the door leading to the main level, then continues. "The staircase up is across the hall. So far it looks clear, but as soon as the staff realize they aren't going to be able to get the electricity back on, they might come back."

"Do you know how many are here?" Maverick asks, joining him by the window.

"Seven, I think. Three to guard the room the research is stashed in, two at the main entrance, one at the back entrance, and then the one outside the room you guys were stuck in—but he shouldn't be a problem for a couple of hours, at least."

"It doesn't take six people to flip a breaker, so I'm sure we'll run into a few of them soon," Maverick says.

"Definitely. Which is where this might come in handy." Angelo reaches behind his back and slides a dart gun out of his waistband. "There are only three shots left, but if you have good aim, that gets rid of half of them."

Maverick takes the gun, tests the weight in his hands, then flips the safety. "Perfect."

Angelo peers out the window again. "I think it's clear for now. We need to go up, then to the right—the research stash is in the room directly above where you guys woke up. Ready?"

Maverick nods, and when Angelo turns his flashlight off, I follow his lead. There's a tiny bit more light up here on the main level, pooling in from the windows and casting a dim glow over everything, but it must be dark outside already, so it isn't much. It'll have to be enough, though.

Slowly, Angelo pushes the door open. I wince as it creaks on its hinges, but we get moving before I can think about who might've heard it. Maverick takes up the lead, then Angelo, then me. We jog across the hall, then slip into the next stairwell and start climbing in a matter of seconds.

When we get to the top, Maverick pauses to look through the small window. Once he determines the coast is clear, he pushes the door open, then leads us across the hall until we're pressed up against the wall. Slowly, we inch toward the bend in the L-shaped building, and Maverick pokes his head around the corner briefly.

"Who's there?" a voice calls, too close to us. My heart thunders as the footsteps approach, but as soon as the figure makes it around the corner, Maverick lurches forward. The woman is close enough that he manages to grab hold of her before she even spots us. He opts to use his power instead of the dart gun, and the second he presses two fingers to her neck, her eyes gloss over. Slowly, her consciousness fades, and Maverick slides her to the floor gently.

"Alana?" a male voice calls from further around the corner. "Did you find anyone?"

Maverick presses his back to the wall again, repeating the same movements as he did with the woman. When the man steps around the corner, Maverick reaches out to knock the weapon out of his hands. It clatters to the floor, and then Maverick grabs him. This guard, however, reacts faster than the last. He slips out of Maverick's grip with little effort, giving Maverick a solid jab in the ribs at the same time.

"Carson!" he calls out. Another pair of footsteps approaches.

As Maverick regains his bearings, he reaches out, trying to find an inch of exposed skin to make contact with, but the man leans back, keeping his face and neck out of reach.

"Use the gun!" I call softly, and Maverick obeys, firing it at the man with a click. The man stumbles back, slamming into the third guard as he rounds the corner. Maverick rushes toward them both, snatching the gun out of the last guard's hand before closing his fingers around his wrist. Simultaneously, both men's eyes roll back, and they fall to the ground in a heap.

In the silence that follows, I find myself panting. Even though I barely moved the whole time, adrenaline courses through me as if I'd been the one to single-handedly take all three guards out.

"I think that was everyone up here," Maverick says, dusting his hands off on his thighs.

"With two sleeping darts to spare," I add.

"Should've been three, but I didn't want to get too risky there. Especially since you pointed out that most of the time, I'm the one that gets knocked out first," Maverick replies with a wink.

I roll my eyes. "Thanks for being so considerate."

"The rest of the floor looks clear, so we should get moving," Angelo says. We snap our attention back to the task at hand, following as he slips around the corner.

When we get to the room at the end of the hall, Maverick pokes his head inside first, checking to make sure no one else is there. Then he waves us in.

"I'll keep watch," he says, taking up a stance by the door and fixing his gaze in the direction we'd just come from.

Slowly, I take in the room. It reminds me a little bit of the chemistry classroom at school, with walls full of beakers, test tubes, and various lab equipment. But this isn't a classroom, so the bulk of the tables are covered in additional equipment—microscopes, bunsen burners, computers—rather than textbooks and worksheets. And there, at the back of the room, is a row of cabinets. They appear to be locked, but the doors are made of glass, so I can see what's inside them.

Plastic boxes. Just like the one Alice pulled out when she'd interrogated me back in the ACA. It had five syringes inside, and she'd threatened to use them if I didn't answer her questions.

I cross the room to peer into the cabinets. I can't tell what's inside the boxes just from looking, so I tug on the door handle. When it doesn't budge, I shield my face and lift my foot to the glass, kicking hard. It shatters, the sound crashing through the quiet room, but I don't even care. I turn my attention to the box closest to me and pull it out, fingers trembling as they search for the latches.

When I finally get it open, a sigh escapes me, long and heavy, as if the weight of everything we've been fighting against is coming out in this one, single breath.

There are five syringes inside.

And there are dozens of boxes.

"They're really here."

Angelo's shoes crunch on the broken glass as he joins me by the cabinets to get a closer look. "It looks like they're all labeled, but how do we know what the serial numbers mean?"

"She must have some kind of labeling system, right? Maybe there's a chart somewhere."

Angelo nods, scanning the room. He spots a computer a few feet away and goes to it. Even with the power still off, it hums to life as soon as he touches it. "I'll see if there are any records on this."

I nod, setting the box back inside the cabinet and turning my attention to the room around me. "I'll see if there's anything else here."

As I search, I quickly realize that the place is pretty well organized. Each drawer I come across is labeled, and nothing appears to be out of place. I open drawer after drawer of various equipment, but I don't find a single notebook or scrap of paper.

"Either she keeps all of her records digitally, or they're in another room," I declare as I move to the last storage cabinet near the front of the room. Inside it, I find a rack full of white lab coats and a couple of drawers stuffed with safety goggles and gloves. Nothing interesting, except… "A safe?" I say out loud when I spot it, puzzled.

"Why would Alice need a safe if this whole place is already hidden?" Maverick asks from by the door.

"I don't know," I reply, crouching down in front of it. "But it's a digital lock."

On cue, Angelo appears by my side, bending down to inspect it. He runs his fingers over the keypad, and it flashes green. Like magic.

I pull the door open, and when I find a red plastic box inside, my eyebrows furrow. I pull it out, undo the latches on the sides, and flip the top open.

Inside, there are more syringes. They're almost identical to the ones in the boxes across the room, except that these ones have red caps.

Carefully, I lift one out of the box to peer at the clear liquid inside. "What do you think makes these ones special?"

Angelo tilts his head. "I have no idea," he says, "but I think I found the database." He jogs back to the computer and types something on the keyboard. "Read the serial number off to me and I'll see if it's in here."

"B94Q8L," I read. Then I join him by the computer, and when he pulls up a PDF with the same sequence of letters and numbers at the top, I read the first couple of lines aloud for Maverick to hear, too.

"Serum B94Q8L: Anomaly Neutralizer. Neutralizes the corrupted DNA of anomalies, permanently preventing the use of their abilities." I pause, scanning the rest of the page. Beneath the description, there's a bunch of additional information—properties, dosage, effectiveness. I skim over it, but my eyes keep drifting back to the phrase at the top.

Permanently preventing the use of their abilities.

"It's like the suppressors," I finally say. "Except permanent. She figured out how to do it—how to take away our abilities. Forever."

Angelo frowns. "But she's keeping the serum here, locked in a safe."

"Because she doesn't want anyone to know about it," Maverick says.

"Of course not." I set the box down on the table in front of us, almost afraid to keep holding it. I wring my hands, remembering the echoes I'd heard in Dr. Shaw's office.

"*Anomalies shouldn't be allowed to leave unless their abilities have been permanently suppressed,*" the woman—Katherine—had said. So instead of releasing anomalies, the ACA decided to make room for new arrivals in a different way: by getting rid of them. And Alice has the solution they've been looking for—a permanent ability neutralizer—right here. For how long? How long has the ACA been killing innocent people simply because of what they are, and Alice has been sitting on this discovery, just letting them do it? Why would she keep it a secret?

The answer becomes suddenly clear to me. "She's afraid someone might use it against her."

"The ACA could destroy her plans with this," Maverick adds.

My chest tightens with sudden rage. "She'd rather let anomalies *die* than give it up to them. Than risk losing power."

The room goes eerily quiet as we let that thought settle in. It doesn't come as a huge shocker, because Alice has never cared about the well-being of her test subjects. But because of her, lives have been lost. Penny's bubbly voice echoes through my head, excited to finally be going home after five years.

But did she get to?

Angelo's voice rips me out of my thoughts. "That reminds me," he begins, his gaze sliding between me and Maverick warily. "The bad news."

The rage boiling inside of me turns to ice. "What is it?"

"We're running out of time."

"What do you mean?"

"When I stole the car Alice's men were driving, I was able to tap into their communication system. In the few hours it took me to track you guys down, I listened in and learned a few things."

"What did you hear?"

"Alice is planning an attack on the ACA."

"An attack?" Maverick asks.

"Some kind of coup," Angelo explains. "I only caught a few details, but it sounded like she's got a bunch of people in on it. They're going to overthrow the ACA."

My stomach sinks to lead. "How?"

"She's planning to do what she did to us—except to the whole ACA. They're going to alter everyone's memories, convincing them that they're loyal to Alice."

I run a hand down my face. "Why? And what is she going to do with all the anomalies?"

Angelo just shrugs.

"When is this supposed to go down?" Maverick demands.

Angelo's expression turns grave.

"Tonight. Probably any minute now."

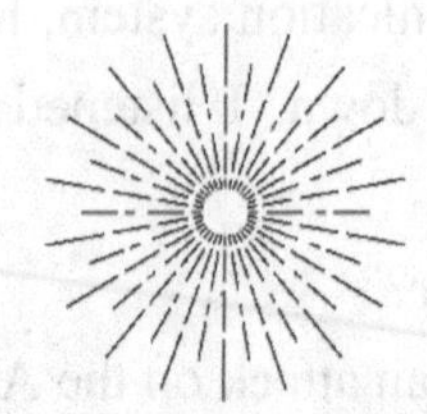

CHAPTER 29

WE'RE TOO LATE.

Always too late.

In the dimly lit room, I reach for something—anything—to ground me. My hands land on a desk, and I press my weight into it, hanging my head in defeat.

What are we going to do?

Against all odds, we made it here. We found Alice's stash of replications. Things didn't exactly go as planned, but somehow, we still managed to push through the setbacks. Only to find out that Alice has been two steps ahead of us this whole time.

I shouldn't be surprised. When have we ever gotten close to outsmarting her? Every time we thought we were about to, she's proved us wrong. It was crazy to think that this time would be any different.

It was foolish to think that we ever stood a chance.

"We have to stop her." My voice wavers around the words. They feel empty, like a wish on a star. Like a dream that could never come to fruition. Something so implausible it's pointless to dwell on.

"What if we… *don't?*" Maverick's suggestion pulls my gaze to him. He's still standing by the door, staring out the window into the dark hallway.

"Don't?" I echo, eyebrows furrowing.

He glances up at me, mouth twisting to one side. "The ACA is killing anomalies. Which is really, really bad. But as long as I've known her, Alice has never had intentions of *killing* anyone." He brings a hand to his mouth, rubbing his knuckles along his chin thoughtfully. "She manipulated people, sure, and she made me cover up her kidnappings to keep people from finding out what she was doing, but as far as I know, she at least never ended a life. And that's better than what the ACA is doing, right?"

I cross my arms, considering the thought. Maverick has a point. I don't believe that Alice has our best interests at heart, either, but she might do less damage than the ACA at this point.

"So… we just let her take over?"

Maverick nods. "We could. At least for now. Until we figure out what to do."

It makes sense, but the idea still makes my stomach churn. "If she goes in there and manipulates everyone's memories—if she makes everyone loyal to her, how are we going to fix that?"

"The same way you restored my memories?" Maverick suggests.

I turn around, my eyes drifting over the boxes full of syringes behind me. Angelo has already pulled one of them out and is typing the serial number into the computer. "If there are enough of them," I say quietly, almost to myself. Then I join Angelo by the computer. "What do we have?"

He hits the enter key on the keyboard, then scans the page that comes up. "This box has replications of Sara's ability."

Sara. I didn't have long to get to know her, but she had become an easy friend and someone I could count on. An image comes to mind of a glass of water boiling one second and turning to a block of ice the next; she could change the temperature of water at will.

It's a cool ability, but unless we can corner her in a pool, I don't imagine it'll be very useful in fixing the whole Alice problem. I turn back to the open cabinet, comparing the serial number on the box next to Angelo with the ones still in the cabinet.

"Looks like these are all the same, too," I say. I move to the next cabinet, break the glass like I did with the first, then pull out a box with a different serial number. I read it off to Angelo, and he punches it into the computer.

For the next several minutes, we repeat the same process, going through all of the boxes in the cabinets and sorting them into groups. I find a pad of sticky notes and start labeling them, and when we finish, I take a step back to process the grim findings.

Twenty-six plastic boxes, each of which can hold up to five syringes.

Seven boxes with Sara's ability to change the temperature of water instantly.

Six with the ability to see through the eyes of any creature nearby—from the boy named Aaron I never knew very well.

Four with Brent and Dahlia's abilities. Teleportation.

Three from a girl named Marian who can phase through solid objects.

Three with emotional manipulation from Veronica.

Two with Gabe's ability to hear people's thoughts.

And only one with Alice's ability to heal.

I reach for the box of syringes with Alice's healing abilities, and when I open it, I frown.

It isn't even full. Two syringes.

Two.

That's it. That's all that's here.

And the rest of these abilities… some of them could possibly be useful. But they aren't going to guarantee our victory.

Maybe, if we had more replications of Alice's ability, we could stand a chance at fixing things once she puts her plan into action. But two… two isn't enough. We can only give two people their real memories back. Show two people the truth about Alice. But two people against… how many? How many would we even need?

I swallow hard, the reality of our situation washing over me. If we had found replications of Maverick's ability, or Wyatt's, we might be able to prevent this from happening in the first place. We could leave now, sneak back into the ACA, and give the syringes to the anomalies trapped inside. Then they could fight back and stop everyone working for Alice. Manipulate *their* memories before they get to everyone else.

But we don't have those replications. It's just the three of us.

Angelo can help us get back into the ACA. Maverick can wipe people's memories, possibly stop a few people working for Alice from executing the plan. But we don't know what other abilities they might be packing, and I doubt he could get to *all* of Alice's people without getting stopped.

So what are we going to do now?

I squeeze my eyes shut as my thoughts race, and when I open them again, my gaze snaps to the red box still resting on the desk where I left it.

Anomaly Neutralizer.

I reach for it, undoing the latches and opening it back up. It's a bigger box than the other ones, and I count fifteen syringes inside.

"How many people do you think Alice is sending in for the coup?" I ask, looking over at Angelo.

He shrugs, biting his lip. "Fifteen? Maybe twenty?"

The tiniest flicker of hope lights inside my chest. "We might be able to stop her still."

Maverick glances in our direction, taking in the red box in my hands. "Of course."

I start to nod, a plan forming in my mind. "These could prevent everyone from using the abilities Alice gave them. We have fifteen, so we could take out the majority of them with the neutralizers. Then there would only be a few we'd have to deal with on our own."

Angelo's eyes dart around the room while he thinks. "Alice won't be able to execute her plan."

"What about the ACA, though?" Maverick asks, narrowing his eyes. "We can't let them keep doing what they're doing."

"And they won't have to anymore," I reply. "In the echoes I heard, the reason they started disposing of anomalies in the first place is because they didn't have this." I raise the red box up for emphasis. "A way to block our abilities permanently. If I can get one of them to Dr. Shaw, she might be able to make more. Then they can actually start releasing anomalies safely. This is the solution they've been looking for."

Silence fills the room as the words sink in. As the plan calculates. And then Angelo speaks, his voice suddenly smaller, more tentative than before.

"Do you think they'll take everyone's abilities away?" he asks. I meet his wide gaze, take in the sudden sadness scribbled across his features.

"I… don't know."

"I'll happily let them take mine," Maverick says quietly, looking down at his hands.

I open my mouth to reply, but hesitate, wondering. If I'm given the option, would I choose to get rid of my ability? Knowing what I know now about it?

Just a few weeks ago, I would've answered in a heartbeat: of course. Because all I'd ever wanted was a shot at normal, a chance to live a life free from the burden of the echoes. Without them, I could go to movies, to concerts, to school without having to constantly listen to the past noise piled up around me. I could actually fit in, actually do the things my friends wanted to do with me.

But… is that what I really want? After everything?

Grace and Leo know the truth about me now. And they seem to have accepted it just fine. Grace and I's relationship had been strained before, but that was because she didn't know how much

I was struggling. I thought I couldn't tell her because she would never understand. How could any of it make sense when I was the only one with this strange ability?

But I'm not the only one. I'm not alone anymore.

And Maverick. I don't remember everything yet, but from the echoes I've seen of our relationship, my doubts were never about him. They were about me. My ability. How he would react if he found out. What he was thinking when I couldn't explain why I just didn't like doing certain things, why I could only tolerate so much. But even back then, hadn't he stuck by my side through it all? Hadn't he loved me anyway, even without knowing anything about my ability?

And now we both know the truths we kept hidden for so long. We understand each other in a way that those past versions of ourselves never could have.

The echoes have brought me so much pain and heartache over the years. But for the first time ever, they've also brought me comfort. Peace. Belonging.

And all along, all I ever really wanted was to be understood. Isn't that the truth?

It wasn't the echoes making me miserable. It was my inability to see past them. My inability to accept them as a part of me. I wanted to be like everybody else, and the echoes prevented that. They made me feel like an outsider.

But what if I had just accepted them? What if I had realized that it's okay to be different, that I wasn't worth less just because I wasn't the same as everyone else?

I see that now. And I know that without this ability, I might have lost Maverick. And my parents. I might have lost everything. Forever.

And I didn't.

I stare down at the red box in my hands, considering it.

Alice has kept this hidden from the ACA despite what they're doing to anomalies. She must know that she has the power to put a stop to it, and yet she's chosen not to. She's chosen to fight against the system instead of giving up her power.

And in some strange way, I understand that.

The ACA isn't on our side. They don't care about what we—the anomalies, the ones who were born with and have to live with these gifts or burdens or whatever they are—want.

But Alice doesn't, either.

No one does.

Which is why we have to fight for ourselves. For the choice.

And we might not win. We might not get to choose in the end. But if it's between losing our abilities and being exploited by Alice for the rest of our lives, I know which one I'd rather do. And I think that the rest of the anomalies would agree with me.

Slowly, I close the box, setting it down on the desk. I look between Maverick and Angelo, knowing that whatever happens next is going to change everything for anomalies.

"We should do it," I decide. "We should try to stop Alice."

Maverick nods. Slowly, Angelo does as well.

"We'll find a way to stop the ACA, too," I say, glancing at Angelo. "To give anomalies the rights they deserve."

And I can only hope that somehow, we'll be able to do both.

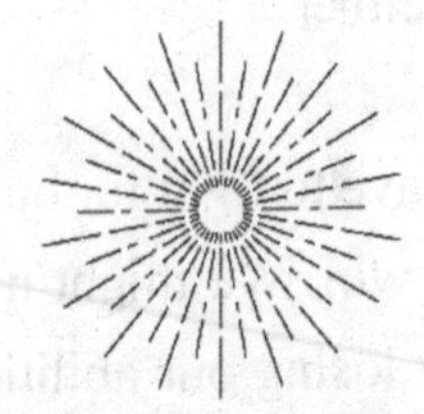

CHAPTER 30

"WE NEED TO GET moving," Maverick says, his tone turning urgent. "How long do you think we have before Alice moves in on the ACA?"

Angelo shakes his head. "I don't know. They didn't give an exact time, but it sounded like everyone was getting ready to act soon. We'll be able to listen in again once we get back to the car."

I scan the room, my gaze landing on a trash can along the back wall. I move to it, then pull the plastic liner out. Luckily, it's empty, so I don't have to dump it before I return to the wall of syringes and start tossing the plastic boxes into the bag.

"We'll take all of these with us," I explain. "We might not find a use for them, but if anything, at least Alice won't have them anymore." I keep the replications of Alice's ability and the neutralizers separate from the rest of the boxes, tucking them into the pocket of my jacket instead.

Angelo turns back to the computer, typing something into the keyboard rapidly. "I'm going to back all of this data up to the cloud. There's a lot more research being stored on this computer, and I'm sure some of it will come in handy for the ACA."

Less than five minutes later, we gather by the door. I toss the bag of syringes over my shoulder and nod at Maverick, who leads us into the hallway. We head back the same way we came, passing the still-unconscious guards Maverick had taken out.

When we get to the main floor, Angelo instructs us to make a right and leave from the back door. Maverick scans the hallway first, then waves for us to follow him. We slip through the empty building quietly, and it isn't until we make it to the back door that we run into anyone. As soon as Maverick pokes his head through it to check if the coast is clear, they spot us. Two guards, probably waiting there specifically in case anyone tried to leave this way.

"Stop!" one of them calls as Maverick tugs the door closed again. We back away from the exit, sinking into the shadows of the hallway. When they barge in after us, Maverick aims the dart gun at the doorway, and with two clicks, manages to take out both of them. Within a few seconds, they both crumple to the floor.

Maverick looks down at the dart gun in his hands, frowning. "I should've saved those for later."

I bend over one of the unconscious guards, reaching for the identical gun at his belt. When I wedge it free, I release the clip, counting the darts left.

"Well, here's five more," I say, holding the gun out to Maverick.

Angelo grabs the gun from the other guard, checking its clip, too. "And another five."

"I should've checked the other guards," Maverick says, glancing back the way we came.

I shake my head. "It's too late now. We need to move."

So we do.

Outside, the sky is overcast, and there's a distinct chill in the air that reminds me of the first snowstorm I'd experienced in Shorewick. It's dark, but the grayish glow of the sky makes it easier to see than it was inside the building, so I click my flashlight off. Maverick checks to make sure no more guards are waiting along the sides of the building, and then we slip into line behind Angelo as he jogs into the woods.

By the time we reach the car, we're all panting, our breath coming out in large clouds of mist. I swing the bag of syringes off my shoulder, tossing them into the back before I slide into the passenger seat. Maverick gets in on the driver's side, cranking the car up, and Angelo scoots into the middle seat of the back row, a tablet already in his hands, flickering as he works his magic.

The car's radio turns on, blasting static. "This is the channel they've been communicating through," Angelo explains. "Seems quiet now, but we'll keep an ear out."

Maverick puts the car into drive, pulling us out of the parking lot and onto the main road. I crane my neck, getting a glimpse of the laboratory in the rearview mirror, and a strange sense of *déjà vu* washes over me. It looks almost exactly the same as the last time I drove away from this building in the darkness, minus the smoke billowing out the top. And minus the group of kids I'd rescued piled into the car. Now they're all trapped in a place that may or may not be worse.

That night feels so long ago, but the memories are so vivid it could have happened yesterday. Maverick and I had come here after Alice had kidnapped my parents, hoping we could slip in and find them without her spotting us. Then she'd caught us, and I'd watched her guards drag Maverick away. I'd managed to get Alice's right hand man—Dave—to turn on her after showing him a photo of the family Alice made him forget, and he'd helped me escape. Told me where to find Maverick and my parents. But at that point, it was too late. Their memories had already been erased.

I close my eyes, my fingers curling around the two syringes with Alice's ability tucked deep into my pocket.

Mom. Dad.

These syringes can give them their memories back. But there are only two.

Alice probably has more, though. Right? Maybe she gave them to the people helping with the coup tonight, just in case. Or maybe she's storing them somewhere else. Even if she isn't, she'll be able to make more. We'll make her. Because there are so many people who still need to have their memories restored: the rest of the anomalies that were with me and Maverick that day in the barn, all of the families that don't remember them anymore, and everyone I'd asked Maverick to erase memories from—my grandparents, my school teachers, a few classmates. We're going to need a lot more than two of these syringes.

But in order to survive tonight…

I pull the syringes out of my pocket, holding one out to Maverick and one out to Angelo.

"You guys should keep these with you," I say. "If Alice or anyone else tries to mess with your memories, you can use these to prevent them from doing it."

Angelo takes the syringe from me, but Maverick just keeps his eyes fixed on the road, shaking his head slightly. "You should keep it instead."

"I don't need it," I reply. "Alice can't mess with my memories, remember?"

"But what if something else happens?" His gaze flicks away from the road to meet mine briefly, his eyes full of worry.

"Then you should have it," I insist. "Statistically speaking, you've been shot more times than me. So if the trend continues, you're the one that's going to need it."

Maverick rolls his eyes. "Or maybe I've already done my time."

"Either way," I reply. "Take it." I keep my hand out, unwilling to budge.

After a long moment, Maverick finally sighs and takes the syringe.

"When we get there, we should split up," I continue. "We won't be able to stop all of them on our own, so you two should go find the other anomalies and get them to help out." I reach into my other pocket, pulling out the neutralizers. I take three for myself, then give six to each of them. "I'm going to find Dr. Shaw and give her one so she can analyze it and create more. I'll warn her of Alice's plans, and then I'll find you guys and help out."

"Are you sure splitting up is a good idea?" Maverick asks.

I swallow. "No. But we need to move quickly, so it's probably the best option."

"We haven't heard anything on the radios, though. We might have more time than we—" Maverick begins, but before he can finish, a sound crackles over the speakers. Then a voice comes through, scratchy but audible.

"Katherine Richardson has just entered the building," a woman says.

"Send her my way," another voice replies, and the sound of it makes my blood run cold. *Alice*. "I'll let you know when she's taken care of, and then we make our move."

"Roger," the first voice says.

Then there's only silence. We wait for several seconds, listening to the hum of the car's engine beneath us, wondering if any more information will come through. When it doesn't, I shift in my seat.

"How far out are we?" I ask, glancing at Maverick.

He swallows, expression grim. "About forty-five minutes."

The number swirls in my head, calculating. How long will it take for Alice to deal with Katherine? And after she gives the signal, how long before everyone's memories are altered? Or at least too many people for us to get through to stop her?

I run my fingers up and through my hair as my knee bounces in place. The longer I process it and try to guess if we'll have enough time, the more helpless I feel.

Forty-five minutes is too long. We'll never make it in time.

But we have to make it in time. If we don't, if Alice already has control of the ACA before we get there, what chance do we stand against her? How will we fix this?

I press my palms to my eyes, trying to blot out this feeling that the world is about to explode and there's absolutely nothing I can do about it.

And then an idea slams into me.

"Angelo," I say, my eyes flying open. "Pass me the bag of replications."

When the flimsy trash bag full of boxes lands in my lap, I dig through it like a dog trying to find its bone. I find the box I'm looking for, then let the bag fall to my feet, not even caring when one of the other boxes flies open, syringes spilling onto the floor.

"We might be able to get there faster," I say, ripping the box open and pulling out a syringe. After tugging off my coat, I uncap it, holding it upright to tap the bubbles out. Then I roll up the sleeve of my left arm.

"Wait, what if—" Maverick begins, but before he can finish, I plunge the needle into my bicep and empty the contents of the syringe into my muscle.

"What are you doing?" Angelo asks, leaning forward to gape at me.

"Brent and Dahlia's ability. To teleport," I explain.

"They can only teleport to each other, though, right?" Maverick asks.

"Maybe," I say, putting the cap back over the needle and tossing it to the ground. "But maybe not."

When I'd gone to look for Maverick, Wyatt, Dahlia, and Angelo the night they got captured, I'd run into the bald man. He'd taken out Sara and Veronica, and I'd managed to get the syringe with Alice's healing abilities away from him. But he'd used another syringe before I could stop him. And then he'd grabbed Sara and teleported out of there.

So maybe, with the replications Alice has developed, there doesn't need to be another person to teleport to. Maybe it can stand on its own.

Or maybe, Brent and Dahlia are capable of more than they thought.

There's so much more to your ability than you realize.

Hadn't that been the case with Wyatt, too? He thought he could only control a few minds at a time, and then somehow, he'd created an illusion for everyone in the vicinity. He allowed us to escape.

Dr. Shaw told me he was in a coma now, though. The phrase *permanent brain damage* races through my head like a warning, but I shake it away.

My ability wasn't what I'd originally thought, either. It has saved me from having my memories altered several times now, and I haven't run into any problems from using it. As long as I don't over-exert myself, I'll be fine.

"Pull over," I tell Maverick, and he obeys. As soon as the car rolls to a stop on a patch of dirt along the side of the two-lane highway, I grab his hand. Then Angelo's.

"Are you guys ready?" I ask, gaze flicking between them.

"Are you sure it's going to work?" Angelo replies.

"Yes," I say firmly. Because it has to.

It's the only way.

I squeeze my eyes shut, concentrating. Aside from the small sting when I'd inserted the needle, the injection doesn't make me feel any different. I have no idea how to make it work or what I should expect to feel, but I know that we need to get to the ACA right now. I know that if we don't make it, the hole Alice has been digging since the beginning of all of this is going to get too deep for us to climb out of.

I picture the ACA. The beige hallways, the noisy cafeteria. The faces of my friends, new and old, sitting in class or laughing by the lockers. My dorm room, dark and cramped and somewhat quiet.

And to my relief, when I open my eyes again, we aren't in the car anymore.

CHAPTER 31

"YOU DID IT." Maverick whispers into the dark.

I blink, disoriented. I'm suddenly standing instead of sitting, and though the floor is solid beneath me, my knees wobble. I let go of Maverick and Angelo's hands, reaching out to steady myself on the solid wooden object in front of me. A bed frame?

Slowly, I run my hands along the wall, taking small steps as I work my way across the room. My fingers find a light switch, and when I flip it on, I let out a steadying breath.

My dorm room. We did it—*I* did it. And now we're back in the ACA.

The relief only lasts a few seconds before the urgency kicks in.

Even though my mind is still spinning from the jarring shift in our surroundings, I whip around and head for the closet on the other side of the room. I open it, scanning the hangers holding several sets of beige scrubs that were issued to me when I first got here. I grab a pair for myself, pull out another for Maverick, then find one of Georgia's smaller sets for Angelo. When I hand the clothes to them, they both head for the bathroom without a word, understanding. We'll blend in better if we change out of the street clothes we'd put on at Maverick's apartment.

I quickly pull the scrubs on and am transferring the three neutralizers I took to my new front pocket when Maverick and Angelo return.

I glance at the clock. "Everyone's probably still at dinner," I say. "It's a good time to slip into the crowd, but the guards might be on high alert looking for us, so we should still be careful."

Angelo nods and taps the screen on his tablet. "I'm going to freeze and loop all of the cameras," he tells us. "We'll be able to get around without being spotted, but someone is bound to notice eventually. And I'll disable the palm scanners at the elevators. That way we can move between floors as needed, even if we're split up."

"Perfect," I reply, always grateful for Angelo's quick thinking. "If you two can find anyone from our original group, I'm sure they'll be more than willing to help. Gather as many as you can and when Alice's people make their move, do everything you can to stop them."

Maverick nods, but then his eyes are on me, searching my face. "You're going to go look for Dr. Shaw, then?" he asks.

I swallow, knowing both that I can't lie to Maverick and that he won't be happy with my answer. "I'm going straight to Alice,"

I tell him. "Katherine Richardson—she's the head of the ACA. If she's with Alice right now, Alice could make her move any second. I'm going to find her and stall as long as I can to buy you guys some time. Maybe even stop her from messing with Katherine's memories if I can."

Already, Maverick is frowning. "You can't go in there alone," he argues. "I'll come with you."

"No. You need to go with Angelo."

He starts to shake his head. "What if Alice—"

"No," I repeat, cutting him off. "She can't mess with my memories, which makes it safer for me to go than for either of you. Sure, there are a million other ways she can ruin this. Sure, there are a million things that can go wrong. But this is the only way we might win."

When I finish, Maverick just stares at me, his hazel eyes soaking in every inch of me as if this is the last time he's going to see me. Then he pulls me into a hug, his fingers bunching into the fabric of my shirt as he tightens his grip.

"I never wanted you to get involved in any of this," he mumbles over my shoulder.

"I know," I say, pulling back to look him in the eyes again. "But you never had a choice. This is my fight, too."

He nods. "I know that now." He lifts his hand, slowly tucking a strand of hair behind my ear. "And Laura, I want you to know—"

I press a finger to his lips, stopping his words. "Tell me later," I say. "This isn't goodbye."

But the way he's looking at me now makes it feel like one, so I look away, refusing to accept it. I release my hold on him, taking one big step back. Then another. Then I squeeze my eyes shut, blotting Maverick's terrified expression out. Focusing.

Alice.

Where is she? In her office? The one on the first floor that I've only ever seen via four camera lenses when my friends snuck into it? Or would she have another room near Dr. Shaw's office on the same floor as the medical wing? Maybe they're in one of the interrogation rooms or she's confronting Katherine in her own office as a display of power. I don't know, and I can't picture any concrete places except for the last one I saw Alice in—the empty interrogation room. So that's where I channel my focus.

THE TELEPORTATION STILL leaves me slightly disoriented, but it seems to be getting easier every time. I pause for a few seconds and take in the interrogation room—completely empty— to ground myself in my new surroundings, and then I'm ready to move.

Alice isn't here. Which means I've lost the precious time it took to get here—only the blink of an eye thanks to teleportation, thankfully, but the sand is quickly falling to the bottom of the hourglass and I have no idea how much I have left before it's gone.

For a moment, I consider attempting to teleport again. I could bounce around between rooms, searching for her faster that way, but I'm still new to using this ability. It seems to take me a minute to get the teleportation to work, and my focus is quickly slipping. So instead, I decide to use my legs.

I crack the door open, peering into the hallway, then poke my head out, scanning the opposite direction. It's clear, so I move, breaking into a jog as I head for the main lobby. I retrace the path Dr. Shaw took me down when she brought me to her office, grateful when I don't run into any guards. As I rush down the hall, I scan the doors I pass, searching for either Alice or Katherine's names on the nameplates. I never find them though, cursing under my breath when I make it to the very last door and it isn't what I'm looking for. More time wasted.

I head back the way I came but pause at Dr. Shaw's office, testing the door handle for good measure. It's locked, so I give it three rapid knocks and press my ear against the cold metal, listening for signs that she might be inside. None come, so I turn and hurry back to the lobby.

There are still two more hallways that branch off from the lobby: one that leads to the medical wing and one I've never been down before. I opt for the latter, heart racing as I urge my legs to move faster beneath me.

This hallway has fewer doors even though it's the same length as the others, and as I scan the labels *Lab 1* and *Lab 2* beside them, I can guess why. These rooms must be bigger, filled with research equipment similar to what we'd seen in Alice's secret lab. I take a few more steps, but pause, debating. Alice probably wouldn't meet the head of the ACA here, in one of the labs, right? I could make my way down the hall, peeking into every door I pass just to make sure, but then I'd risk getting spotted. And if she's actually in her office like I suspect, that's only more time wasted.

I've just decided to turn around and head upstairs when in front of me, a door opens.

I flatten myself against the wall, knowing that as soon as the person steps into the hallway I'll be in plain sight anyway. But when they come into view, I realize it doesn't matter.

"Dr. Shaw!"

Her arms are full of paperwork that promptly drops to the floor the moment her eyes land on me. She doesn't move to pick it up, though. Instead, she scans the hallway around us, immediately on high alert. Then she turns back to the room she was just exiting, beckoning for me to follow.

I slip through the door behind her, and she closes it, pressing her back against the wall while panic takes over her features.

"What are you doing?" she hisses.

I swallow hard, panting. "Looking for Alice."

"Why? And why are you out in the open like this?" She gestures vaguely with her hands, clearly frustrated.

"Angelo looped the cameras, so it's fine," I explain. "But I need to find Alice. Fast."

"Why?" Dr. Shaw demands. "What happened out there?"

"We found her stash of replications, but she'd already cleaned most of it out. She's staging a coup to take over the ACA. Right now."

Dr. Shaw's eyes widen.

"I need to find her so I can stall. Maverick and Angelo are going to try and stop it, but they need more time."

"How are they going to stop it?"

"She's sending people in with abilities that will allow them to manipulate memories. She's going to make everyone in the ACA believe they're loyal to her," I explain. I reach into my pocket and pull out one of the neutralizers, handing it over to Dr. Shaw. "We also discovered that Alice figured out how to permanently suppress anomalies' abilities. We found a stash of these, and we're going to use them on the people working for her so they won't be able to mess with anyone's memories. But I need to find her. Right now."

Dr. Shaw just stands there, looking shell shocked. She stares down at the syringe in her hand, blinking like she has no clue what to do.

"I don't have much time," I say, impatient.

Dr. Shaw's eyes finally clear, then focus on me. "I know where she is," she says quietly.

"Where?"

"Upstairs, in one of the conference rooms."

"Thank you," I say, moving for the door, about to break into a sprint. But Dr. Shaw's next words make me pause.

"She just called me."

I search Dr. Shaw's face, chewing on my lip. "What did she say?"

"She invited me to meet with her and the head of the ACA. To discuss a few things."

A chill runs through me. "She wants to deal with both of you first," I say, mostly to myself. If I had gotten here just seconds later than I did, I wouldn't have run into Dr. Shaw. She would have been on her way up to visit Alice, and her memories might have been wiped clean long before I found her.

I sigh, contemplating. "You need to stay away from her. Get somewhere safe—and put that neutralizer where Alice can't find it," I tell her. "When this is all over, you'll need to analyze it and replicate it. So the ACA doesn't keep killing anomalies."

Dr. Shaw's eyes snap to mine, obviously shocked that I know this bit of information. "I never—"

"I know you never wanted to do it. But it isn't okay," I say. "It has to stop."

Dr. Shaw shakes her head. "I never let anyone kill the anomalies," she tells me. "I faked their deaths. Then I let them go, just like the ones before that policy was introduced."

Something loosens in my chest, something I hadn't even realized was wound so tight. "They're alive?"

Nodding, Dr. Shaw moves away from the door and toward a storage cabinet. She opens it, tucking the neutralizer into one of the drawers. "Only a few anomalies have ever passed away on my watch, and always because of some experimentation Dr. Wight was doing. She was obsessed with testing the limits of their abilities, and many of her subjects ended up in comas similar to your friend Wyatt. ACA protocol doesn't let me keep them on life support for very long."

I swallow. "Is Wyatt...?" I can't even finish the sentence.

Dr. Shaw turns back to face me. "He's alive. Barely. But he may never make a full recovery."

I squeeze my eyes shut, flashes of Maverick bleeding and on the brink of death racing through my head. Miraculously, I'd managed to save him. And I'm going to find a way to save Wyatt, too.

I shift my gaze to the door. "I need to move," I say. "I need to stop her."

"I'll come. I can help you stall," Dr. Shaw tells me. "I have questions for Dr. Wight that need answers, anyway."

I open my mouth, about to argue that she needs to leave instead. She's potentially our only ally in the ACA, and if Alice messes with her memories, she won't be able to help us anymore. But the idea of going after Alice with Dr. Shaw by my side instead of alone—especially after learning that Dr. Shaw has been protecting the anomalies that the ACA wanted to get rid of—calms me. So I close my mouth instead, nodding. Then I reach into my pocket and grab another syringe, holding the neutralizer out to Dr. Wight. "This one's for you to use. In case you need it."

She takes it, offering a grim smile.

I reach for the door handle.

"Let's go end this."

CHAPTER 32

THE ENTIRE ACA APPEARS to be deserted. As Dr. Shaw and I jog to the elevators, then make it to the top floor and start for the conference room, we don't run into a single person. No guards, no employees, *nobody*.

I hope it's a sign that Alice's plan hasn't been set into motion yet, and not a sign that things are already over.

When we finally come to a stop in front of the conference room's double doors, I take a deep breath. Dr. Shaw and I share a glance, and with a final nod, she tugs the door handle.

"Ah, there she is!" Alice's pleasant voice rings out from inside. "Gloria, thank you for coming."

Dr. Shaw steps into the room, moving out of the doorway where she'd been blocking me from view. Across the room, Alice glances up and notices me standing there, and her eyebrows lift in genuine surprise. But she doesn't appear startled or even the slightest bit worried, like I want her to.

"And Laura Jones," she says, flashing her signature smile. "How fitting that you should join us. Please, come in."

Hesitantly, I step into the room, letting the door slide closed behind me. I take in the space—a conference table with eight chairs around it, a water station in the corner, and a wall-mounted screen behind Alice, who's standing at the head of the table. Dr. Shaw takes a seat on the right side near the middle of the table, and in the seat directly to Alice's left, there's another woman who must be Katherine. Her light brown hair is chopped into a bob that gives her a stern look, and she's wearing a navy blazer over a plain white dress shirt.

She frowns at me, then shifts her gaze to Alice. "Who is this?"

"Miss Jones is one of our recent escapees," Alice tells her, and Katherine's lips pull into a thin line. "But don't worry, she's here where we can keep an eye on her now. And she's actually somebody I wanted to discuss with you both."

Dr. Shaw narrows her eyes but doesn't say anything. Katherine just watches Alice expectantly.

"As you both know," Alice continues, pulling a chair out to take a seat at the table, "the search for a method of permanently inhibiting the abilities of anomalies has been unsuccessful for some time, and the chances of discovering one are slim."

I fold my arms across my chest, feeling the reassuring bulge of the plastic syringe in my pocket. I consider calling Alice out on the lie, but I don't want to show my hand too soon, so I decide against it. Dr. Shaw, too, keeps her mouth shut.

"But I've learned something recently about the nature of anomalies that has changed my perspective on how we have been handling the issue, and I believe it might change yours, too." Alice pauses, glancing between the three of us. "We've known for a while now that anomalies exist because of a genetic mutation in the maternal grandmother, who was likely exposed to something that caused the mutation," she says, and I get the sense that the explanation is directed mostly at me. She doesn't realize how much I already know, which is good. "However, for the longest time, we haven't been able to figure out *what*. But thanks to you, Laura, I've made some progress and believe I've discovered the source."

Me. It always comes back to me. *You're different, Laura. You aren't like the rest of them*. But why?

I ball my hands into fists, suddenly angry. "This has nothing to do with me."

"It has *everything* to do with you, Laura."

I shake my head, taking a step closer to the conference table. "No. It doesn't. This is all *your* doing," I say, pointing my finger at her accusingly. "You created anomalies. *You* started all of this."

Alice just tilts her head at me, unfazed, her eyes gleaming with concern as if I'm a small child throwing a tantrum and she's the calm parent, waiting for me to finish. I drop my hand to my side, hating the way one look can make me feel so small.

"Alice is an anomaly," I continue, shifting my attention to Katherine. "She can heal from any wound instantaneously. She's been hiding it from the ACA, and I think I know why."

Katherine shifts in her seat, her frown deepening.

"The source that you've been looking for—whatever everyone was exposed to back when the mutation first happened—was Alice's doing. She created it, and she must have mutated herself, too."

My words, directed at Katherine, seem to have little effect. She just studies me, looking unconvinced.

And then Alice laughs, and the sound makes my stomach sink. "Your attempts to discover the truth are admirable, I must admit," she says, shaking her head. "But also pitiful."

"You're lying." I try to keep my voice even despite the fact that her denial is making my blood boil. "You're trying to play it cool, pretending you don't know what I'm talking about."

"I know exactly what you're talking about, Laura," she replies, her eyes going serious. "But I can assure you that I didn't *create* anything. I was simply born with a gift. One that I spent far too long believing was a curse."

I open my mouth, wanting to accuse her again, to demand that she explain everything to us. But I can't seem to find the words.

Alice stands, her steely gaze never wavering from my face. "You understand that, Laura, don't you? You know what it's like to not understand yourself. To believe that something about you is wrong. Or a mistake. To feel like an *anomaly*."

I close my eyes, frustrated. She won't give me straight answers, won't tell me the truth. And the worst part is that her words still hit a nerve inside me. Because it's true. I know exactly what that feels like.

"That, my dear, is because you and I are the same."

"We are *not* the same."

"But we are," she insists. "And that's what made me realize that we—anomalies—are not just a fluke. We're a new species. An evolution of humanity, created by nature herself."

I shake my head. "By nature? Or by *you* in order to gain power?"

"You're mistaken," Alice says, almost gently. "I was born this way, Laura. And it wasn't until years later that I realized how significant that was."

I glance between Dr. Shaw and Katherine, gauging their reactions. Katherine's expression is stony, void of any emotion. Dr. Shaw, however, appears to be intrigued. She's watching Alice with wide eyes, like she's ready to drink in any more information Alice is willing to give.

I let a sigh out through taut lips, wishing Alice would make it all make sense. But also grateful, because we really are stalling. And the longer we can keep her talking, the more of a chance my friends will have at saving everyone.

"Why?" I demand. "What do you mean?"

Alice's eyes drop to the table, her features softening. When she speaks again, her voice takes on a new, haunted quality, almost like the story is painful to tell.

"I didn't understand it, at first," she says quietly. "My family didn't, either. They thought I was a freak. That something was wrong with me—even though now, I see how ridiculous that notion was. I could never be injured. My cuts and my broken bones would disappear as quickly as they came, and no one could explain why. And instead of embracing it, instead of being grateful for it, they feared me. They treated me like something about me was broken.

"I spent years—too much of my life—trying to figure it out. Trying to understand my own existence. I eventually figured out how it worked, but I couldn't figure out why. Why me? Why now? It was just a random mutation. A mishap with no explanation. And I was alone. There was no one else like me... at least, not at the time.

"Then, almost forty years later, I stumbled across a case study published by Dr. Gloria Shaw," Alice continues, glancing over at Dr. Shaw with a small smile. "About a young boy who could move objects with his mind. It seemed impossible, but I knew that impossible things can happen. And when I reached out, I learned that he wasn't the only one. That there were more people out there with similar talents.

"It took a while to prove myself to the ACA and to be accepted as part of their team. But when I finally got access to the research, I realized something terrifying." Alice pauses, swallowing. "It was me. *I* was the catalyzing agent you were looking for—the thing that caused the original mutation. The mutation inside of me is different from the others. It gives my cells the ability to regenerate at a faster rate, but it also has an effect on the people I come in contact with."

"Like a virus," Dr. Shaw says quietly. "It infects everyone you touch."

"More like a force field," Alice corrects. "I simply have to be close enough to them for their cells to react." She closes her eyes, a pained expression taking over her features. "The people I went to school with, the places I traveled growing up, everyone in my community that I might have shaken hands with or even passed by throughout my life—they all likely carry the mutation.

Then some of them had children, passing the mutation on. And the next generation became our anomalies."

"All of the anomalies we've discovered have been a direct result of your original mutation," Dr. Shaw says, almost to herself.

Alice's gaze cuts to me. "All of them except for one."

And then the penny drops. All of the times Alice has hinted at this moment echo back to me, suddenly making complete sense.

But you, Laura, are special.

You're different, Laura. You aren't like the rest of them.

There's so much more to your ability than you realize.

I'm not like the rest of the anomalies, because the mutation in me has nothing to do with Alice's. I'm not originally from the Pine Springs Valley, where Alice must have grown up and spent most of her time, where the rest of the anomalies have roots. Which means my mutation wasn't passed down from my maternal grandmother.

It's new. It's different.

The realization has me reeling, and I stumble forward, pressing my hands into the table for support. My breaths come out in short gasps, and my vision starts to blur.

But why? Why does learning this make me feel sick, like I've done something wrong? It shouldn't matter. It shouldn't change everything.

I look up, meeting Alice's satisfied gaze. A sickening smile plays on her lips, twisting my stomach into knots. When she finally speaks again, I understand why knowing the truth is suddenly making me feel so *wrong.*

"You and me. We're the same, Laura."

CHAPTER 33

THE ROOM FALLS QUIET for a long time. I stare down at my hands, pressed into the wood table to keep me from sinking to the ground under this new weight. I feel Alice's eyes on me. Dr. Shaw's. Katherine's. They're all studying me. Waiting for my reaction.

But how am I supposed to react? What am I supposed to do with this information?

Me. Different. Not like the other anomalies.

Like Alice.

If the mutation in me is like Alice's, then it affects those around me, too. It spreads the mutation that creates more anomalies.

But no. I'm not like her. I can't be like her.

"We are not the same," I finally manage to say, an echo of the same words I'd spoken only moments ago. I cling to them, desperately needing them to be true.

"But we are," Alice says, shifting on her feet. She begins to pace on the other side of the table, but slowly. Calmly. "You and me, Laura. We're the original anomalies. Truly random acts of nature. Because of me, so many anomalies were created. And because of you, even more will be given the opportunity to exist."

My gut twists, and I squeeze my eyes shut, trying to picture all of the people I've ever come in contact with. My friends, my classmates, my teachers. People I passed in grocery stores, in restaurants, in the park. How many people carry the new mutation? How many of them will have children, and how many of those children will pass on the gene that makes the next generation of anomalies? Definitely not all of them, which is good, but still too many.

"I understand why you're conflicted." Alice's voice pulls my attention from my racing thoughts. "I spent so long feeling guilty. I watched these anomalies—these *children*—suffer because of their abilities. So many of them were treated like outcasts. Tossed from their families, blamed for things that they had absolutely no control over. And then they were brought here and put into captivity. Even *killed,* simply because they existed." She pauses her pacing, grimacing. "And all along, I knew it was my fault. That if I hadn't existed first, none of them would have. None of them would be suffering."

Her words swirl in my head, sinking under my skin and making me feel ill. More anomalies will exist because of me. More people who will grow up misunderstood. Who'll be hunted by the ACA or by Alice, then killed or exploited because of their abilities.

"But then you came along, Laura," Alice continues. "You opened my eyes. You made me realize that this wasn't an isolated incident or some freak accident. We—anomalies—are something nature intended to create, not a mistake. We've been given a gift, one that will change the course of humanity forever."

A gift.

Is it a gift?

Maybe, for some of us. Angelo's sad eyes when he'd asked me if the ACA was going to take everyone's abilities away flash through my mind. Clearly, he sees his ability as a gift. The way he's always tinkering with technology and gets excited about the things he has made is easy to recognize. And I've seen the same spark in other anomalies, too. Sara when she turned Maverick's pool into a giant hot tub. Brent and Dahlia, who always know they can get back to each other. Even Georgia, who has been in the ACA for more than four years, lit up when she reminisced about being able to use her telekinesis.

But on the other hand, so many anomalies have abilities that are burdens, too. Gabe always having to hear people's thoughts. Ash, for years haunted by the fears of anyone she touched. Veronica, who could never quite gain control of her ability. And Maverick, riddled with guilt after being forced into doing things he never would have unless he thought he had to. Terrified that his ability might be affecting the people he loves.

It isn't so black and white.

"Think of what we could do, Laura," Alice says, her eyes almost sparkling as they dart to the ceiling, seeing some future off in the distance. "There are already dozens of abilities that will be useful to the public on their own. But we can combine them, too. I've barely scratched the surface of what's possible." She closes her eyes, relishing in the idea. Then she opens them, fixing her gaze on me. "Think of the lives we could change with what we've been given. We'll prove to the world that we aren't something to be cast out or locked away."

I swallow, hating the fact that in a way, she's right. Anomalies *could* impact the world in a lot of amazing ways, and we shouldn't be treated like outcasts. But there's more to her plans than just the appealing idea of a brighter future for anomalies.

I lift my chin, narrowing my eyes at her. "How do you plan to make this happen? What are you going to do with the anomalies?"

"I believe that most of them will be more than willing to cooperate."

"And if they aren't? If they *don't* want to be a part of this?"

Her lips turn down. "Then we'll have to fix that, won't we?"

"You're going to brainwash them," I say bitterly. "You're going to take away their choice."

"I'm going to do whatever is necessary to ensure a better future for them."

"A better future for *them?* Or a better future for *you?*"

My spite-filled words hang in the air for a long moment. Alice's eyebrows pinch together the tiniest bit, and she folds her arms across her chest, but she doesn't say anything. I can't tell if she's actually being affected by my words, or if she's just frustrated that I won't agree with her. Either way, it leaves me with an odd sense of satisfaction.

"You're wrong," I say quietly. I push myself away from the table, straightening my back. "You and I are not the same. Because I would never *use* people like you do."

Alice shakes her head, tsking at me. "You won't allow yourself to see what could be."

"That's not true," I fire back. "I think you're right. Anomalies *could* change the world. Our abilities—yours, especially—could help so many people. But forcing people to be pawns in your game is not the way to do it."

Alice leans into the table, her lips curling. "Then you don't understand what's at stake here. You don't understand that I have no other choice."

"I do understand." I fix my gaze on Katherine, who hasn't said a word throughout this entire confrontation. "And what the ACA has been doing to anomalies is horrifying." I pause, trying to judge her reaction, but she just stares back at me, her emotions locked behind a mask of stone.

"But you found a solution," I continue, turning back to Alice. I reach into my pocket, fingers curling around the syringe with the red cap still tucked inside. When I pull it out and place it on the table, Alice's hands tighten into fists and she straightens, looking almost frightened. But then her expression darkens.

"Anomalies shouldn't have to give up their powers just to walk free."

"No," I say. "They shouldn't. But they shouldn't have to *die*, either."

Dr. Shaw stands suddenly, kicking her chair out behind her. "How long have you been keeping this from us?"

Alice's gaze sweeps between me and Dr. Shaw, realization settling over her. "So you've been working with one of your patients. And how long exactly have you been going against the direct orders of the ACA?"

"As long as I've known that you were doing the same," Dr. Shaw snarls. She takes a step toward Alice, seething. "You could have saved lives!"

"But didn't you save them already?" Alice asks, her voice even despite Dr. Shaw's outburst of emotion. "I've seen you getting them out. I knew you wouldn't have it in you to actually follow through with those orders."

Out of the corner of my eye, I see Katherine shift in her chair, frowning. "Is this true?" she asks.

Dr. Shaw's frame goes rigid across the table. "I knew Alice was hiding something. I knew that there was a way that didn't involve harming anyone. I couldn't let myself be responsible for the loss of innocent lives."

Katherine studies her for a long moment. "You know the consequences of disobeying direct orders."

"And what about Alice?" Dr. Shaw demands. "She's been going against the mission of the ACA, hiding research from us, and she's an anomaly. She just admitted to being responsible for the existence of anomalies in the first place!"

Katherine doesn't reply. Just maintains her cold stare, which somehow puts me even more on edge than if she were storming around the room, angry and shouting.

Dr. Shaw's gaze cuts between Alice and Katherine, horror pulling at her features. "You've brainwashed her already," she finally says.

Alice's lips turn up triumphantly. "Katherine understands what needs to happen now, and she agrees with my approach. Luckily, soon you will, too."

Then Alice moves, her steps slow but terrifying as they point her in Dr. Shaw's direction. Dr. Shaw mirrors her movements, backing away to maintain the distance between them. But then her leg bumps into the chair behind her, and she falters for a fraction of a second.

Alice seizes the moment, lunging for her. Dr. Shaw stumbles away, and before I realize what I'm doing, I'm moving, too. I reach out and pick up the syringe from where I'd set it down, then slip off the red cap. I step around the table and move closer to Dr. Shaw and Alice, holding the needle in front of me like a weapon.

But it's already over. Alice's hand snaps around Dr. Shaw's wrist. Dr. Shaw's face goes pale. And for a moment, I swear I can almost see Alice reaching into her mind, draining her memories away.

"No!" I call out, rushing forward. But then Alice's eyes widen.

Not because of me, though.

I skid to a halt, noticing Alice's gaze shifting to her left shoulder, which is blocked from my view by Dr. Shaw. When she stumbles backward, though, I see it sticking out of her arm.

The syringe.

In slow motion, I watch the red cap drop to the ground from Dr. Shaw's other hand.

Alice rips the needle from her arm, the panic plain on her face. "No," she breathes, dropping the syringe like it's a hot pan and backing away, stumbling until she hits the back wall of the conference room. "No, no, no, no, no."

Dr. Shaw lets out a heavy sigh, her shoulders slumping. "Now you can't manipulate my memories," she pants. "Now you can't hurt anyone else."

The scene sharpens in front of me, the impact of it finally sinking in.

Dr. Shaw gave her the neutralizer.

She took Alice's abilities away.

Which means she can no longer heal instantly. She can no longer use the replications of abilities she probably pumped herself with minutes before we got here.

And for one tiny slip of a moment, the tension in my body dissipates.

Because we did it. We got her.

We won.

And then I hear a *click*, and cold dread seizes me once again.

CHAPTER 34

MY EYES FIND THE source of the sound: Katherine's gun. Aimed directly at Dr. Shaw's head.

Even though it isn't pointed at me, I go rigid. Dr. Shaw does, too, putting her hands out in front of her cautiously.

"You're going to pay for that," Katherine says. Slowly, her finger moves toward the trigger.

"Wait." It's Alice's voice that stops her. She's still hunched over in the corner, cradling the arm Dr. Shaw injected with the neutralizer, but despite how much she looks like an animal caught in a trap, her command still freezes Katherine in place. "She can still be useful to us."

Katherine's jaw twitches, and she doesn't move for a long moment. But then, finally, the gun lowers.

Swallowing, I glance at Dr. Shaw, unsure of what to do. I could take the opportunity to try and get the gun away from Katherine, but she's several yards away, so the chances of me getting to her before the gun ends up in *my* face are probably slim. Maybe, if Dr. Shaw and I work together, one of us could distract her while the other grabs the weapon, but Dr. Shaw is still frozen, her hands suspended in the air and her face as pale as a ghost.

The moment of uncertainty is short lived anyway. A second later, the door swings open behind me.

I whirl on the intruder, a burly man wearing an ACA guard uniform. He pauses in the doorway, scanning the room until his gaze stops on Alice.

"This one needs to be dealt with," I hear her say from behind me, her voice strained.

Then the man's eyes land on me, and I widen my stance, fingers tightening around the neutralizer I'm still holding. He doesn't appear to be armed, at least not with a gun, so I aim the needle in his direction, preparing for an attack. But then something cold and hard presses against the back of my head.

"Don't even think about it," Katherine says, low into my ear.

The man offers her a small nod, then shifts his attention to Dr. Shaw.

With the gun pressed against my head, I don't dare move an inch when he goes to her. I don't scream or call out when he grabs her by the arm and shoves her into the nearest chair. And I can do nothing but watch, silent with horror, when he presses his palm against the bare skin of her neck and a moment later her eyes roll back, the memories draining away along with her consciousness.

It takes him only a minute. And then he steps back, turning to Alice's attention. Ready for the next order.

Slowly, Alice stands up straight, dusting herself off. She schools her features into composure, setting her shoulders, but I can still see a few cracks in her carefully crafted armor. She's scared. She's powerless on her own now.

That, at least, has to be good for something.

"Did you manage to find the others?" she asks, reclaiming her even, unfazed tone. The guard nods silently, and on cue, the door swings open again.

Two more guards step into the room, but these ones aren't alone. They're each dragging someone.

My mouth goes dry.

Maverick.

Angelo.

Both of them are struggling against their captors and bound with handcuffs. Maverick's eyes land on me and he shouts something, but there's a gag tied around his mouth that muffles it. I reach out for him, but Katherine presses the barrel of the gun harder against my head in warning, and I stop.

The guards shove Angelo and Maverick toward the still-unconscious Dr. Shaw, forcing them to kneel against the wall beside her. When the commotion finally settles down, Alice nods her approval.

"Were there any others?" she asks.

"No," the original guard replies. "But they took out two of our guys before we could stop them. With these," he adds, gesturing at the other guard. The man behind Angelo steps forward, pulling a handful of syringes out of his pocket and setting them on the table in front of Alice.

Alice's eyes drift from the pile to the syringe still in my hand. She glances up at the guard, giving a silent order, and he turns to face me. I tense up as he moves closer, training the end of the needle on him with each movement, prepared to attack. It might not fix the situation, but I'm not about to go down without a fight.

But then I hear a soft click next to my ear, one I can only assume is from Katherine flipping the safety switch of the gun. "Give it to him," she orders.

I hesitate, not wanting to give up. Wanting to test my limits, to fight back and see if she'll actually shoot. But then, across the room, I see Maverick shaking his head, his eyes wide and pleading.

A puff of air escapes my lips, and reluctantly, I replace the red cap and hold the syringe out to the guard. He tosses it onto the table with the others.

Eleven of them left. And only two people down.

And now we're all here, trapped with Alice and her guards.

"It was quite the stunt you three pulled, wasn't it?" Alice smiles, amused. "It was never going to work, of course. But I must commend you for trying."

Her composure, her flippancy, the way she has always so calmly pretended that our efforts to stop her were nothing but small inconveniences sets my insides on fire. "And what are you going to do with us now?" I demand.

Before answering, she pulls out the chair at the head of the table and takes a seat, resting her elbows on it and folding her fingers together. "Well, considering my agents should have secured the loyalty of at least half of the organization by now, I suppose these two will have to soon follow," she says, nodding at Maverick and Angelo. Maverick yells something through his gag, attempting to rise to his feet, but one of the guards puts a hand on his shoulder, shoving him back to the ground.

Alice ignores him, keeping her eyes fixed on me. "However, since you seem to be capable of resisting the memory manipulation, I suppose we'll have to come up with an alternate plan for you."

I'm suddenly acutely aware of the gun still pressed into the back of my skull.

"You won't kill me," I say, hating the falter in my voice that shows how terrified I am that I'm wrong.

"Of course not," Alice assures me, though it does nothing to calm my thundering heart. "You're far too valuable for that. We'll just have to keep you somewhere safe. Where you won't be able to meddle any more."

I start to shake my head, feeling desperate. "You don't have to do this," I say. "It doesn't have to be this way."

Alice smiles sadly. "If that were true, Laura, then none of us would be in this room right now." Then she nods at the guards standing beside Angelo and Maverick. "Let's get this over with, shall we?"

The panic sets in the moment the guards start to move. As they close in, both Angelo and Maverick attempt to fight them off. Angelo, unfortunately, is no match for the six-foot tank going after him. The guard shoves him against the wall effortlessly, and with two fingers to Angelo's forehead, he drains the memories away until Angelo's body goes slack.

Maverick, on the other hand, manages to put up more of a fight. He shoves the guard off of him and makes it to his feet, but the victory is short lived. The third guard comes in to help and throws his weight into Maverick, knocking him to the ground. Maverick ends up flat on his stomach with two guards hunched over him, pinning him to the floor.

"Please," I beg, trembling. "Don't."

But my words hold no weight.

When the guard presses his palm to Maverick's neck, I lurch forward, knowing I have to stop him. Not even caring if Katherine shoots me. Thankfully, she doesn't, but I only get two strides in before she grabs my arm, twisting it behind my back painfully. I fight her, kicking out with my legs, screaming for them to stop.

But it's all useless. There's nothing I can do.

From the ground, Maverick looks up at me, his gaze finding mine one last time. But it isn't filled with fear or desperation. Instead, he almost looks resigned.

Like he's saying goodbye.

I watch, helpless, as the recognition slowly fades.

As his eyes flutter closed.

And then it's all over.

*****

NO.

It's the only word I can think of, the only feeling coursing through me in the seconds that follow.

No. No. No. No. No.

This can't be happening. Not again.

I've nearly lost Maverick too many times already. This can't be the end. I won't let it be.

Distantly, I feel Katherine's grip on me loosen. My legs give out beneath me, and I sink to my knees, hot tears sliding over my cheeks. Then I scramble over to Maverick, kneeling beside his prone body. I tug on his shirt, rolling him over. Pull his head into my lap and shake his shoulders, yelling desperate pleas that I can't even hear over the blood rushing in my ears.

He isn't dead. Somewhere in the back of my mind, I know that. He isn't completely lost.

But somehow, this feels worse than watching blood pour out of his abdomen. Somehow, this feels like the end.

No.

Sobs wrack my body. Tears fall onto Maverick's face as I pull him closer to me, clinging to the futile hope that he'll wake up any second and look me in the eyes. Say my name.

No one in the room seems to care. No one tries to stop me. They all just watch, their cruel gazes boring down on me like weights that are slowly crushing me.

I squeeze my eyes shut, pressing my forehead to Maverick's.

No.

No.

No.

I won't let this be the end.

I have to do *something*.

But the darkness is curling its thick fingers around me, pulling me into its sweet, silent abyss. There's nothing I can do to stop it.

And then, as I'm being pulled down, as I'm giving in to the void, I catch a glimpse of light.

It twinkles above me, the tiniest flicker in front of my eyes.
Just within reach.
So this time, I reach for it.

CHAPTER 35

ONCE AGAIN, I FIND myself somewhere else. Somewhere in my mind, in the space behind my eyes. This time, though, it feels different. Familiar… but also somewhere I've never been before.

My fingers are extended, barely brushing the light glimmering in the darkness. It feels warm under my skin but textureless. Weightless.

And then it brightens, shifting and growing until it illuminates a scene in front of me.

A house. Standing on the front porch, a finger on the doorbell.

Footsteps approach, and the door cracks open. A girl peeks out, offering a soft "Hello?"

It's me. Behind the door. I'm watching myself, just like so many of the echoes before have started.

"Hey there!" a woman to my left greets, smiling brightly.

I don't recognize her tall, thin frame or her silky, almost black hair, but I know I've heard her voice before. And she's holding something that catches my eye: a bouquet of flowers inside a stained glass vase.

"Who is it?" A third voice appears, pulling the door open wider.

It's my mom, I realize. And the woman with the vase is standing on *our* doorstep.

"Hi!" The woman waves enthusiastically. "My name is Annie, and this is my son, Maverick," she says, gesturing in my direction. "We're your new neighbors!"

Two sets of eyes glance over at me, and it's then that I realize I'm not just a spectator in this echo. I'm taking part in it, too. But it isn't one of my memories.

It's Maverick's.

"Oh, hello! It's so nice to meet you! Which neighbors are you?" Mom replies, smiling. But no, not mom to Maverick. *A stranger. A woman with brown curls the same as the girl standing next to her, looking at me warily.*

"Across the street and to the left, the one with the yellow flowers in front." Annie—no, *mom*—points. *We all turn to glance at our house. At Mom's prized flower bushes out front.*

I remember this. It was the first time I heard Maverick's voice, in the echoes from the day we moved into our new house.

The memory continues, accelerating to triple speed as I experience it from Maverick's perspective.

Mom offers our new neighbors the flowers she carefully cut and arranged for them, always so thoughtful and generous. Then she offers for us to help with moving things, and we're all waved inside.

The memory slows down again, the moment Maverick and I spoke to each other for the first time sharpening. I see it through Maverick's eyes, feel his thoughts and emotions as it plays out before me.

I hesitate in the entrance way, making eye contact with the girl, who tucks a curl behind her ear and nods at me. She looks about my age, potentially someone I'll want to get to know, so I rack my brain, trying to think of something funny or witty to say to her. But to my disappointment, all I manage to come up with is a lame, "I'm Maverick." To make it worse, I throw in an awkward wave.

"I heard," she replies, and I wince. A small smirk twists the corner of her mouth up. "I'm Laura," she finally adds, grinning at me.

"Laura," I repeat, committing the name to memory. Trying to keep myself from saying anything else that will make me look like an idiot. "It's nice to meet you, Laura."

After that, the memory dissolves in front of me, scattering into bits of light that fade into the void. I blink several times, wondering whether I'm imagining it or whether the darkness turned the tiniest shade lighter after the explosion.

Then, another light flickers on in the empty space, like a star appearing in the night sky. I lift my fingers to it, embracing the memory that follows.

A cool, foggy morning. I pull my hoodie over my head as I step outside, moving at a quick jog. But as soon as I get to my car, a sound makes me pause. I look up, watching the front door of the house across the street swing open. A girl steps out, the same girl I'd met a couple nights ago when her family moved in.

The girl is me. I'm seeing the memory from Maverick's perspective again.

Despite the fact that Tony is definitely going to kill me for being late again, I raise my hand in a wave. "Hey!" I call out. "Laura, right?"

She looks up, spotting me. "Yeah!" she calls back. Then she tilts her head. "Mark?"

I jog over, stopping a few feet in front of her. "Close. Maverick."

"Oh, I'm sorry," she replies, the embarrassment plain in her voice. But her eyes are sharp, and that little smirk makes an appearance again.

She's teasing me. And for some reason I can't explain, I like it.

The memory jumps ahead, giving me only glimpses of the rest of the conversation—Maverick asking me about school, giving me tips about the teachers and clubs to join. Telling me I should come by Louise's Diner sometime.

I remember this, too. It's another echo I'd heard one morning before school. But why am I seeing it from Maverick's point of view?

The moment the memory fades out of existence, another light appears in the space before me, and I waste no time before grabbing it, slipping into Maverick's head once again.

Days pass. The week drifts by at a crawl. Work. School. Repeat. Try not to think about Laura, the intriguing girl who just moved in across the street so much. Try not to get my hopes up every time the bells on the diner's door jingle as a new customer enters.

And then, one afternoon, as I'm wiping down the counters at the end of my shift, she finally comes.

I can't suppress the sloppy grin that pulls at my lips when I see her standing in the doorway. She pauses for a long moment, her eyes darting around the mostly empty diner, taking it in. Then she glances my way, spotting me through the window into the kitchen. I lift a hand in a small wave, then toss the rag into the hamper and slip my apron off, hurrying to greet her.

I don't remember this one. But I watch it unfold through Maverick's eyes, drinking in every moment.

Us slipping into a booth by the window. Maverick introducing me to Penny, the waitress and owner of the diner. Two plates of food that almost get ignored because we're both too focused on the conversation about nothing and everything at the same time.

I'm seeing Maverick's memories now. Somehow, I must have slipped into his head, and now I'm pulling out his echoes. And before I can process what that means, how it might change things, it all starts to happen faster. One memory after another, tipping into each other like dominos.

Maverick and I, climbing into his car to go on our first date.

Maverick tapping on my window late at night to go stargazing.

Halloween, holding hands at a haunted house, laughing. Kissing under the porchlight at the end of the night.

Going to *Coffee and Cream* for the first time.

Thanksgiving dinner at my house.

New Year's Eve.

Some of them I remember from the echoes. Others are new to me. But it doesn't just stop at memories of us.

I see Maverick and his mom in a doctor's office, too. Their heads hanging in despair as the doctor gives them the verdict.

I see Maverick moving things around in his life, working hard to take care of his mom as her health begins to decline. And then I see Alice, offering miraculous solutions from behind a desk. Asking for things in return that make Maverick's gut twist with guilt, but that he's desperate enough to agree to anyway.

I see dark alleyways. Movement in the dead of the night.

I see me. More of me. The bright spot that Maverick clings to when things get worse. When he loses his mom. I feel the terror gnawing at him when Alice sends threats. I feel his fierce determination to protect me, no matter what it takes.

I see him coming to a decision.

I see him curled up in a ball, wracked with guilt.

I see him watching me from a distance, following me into an alley.

I see, I see, I see.

All of his memories. His entire story, flashing before my eyes at lightning speed.

The echoes burst in front of me like fireworks, sending out sparkling, glittering light. Brightening the darkness of his mind.

And I realize then what's happening.

I'm giving him his echoes back.

I'm restoring the truth.

And it doesn't stop there.

When I sense that Maverick's mind is whole again, when there is only light, I look out into the distance, sensing more pockets of black around me. More people with memories that have been stolen and twisted.

When I focus on them, willing them to light up, pain shoots through my skull. Warning me that I shouldn't test my limits.

But I do anyway.

I push deeper into the spaces outside of myself, reaching out, finding endless chasms of darkness. I hold my hands out, channeling every ounce of my focus, willing the echoes to appear. And slowly, one after another, little flecks of light flicker into existence, dancing before my eyes.

I feel my body resisting me the harder I focus on summoning the lights. Each second it takes seems to drain more life out of me, sending pain shooting down every nerve ending.

But I refuse to let go. Refuse to stop until there are thousands of lights glittering before my eyes.

For a moment, I just stare at it, in awe. It's like a starry night sky, one that can only be seen from the most remote places on Earth. Too many stars to count. Too many galaxies to even fathom.

Echoes of the past—echoes of the *truth*—everywhere.

And finally, I reach for them, dipping my hands into pockets of light, pulling them into me.

I pull until the stars glow brighter.

Until they are all as bright as the sun.

Until there is no darkness left.

CHAPTER 36

AND THEN THERE IS NOTHING.

CHAPTER 37

WHEN MY EYES FINALLY crack open, a dark shadow looms above my head. I jerk upright, startled, sucking in giant gulps of air while I blink rapidly, trying to clear my vision.

"Easy," a steady voice says. A hand settles onto my shoulder reassuringly. "You're okay."

Slowly, I regain my bearings. I shift my gaze to the figure standing over me, taking in his tall, lean frame and the dark hair falling into his eyes. His hazel eyes.

"Maverick."

He nods, a small smile forming on his lips.

I stare at him for a long time, too many words tumbling through my head, creating a traffic jam in my mouth. But finally, three of them manage to slip through.

"You remember me?"

He reaches out, intertwining his fingers with mine. "Thanks to you, Laura, I remember *everything*."

My mouth hangs open for a moment while I process his words. "What happened?" My eyes dart around the tiny room with no windows. A room eerily similar to the one I woke up in when I was first brought to the ACA. "Where's Alice?"

Maverick squeezes my hand. "She's gone. Locked up."

"Gone?" The word barely makes any sense. I shake my head, swinging my legs over the side of the bed, ready to move into action. "What about the guards? The rest of the anomalies? We need to—"

"It's over," he interrupts, his other arm shooting out to steady me.

My heart thunders in my chest, unconvinced. "I don't— I don't understand."

"You saved us," Maverick says, staring at me with something akin to wonder. "You saved all of us."

"How?"

"You gave everyone their memories back."

"*How?*" I repeat. Nothing that he's saying makes any sense.

"I don't know," he answers simply. "You used your ability somehow. It sent out a blast that affected everyone in the ACA. And then we all woke up, our memories completely intact. You reversed everything Alice did."

For a moment, I still don't understand. I can't figure out how that would be possible. But then, slowly, the memories come back to me.

The darkness.

The glittering stars, giving way to light.

Pain splitting through my skull as I focused harder.

"Whatever you did drained you," Maverick continues, tightening his grip on my hand. "You've been out for two days."

My eyes widen. "*Two days?*"

He nods, frowning. "They told me that if you didn't wake up this morning, then you might not wake up at all. So I kind of… took matters into my own hands." I follow his gaze down to the table beside us, spotting the empty syringe resting on it.

"Alice's healing ability," I whisper.

"Yeah." Maverick smiles grimly. "After what you did, all of the people working for Alice realized they'd been brainwashed, and then it wasn't very hard to stop her. She wouldn't tell us where to find the rest of the replications, but luckily a few of her guards remembered and led us to her stash of them."

"Wow," I say, still in disbelief.

Maverick's eyes drop to the ground. "But there were only sixteen with Alice's ability in them. And we won't exactly be able to make more now that she's been neutralized. So everyone wanted to wait and see if you'd recover on your own first to conserve what we have left." He takes my other hand in his, rubbing his thumb along my knuckles. "I couldn't wait any longer, though."

"You saved me," I say, blinking away the tears that well in my eyes. Not sad tears. Not even happy ones. These tears are from relief. Because finally, this is all over.

Maverick looks into my eyes, then lifts his thumb to swipe away a rogue droplet sliding down my cheek. "You feel okay, though?" he asks, eyebrows pinching with concern. "Like the syringe worked?"

I nod, stretching my limbs, wiggling my fingers and toes. "Not a scratch on me."

His concern remains, though. And I don't understand why until he adds, "And your memories?"

My memories. Not memories Alice might have messed with, because he knows I figured out how to resist her. He wants to know if the memories *he* took from me are back now.

And with a startling jolt, I realize that they are. It all spreads out in front of me, and for the first time, I see the complete picture of our relationship. The echoes I'd heard or seen glimpses of in the last few months are whole now, colored in with my thoughts and feelings and all the things in between.

And there's more. So much more.

Dates we went on. Hours we spent together, hanging out, laughing, just enjoying each other's company. The progression of our relationship, from friends to hesitant lovers to two people who truly, deeply cared about each other. There are no dark spots in my memory anymore. Just light.

But even in all the light, I can see exactly what pulled us apart. It wasn't just that stormy day when Maverick showed up on my doorstep and took my memories away to protect me. It was in all the moments before that, when we were both too afraid to tell each other the truth. Too caught up in our own insecurities to believe the other would understand.

And now, here, after everything that has happened, there's nothing left to hide from each other.

"I remember it all," I say, lifting my gaze to Maverick's. He nods, relieved, but a question still lingers on his face. He doesn't ask it out loud, but somehow I understand.

I shake my head. "None of the memories that came back change how I feel about you," I tell him. "Because I have always loved you, Maverick. And I'm pretty sure I always will."

He doesn't say it back. But he doesn't have to, because after everything he's done for me, I already know how he feels. So instead of speaking, he just takes my face in his hands and brings his mouth to mine, kissing me with a tender passion that leaves no room for doubt in my mind.

Until a knock raps against the door, interrupting the moment. Maverick ignores it, though, lingering for a few seconds longer and grinning against my lips.

"That," he finally says, "must be your entourage."

He pulls away from me and heads for the door, tugging on the handle.

"Is she awake?" A familiar voice asks. Then Angelo steps into the room, his face lighting up when he spots me. "You're awake!"

Behind him, more familiar faces appear. Brent and Dahlia. Sara. Gabe. Veronica. They file in one after another, each one making my grin impossibly wider.

Then, last, a large figure with a head of blonde hair slips through.

My eyes widen. "Wyatt! You're okay!"

He smiles, slipping in next to the others, who all spread out across the tiny room, forming a circle around me. "Yeah, I heard that your crazy mind powers did a better job at saving everybody than mine did."

A burst of laughter escapes me, but when it fades, I stare at him, serious. "What you did…" I begin, trailing off because I can't find the right words. "Thank you, Wyatt."

He reaches out, squeezing my shoulder. "I think I'm the one that should be thanking you."

"We all should be," Veronica adds. "And we're so glad you're okay."

"I'm glad *you guys* are okay," I reply, scanning each of the faces around me, feeling suddenly full of emotion.

"Oh, don't get all teary on us now," Gabe groans. "No one wants to see you ugly cry."

Laughing, I reach out and slug him in the arm. I cover my face with my hands, using the sleeves of my shirt to dab my eyes dry. Then I look around the room again. "So… what happens now?" I ask.

"Well, a few things have already happened," Maverick answers. He sits down on the edge of my bed, launching into his explanation. "The head of the ACA stepped down yesterday. I guess she couldn't handle the pressure of the job, so she called it quits."

My eyebrows furrow. "So who's going to take over?"

"Our very own Dr. Shaw."

"Yeah, and she's going to be making a lot of changes around here," Angelo adds.

Maverick nods. "Including giving the ACA a new name."

"Oh?"

"It will now be the A*P*A," he tells me.

I drum my fingers against my thigh thoughtfully. "Anomaly… Placement Association?"

He shakes his head.

"Hmmmm. Anomaly *Provision* Association?"

Another no.

I twist my lips to the side, fighting a smile. "Maybe it has something to do with the new mission of the organization. Maybe we're going to stop being so secretive. So we'll be the straightforward, no-nonsense Anomalies Providing Answers."

Someone snorts.

"Or… I know! Alice's Pesky Adversaries!"

There. That one gets me a good laugh.

"Okay, but seriously. What does the *P* stand for?"

"We are now officially going to be," Maverick starts, pausing for dramatic effect, "the Anomaly Protection Association."

"Protection," I repeat, nodding. "Good. So does that mean we'll get to go free?"

"That's the plan," Maverick replies. "I think Dr. Shaw still wants to have some kind of regulations—we'll have to sign some non-disclosure agreements and keep up with regular check-ins—but we won't be trapped here. And she isn't going to enforce the use of the neutralizers."

"So we get to keep our abilities?"

"Only if we want to," Veronica answers. "I, for one, will be demanding that shot the second they're available."

I nod, certain she won't be the only one. There was a time when I would've been right behind her, but due to recent events, I've had a change of heart.

And it seems like I'm not the only one. Gabe frowns, eyebrows furrowing. "I thought that maybe I would, too. But honestly, these last few weeks of not being able to hear people's thoughts have been kind of boring. And the silence is driving me stir-crazy."

"I think we should make a special exception for you," I say, smirking. "So you can't keep invading everyone's private thoughts."

"Or maybe everyone should just stop being so angsty about everything," Gabe fires back.

"But that would make your life way less interesting."

"And that, unfortunately, is a very good point."

We all join in laughter. When it fizzles out, I look around the room once again, feeling suddenly cramped in such a small place. "So, when do we get to go home?"

There's a moment of hesitation, and everyone in the room shares awkward glances with each other. My heart sinks a little bit, though I don't know why yet.

"Well," Maverick begins slowly. "Some of the anomalies have already left. But some of them, the ones from our group, at least, don't exactly have anywhere to go."

Right. Because Alice made Maverick erase the memories of all their families and friends before she locked them away. So no one remembers them.

"There are only thirteen replications of Alice's ability left," he continues. "We used one of the original sixteen on you, one on Wyatt, and Dr. Shaw wanted one to study. She thinks that there might be a way to extract the DNA from it and find a way to make more, but she didn't sound too hopeful. Which means we don't have enough to fix *everyone's* memories."

"But we've all agreed that you should have two of them," Angelo adds. "For both of your parents. Since you're the one that saved all of us."

"We just... haven't figured out how to distribute the rest yet," Gabe finishes.

I blink at them, realization dawning on me. It's a sucky situation, but the solution to it shines bright behind my eyes, clear as day.

"We might not even need to use the replications to restore everyone's memories," I tell them. "I might be able to do it."

Because of the echoes. The answer is the echoes. I just couldn't see it before. I thought I'd been sentenced to a life of never being able to find silence. But I was always capable of so much more than that.

Maverick starts to shake his head. "I don't think—"

"I can," I insist. "I just restored everyone in the ACA's memories, didn't I?"

"Yeah, but then you almost *died,*" Maverick replies, the fear evident in his eyes. He doesn't want to see that happen again. He still wants to protect me.

"That was also my first time trying it," I argue. "And if I do it in smaller increments, instead of one giant blow, I'll probably be fine."

Maverick holds my gaze, looking unconvinced. But around the room, everyone else starts nodding, their eyes lighting with hope.

"Do you really think you can do it? Without hurting yourself?" Dahlia asks, her quiet voice filling the silent room.

I have answers to neither of those questions, so I just shrug.

"Let's go," I say instead, tossing the blankets off of me. "Let's go find out."

CHAPTER 38

MAVERICK AND I GO together, just the two of us, but the others make us swear to call them the second we know for sure if this is going to work. They're all hopeful. They're all counting on me. And although he seems wary about attempting this—even making a point to grab one of Alice's replications before we left, *just in case*—I know that Maverick is counting on me, too. I'd seen his memories and felt his emotions as if they were my own, and I know he's still wracked with guilt because of the things Alice made him do. So he needs this to work just as much as we all do.

The drive is long. Quiet. The anticipation and the uncertainty surrounding what I'm about to attempt reminds me all too much of the drive from Maverick's mansion to my house all those weeks ago when we'd first escaped from Alice's laboratory. On that terrible day, Alice had just erased both of my parents' memories of me, and I'd asked Maverick to take them home and make them forget about the whole thing. It had seemed easier than trying to tell them the truth, trying to convince them that they didn't remember me because things that I couldn't fully explain had happened to them.

It wasn't easier, though. At least not for me. Losing them— losing my life like that—had ripped my heart in half.

But now, I'm going to fix it. I'm going to get it back.

When we roll to a stop in front of my house, my hands are shaking. Maverick turns in his seat, reaching out over the center console to clasp them.

"You don't have to do this," he tells me gently.

I shake my head, sucking in a deep breath and letting it out through my nose. "No, I do."

"Just… be careful."

"I will," I assure him. "I know this is going to work. I know I'll be fine. I'm just…" I trail off, glancing up at my house. What used to be my home. Then I drop my gaze. "What are they going to think? What are they going to say when I tell them what happened?"

"I think they're going to be so proud of you."

I squeeze my eyes shut, unconvinced. For so long, my ability was such a point of tension with them. They didn't understand it, couldn't figure out what was wrong with me. And they didn't even believe that the echoes were real for a large portion of my life.

Things got better in the last couple of years, and we finally found a good rhythm of dealing with it. But they always seemed to tiptoe around the topic, still unable to come to terms with the fact that I was different from the rest of the world.

I know I wasn't the normal, happy kid they wanted. I know I made their life harder in so many ways. And for a moment it makes me wonder if maybe, they would be better off if I just left them this way. Free to live their lives without having to worry about me all of the time.

"Hey," Maverick says, reaching up to swipe away the tears that are suddenly sliding down my cheeks. He pulls me to him, circling me in his arms as I bury my face into his chest, giving in to the sobs. And for a long time, he just holds me while I cry, silently being there while I release all of the emotions swirling inside of me.

When my sobs finally subside into sniffles, Maverick gently tilts my chin up to level my gaze with his.

"You know they love you more than anything, right?" he says, his eyes serious.

I swallow, nodding slowly. I open my mouth to reply, but at that exact moment, someone knocks loudly on the window, startling me. I lurch in my seat, facing the intruder, and then I freeze, my jaw falling open.

A girl with long, jet-black hair stands just outside of the car, a boy with bright red curls behind her.

"Grace?" I call through the window. "Leo?"

I reach for the door handle, shifting my legs to scramble out of the car, but I get tangled in my seatbelt in the process. By the time I break myself free and step out into the cold air, Grace and Leo are just standing there, watching me with wide eyes.

"Laura Freaking Jones." Grace drags out the words, shaking her head in disbelief. Then she throws her arms around me. "Oh. My. Gosh. What happened to you?!"

"You guys!" I reach for Leo over Grace's shoulder, beckoning him to join the embrace. And even though he's never been much of a hugger, he wraps his arms around both of us anyway. "What are you doing here?"

"Ummm, I asked you a question first," Grace says, releasing me from her tight grip and taking a step back. "Where have you been?!"

I run a hand through my hair, shaking my head. "It's... a long story," I tell her. Then I glance up at the house. "I can tell you soon. But there's something I need to do first."

Grace follows my gaze up to my own front door, a sadness slipping across her features. "We've been coming here to check up on them, like you asked."

My heart leaps into my throat. "Really?"

Grace nods. "We came by one day and told them we had just moved in down the street," she says. "I told them that we loved board games and asked if they wanted to get together sometime. So they invited us over, and we've been playing with them every week since."

"Seriously?"

"Yep," Leo answers. "And I've had to suffer through way too many rounds of *Clue* this month."

A laugh escapes me. "*Clue* is their favorite."

"I know," Grace replies. "We figured it would help cheer them up."

My eyebrows furrow. "What do you mean?"

Grace bites her lip, sharing a glance with Leo. "They haven't been doing so well, lately," she explains. "They've just been… lonely. They keep talking about how they wish they'd had a son or daughter like me or Leo."

My insides lift with sudden hope. "They do?"

"Yeah. They just seem sort of down. Like they're missing something. I thought that—" Grace keeps talking, but I don't hear the rest. Because in the next moment, I'm already making a sprint for the door.

When I get there, I test the handle, shoving it open when I realize it's unlocked. I step into the house, pausing for just a breath to take in the familiar scent of home, to let the warm, cozy air wrap around me. Then I race through the house, scanning the hallways and rooms as I pass.

I find them in the kitchen, Mom at the sink working on the dishes and Dad at the table typing into his laptop. They both look up at the sound of me entering, their eyes going wide, suddenly on high alert.

They don't know who I am. I'm an intruder, someone that shouldn't be here.

Dad's chair scrapes against the floor as he stands, putting his hands out in front of him warily. Mom presses the plate she's holding against her chest defensively.

Dad starts to say something, but I just close my eyes, tuning him out. Focusing. Searching for that space behind the eyes, that somewhere in between.

It's easier this time. The difference between riding a bike as a wobbly child and hopping on one years later, after you've found your balance.

I find the dark spots inside their heads. See the stars twinkling to life.

I grab them. Pull the echoes closer and watch them fill everything in with light.

And when it's over, I open my eyes. Find their gazes, slowly filling with recognition.

Grace, Leo, and Maverick step into the room, panting. They freeze behind me, watching as Mom and Dad stare at me, processing.

Mom is the first to move. She drops the plate and it shatters, but she doesn't even notice. In three strides, she reaches me, then throws her arms around me, repeating my name over and over while hot tears drip onto my shoulder. Then I feel Dad's arms over hers, hear his sobs as he buries his face into my neck.

And as the three of us stand there, locked in an embrace, I feel the weight of the past wash away.

The struggles, the misunderstandings, the confusion. None of it matters anymore.

They love me. They love me wholly and completely, no matter what I am. No matter what I can or can't do.

Over the years, my parents did the best they could with the information they had—which wasn't much. None of the specialists I'd seen growing up knew what an anomaly was, none of them thought having an ability to hear echoes of the past was even possible. My parents wanted desperately to help me, and they were frustrated because they didn't know what to do, not because I made their lives harder.

All the things we've experienced and all the mistakes we've made have just been lessons to teach us how to step into the future with grace.

Because of Alice, so many anomalies grew up confused, outcast, and lonely. And because of me, whether I like it or not, more anomalies are going to exist. But with what we've learned, we'll know how to treat them better. We'll be ready for them. Ready to teach the world how to show them kindness and how to see them as equals.

There's still so much work ahead. There's still so much we need to learn.

But because of everything we've been through, we'll be able to create a better world for anomalies.

And that, I think, remembering Alice's extravagant but impractical plans for us, *is what's going to make us heroes.*

THE END

AUTHOR'S NOTE

WHEN I FIRST SET OUT writing this series, I didn't realize how much I had woven my own journey into Laura's.

I wanted to tell the story of a girl who felt like she could never fit in. A girl who, even though she managed to find some normalcy in her life, felt like there were parts of herself she had to hide from the world and even those closest to her. Who felt misunderstood, just like I felt for a good portion of my life.

And then, over the course of the books, Laura learned how to accept herself. She learned that she was never truly alone. And even at the very end, though she still battled with her own insecurities, she learned how to overcome them. She learned to recognize her own value and how to tune out those thoughts telling her that the things that made her different made her a burden to those around her. And over the course of the past several years of writing these books, I've learned how to accept and love myself, too.

As I plotted this story over the years, it was never my intention to write about superheroes. While I leaned heavily on some of the tropes of the genre and the existence of supernatural abilities, I made a goal that these abilities would be different. That some of them would be super cool and useful in the ways we think superhero powers are, but that others would be more like burdens. Things that kind of suck… like hearing echoes. And when the title of the third book—Heroes—popped into my head, I fought it for a long time. Because I wasn't writing about heroes, not really. I was writing about anomalies.

But then I really started to stew on the idea. There was a reason my mind kept coming back to this title, and I couldn't shake it. Because what if heroes aren't always the people with amazing superpowers jumping in to save the day? The ones changing the world or fixing everyone else's problems.

What if a hero is just someone who doesn't stop fighting? Whose biggest battle is the one within—the one they have to fight against themself, every single day.

And maybe they never truly win, maybe they will fight for the rest of their life. But they refuse to give up. They refuse to let the world tell them what they are, and they fight to discover their own worth outside of what others say.

Just like Laura, I think that we're all anomalies, in our own ways. We have our gifts and our burdens, and we struggle to make peace with them. But despite it all, we never stop trying to carve out happiness from the cards we've been dealt. We never stop fighting.

And I think that's what makes true heroes.

I hope you've enjoyed reading Laura and Maverick's story, and I hope you've discovered something about yourself along the way. I know I have.

And I can't wait to explore whatever journey I'm about to embark on next!

ACKNOWLEDGMENTS

WRITING THE acknowledgements for any book is hard, but figuring out who to start with will always be the easiest. Because it's you. The person reading this. Whoever you are, wherever you are, I can't thank you enough. If you're here, that means you made it this far, through three books of mine (unless you just skipped ahead, in which case, I hope you'll either have been confused enough or intrigued enough to read the other two!). And I cannot thank you enough for being here, for taking a chance on my books, and for joining me on this journey.

Secondly, I want to give a huge shout out to the most patient and supportive husband ever. Jacob, you've cheered me on since the beginning, you've been my rock through the emotional highs and lows of being a writer, you've done nothing but encourage me to keep going, to keep chasing my dreams. Your constant, unflinching support got me through this trilogy and gets me through every single day. Without you, I'd be a mess, and let's be honest—the plot and characters in these books wouldn't be as cool.

To Bri—without you, I don't think I would have ever been brave enough to share my writing with the world. You're the first person I send my writing to, and you were the first person I ever shared any of my writing with, and for that I will forever be grateful. Your writing inspires me and has always made me think deeper about my own writing, so you've influenced these books probably in more ways that you realize. I'm so grateful to have you as a friend and to share this hobby with you!

Huge thanks to Stephen, whose careful edits improved the readability of this book and whose writing also continues to inspire me. Even though I didn't go the time travel route for the ending of this book, I definitely considered it briefly thanks to you.

Thanks to Donn Marlou for the beautiful cover designs that always take my breath away. And shoutout to my fantastic audiobook narrator, Brogan Werder, who gave my characters a voice. Seeing my books come to life in different ways is my absolute favorite part of being an author, and I'm so grateful to have found such talented people to work with.

To all of my fellow authors I've met on Instagram or TikTok or at a conference or on my podcast or anywhere, thank you. Thank you for being you and for writing books and for being an example to me. Whether we just met once or we chat more regularly, whether we've read each other's books or read in completely different genres, I am so grateful to be surrounded by such an amazing community of storytellers. Every book that goes out into the world inspires me to keep writing, to keep going. And writers are just the best people ever!

Last, but certainly not least, thanks to all of my family and friends for your unwavering support. Whether you've read my book and left a review, shared a post on social media, recommended my books to a friend, bought a copy just to put on your shelf, left a comment or a like on one of my posts, or are just quietly cheering me on, I appreciate you. Every little, tiny bit of support means the absolute world to me.

ABOUT THE AUTHOR

Marissa decided early on that she never wanted to grow up, so she became an author of young adult novels. When she isn't writing her own books or reading everything she can get her hands on, you can usually find her somewhere in the outdoors admiring nature or curled up on the couch playing The Legend of Zelda.

Visit www.MarissaLete.com for updates on her latest writing ventures!

If you enjoyed this book, please consider leaving a review.
Reviews are vital in getting books from independent authors
into the hands of readers.

Some key places you can leave an honest review are:

Amazon
Goodreads
BookBub